TO THE VICTORS THE REMAINS

Book 3 of the Lone Star Reloaded Series

A tale of alternative history

By Drew McGunn

Newsletter Sign Up/Website address:
https://drewmcgunn.wixsite.com/website
V1

ISBN: 198569235X
ISBN-13: 978-1985692350

ACKNOWLEDGEMENT

I'm not sure who *they* are, but I have it on the highest authority that *they* say the third time is the charm. I am humbled by the reception my first two books have received and am happy to release into the wilds my third book in the Lone Star Reloaded series, To the Victors the Remains. Thank you to all the readers who have bought an e-book or paperback.

I would also like to thank my better half, my wife, for the many hours of work she graciously left me alone to work out the details of this series. Without her I don't think I could have stayed on task to complete this story.

My love of writing started when I was in high school. My sophomore English teacher nurtured my creative spark. She assigned creative writing projects each grading period that showed I had some small skill at stringing words together in a way that entertained. Thanks, Mrs. Trest. At least one of your students was paying attention.

Table of Contents

The Story So Far

In 2008, SSGT Will Travers couldn't have imagined how wrong a routine supply run could go, as he counted down the days until his National Guard unit would rotate back stateside. That is, until an explosion overturned his Humvee and propelled him through space and time.

When he woke, he was trapped in the body of William Barret Travis, with only a few weeks to go before his fateful death at the Alamo in 1836. With no way to return to the present, and with no desire to become a martyr for Texas liberty, Will could have fled. He had nearly two centuries of history he could exploit. Instead of fleeing or dying at the Alamo, he chose to do the impossible. He rallied every Texian volunteer between the Rio Grande and San Antonio, and met Santa Anna at the Rio Grande where he stopped the dictator with the help of David Crockett, Jim Bowie, James Fannin and seven hundred more patriots.

As Santa Anna brought up his reserves, Will sent most of his men north, to build new defensive positions on the Nueces River. He stayed behind with David Crockett, Juan Seguin and a handful of brave riflemen and gallant Tejano cavalry. They fought a delaying action, leading the might of Santa Anna's army into the jaws of the trap on the Nueces. The flower of Mexico died on the fields of South Texas, as Will led the Texian army to victory.

Victory over the Mexican dictator was only the first obstacle to overcome. Having won the war, Will was determined that he would win the peace. As a student of history, he knew that without a change in direction, Texas would implement a constitution that would trap thousands of slaves and freedmen in one of the most oppressive slave codes in the American South. Indians, like the Cherokee, who were trying to put the pieces of their society back together after President Jackson's genocidal Indian Removal Act, would be driven out of Texas. Thousands of Tejanos, who had lived in Texas for generations, would be forced from their homes, as men like Robert Potter and James Collinsworth strove to make Texas a welcome place for Anglos only.

Will allied himself with David Crockett and Sam Houston to thwart the worst of the pro-slavery faction, and passed a constitution that gave the Cherokee a path to citizenship, and allowed for freedmen to remain in the Republic and for slave owners to free their slaves. For a man of the 21st century, it seemed too little, but it was a start.

The constitutional convention was still in session when an assassin attempted to kill Will. He killed his assassin, and David Crockett used the shock waves sent through the convention to elevate him to the rank of general.

With a promise from David Crockett that the hard-won gains wouldn't be traded away, Will dives into transforming the army, but he has barely begun before the frontier erupts into violence as the Comanche storm out of the Comancheria, attacking settlements along the frontier. Pressed by the Republic's congress to stop the raids, Will rushes north, and discovers the Comanche are masters at staying one step ahead of his army. Forced to retreat, he refines the tactics and develops new weapons designed to bring the Comanche raids to a stop.

The following year, he returned with an army rebuilt to face the lightning fast attacks from the Comanche and led them into the Comancheria where they burns several villages to the ground and captured more than a hundred prisoners. He offered terms for the release of the prisoners, an end to the raids and release of hundreds of Anglo and Mexican prisoners held by the Comanche. The war chiefs refused and they assembled the largest war band the Comanche had ever fielded and rode to San Antonio.

In an epic battle of civilizations, Will's new model army defends the town and forces the Comanche to seek peace.

In the years that followed, Will helped Texas to find its economic footing, and invested in free labor farming projects and banking. But he never lost sight of his responsibly for the army, and he continued to work with inventors to refine the weapons of war.

By the time President David Crockett's term in office drew to a close in 1842, he ordered Will to lead the army west, to secure the boundary agreed upon by Santa Anna and the Texians six years before. It was a herculean task for the small army, and Will was determined to rise to the occasion.

Chapter 1

3rd May 1841

The young officer swept his black wide-brimmed hat from his head and took a once white handkerchief from his pocket and wiped the grime from his face. The midday sun would have felt hotter if not for the cooling breeze from the north. Even so, the officer thought it warm as he unfastened his tunic's top button. A quick glance toward the sun overhead wasn't as important as the rumbling in his belly. "Alright, Mr. Cavanaugh, let's break for lunch."

A large, barrel-chested man with sunburned face and bright red hair climbed down from a wagon filled with dirt and turned to a group of laborers. "Ye heard Lieutenant Wagner, boys. Cesar's got lunch ready." To the German-born officer, the Irish foreman's pronunciation of his rank as left-enant sounded wrong to his ears. Worse yet, was the way he pronounced the 'w' as 'double u', instead of the correct 'v'. As the laborers received their food from the back of another wagon, the officer watched the men segregate themselves as they ate. The Tejanos were the largest group of laborers. As they found places to eat, the sound of Spanish could be heard, as they ate and chatted with each other.

The second group of laborers were the freedmen the army had hired. Their ebon skin, the lieutenant thought, was a much better protection against the harsh west Texas sun. As they talked and ate, their patois revealed their former status as slaves.

The last group, were the Irish. As English landlords had raised rents across the Emerald Isle, the number of Irish turning up in Galveston had climbed. Nearly a thousand had immigrated to the Republic the previous year. Cavanaugh, unlike the other Irish, was literate. It was the reason, if Wagner was honest about it, why the Irishman was the foreman for the two score workers.

After Wagner had eaten, he climbed atop the wagon and watched the laborers finish eating. The wagon was a custom-built device, constructed by the Republic's small engineering company. A wide, heavy iron cylinder was fixed behind the seat. A team of two horses pulled the contraption. Its purpose was to compact the roadbed, which the lieutenant's crew was building. Again, glancing at the sun, the young officer called out, "Mr. Cavanaugh, get the men back to work. This road isn't going to build itself."

As the men returned to work, Wagner's attention was drawn to a team of soldiers in butternut uniforms, walking across the rolling prairie toward the work crew. Each carried the new breech-loading Model 1842 Sabine Rifle. They were part of the squad of infantry assigned to Wagner's construction crew as guards. With the Comanche war a few years in the past, the lieutenant hoped the guards were unnecessary. The soldier in the lead, with two stripes on his sleeves, saluted. "Lieutenant, sir. There's a band of Indians to our south. They're heading this way."

Wagner scowled as he looked to the south, "How many, Corporal?"

"No more than five or six. They weren't wearing any face paint."

Wagner had not heard of any Comanche bands ranging through this part of the country but having responsibility for forty workers and his own platoon of engineers, taking risks wasn't something his Prussian sensibilities cared to do. "Alright, Corporal, let's see what they're up to."

The four riflemen deployed to the south of the workers, where they waited along with Wagner, until they saw a half-dozen Indians ride over the rolling prairie. The soldiers held their rifles at the ready, waiting to see if the mounted warriors intended any mischief. One of the warriors detached himself from the other riders and approached Wagner's position. When he was still ten yards away, he called out in Spanish. One of the soldiers, a Tejano, said, "He says he was sent by some *hombre* named Flacco. Says they came from Bexar a few days ago. Lt. Colonel Seguin's command will be on the march at the next moon and he has been asked to find out how many more days until we reach the second supply depot."

Wagner realized he'd been holding his breath and as the soldier translated, he let it out. Lipan Apaches, then.

Flacco was a friend of Lt. Colonel Seguin. Wagner's recurring fear was to see Comanche raiding south of the treaty line along the Red River. As he considered the answer, he looked behind his laborers in the direction from which they had come. A narrow, brown ribbon of road cut across the prairie. It traced back to the first depot, almost ninety miles east, on the upper Guadeloupe River, and from there back to San Antonio, another eighty miles away. At the speed they were building the roadbed, another three days were needed to reach the second depot.

As he considered the distance, it was still another four hundred miles to El Paso. At the rate they were building road, Wagner had calculated his crew would get there sometime after judgement day.

After the soldier told the Apache they would arrive at the second depot in a few days, the warrior swung his mustang pony around and joined the other Apache. Then they wheeled around and trotted away, in the direction from which they came.

The breeze blew through the awning, causing the canvas to flap. Will Travers stood next to a support pole, looking to the west. Even at a distance of more than a mile, he could see the lone star flag of the Republic flying above the old chapel of the Alamo. It was a testament to how much had changed over the past five years since he and President Crockett had led the forces of Texas revolutionaries against Santa Anna's veterans.

As the cool northern breeze overcame the warmth of the setting sun, Will still marveled at the circumstances which led him to this place. A little more than five years before, he had been riding shotgun in a military Humvee in Iraq, when their convoy had been ambushed. His driver had driven over an IED, flipping the utility vehicle. When he came to, he'd expected to find himself in a military hospital, not trapped in the body of a nineteenth century adventurer. After five years, he'd long surrendered hope of swapping back into his own body. Whether a trick of fate or the hand of God had played a role in the transference, he couldn't say. But he found more purpose to his life in believing God, rather than random fate, had led him to this point.

Waking up in the body of William Barret Travis had been disconcerting, to say the least. Even after all this time, it stretched his mind to consider how different the world was becoming since he, President Crockett and the army of Texas had won independence on the Nueces River in 1836. In the world living only between his ears, Sam Houston had crushed Santa Anna and Crockett and Travis had died at the Alamo. In the world he now inhabited, Will commanded the Texian army, David Crockett was president, and Sam Houston chose a life of semi-exile among the Cherokee of east Texas, after losing the presidential election of 1836 to Crockett in a landslide.

The wider world wasn't the same either. Henry Clay had won the presidential election of 1840 in the United States and all Western Europe now recognized Texas' independence. Will had no idea when he recommended to Crockett that Mirabeau B. Lamar be appointed chargé d'affaires to France, that the ambitious former

Georgian, would take to Europe like a fish to water, or that Europe would reciprocate.

Other changes had happened much closer to home. He had married Rebecca Crockett nearly two year

earlier and their first child together was due soon. Will couldn't help but smile, as he looked vacantly toward the old fort. *"Not bad for a guy who was supposed to die a martyr."*

The sound of a throat clearing brought Will back to the present and he turned. Colonel Albert Sidney Johnston sat in a rickety field chair across a table from a young officer. "General, I was asking Captain Hays here, how much longer he expected his command to continue their game."

Twenty-four-year-old Jack Hays spread his hands wide and grinned at the Colonel. "Hard to say, sir. Last week, the game continued until almost dawn the following day before the second platoon captured the first's flag. This evening, I think, shouldn't be as long. This time, when one of the boys gets tapped out, he's 'dead' for good."

Will watched his second-in-command and saw the irritation in his body language. Even though a graduate of West Point, Johnston was more innovative than many of his fellow graduates. "We're putting a lot of time and effort into your boys, Captain. Letting the wargame drag into the night raises the risk of injuries."

This wasn't the first time Johnston had voiced this concern. Before Hay could respond, Will interjected, "Colonel, while I agree with you about greater risk for injury at night, the skills that Hays' boys are building, I think outweigh the risk."

As the sun sank below the western horizon, Will said, "Aside from the infrequent noise, it is nearly impossible to hear them as they move back and forth across the field. On our campaign to El Paso these skills could allow us greater control over a battlefield."

Will watched as Johnston pursed his lips. This was a familiar battleground between the two men. Part of Will agreed with the colonel. The risks associated with training at night was higher than during daylight hours. But the benefits, Will thought, outweighed the risks. But he conceded, Johnston's tendency toward conservatism when it came to risking his soldiers' lives was a trait he admired.

As the moon crested the eastern sky, Will heard a noise behind him and he turned and saw two men, dressed in black clothing, with their faces and hands blackened with charcoal. One of them held a checkered flag with a "1" stenciled on it. The other saluted Captain Hays, saying, "Private Watkins, second platoon, sir! I believe first platoon has misplaced this."

The wargame over, the men of Hays' Rangers came together around a sizable campfire as the two lieutenants debriefed their men over the things that went right and wrong for both platoons. After a moment, Will tuned them out and turned back to Hays and Johnston. "Jack, the use of black clothing for your soldiers was a stroke of genius. How prepared are your boys?"

Hays watched the men around the campfire, as the soldiers talked through the game. Finally, he turned back to Will and said, "Every one of them can hit the fly off the back of a bull at three hundred yards under the right conditions and more than a few can hit the center of a bullseye at five hundred yards. Most are tolerably good with a pistol out to a hundred feet but beat all at fifty feet or less."

Hays paused, gathering his thoughts for a moment, "General, you told a story about a Chinese army and how they could fight and kill with just their hands and feet. That's gotten me thinking about ways to train our boys in hand-to-hand fighting. We're still trying to figure out the details, but should you happen to see a Chinaman who knows that way of fighting, send him our way."

Hays' ability to adapt filled Will with hope for the coming campaign. Will had discovered his own tendency to micromanage and had been second-guessing his decision to send Lt. Colonel Seguin as the expedition's commander. The leadership skills Hays had demonstrated as he had drilled his company of Rangers buoyed Will's optimism that Seguin had good officers under his command.

Coming back to Hays' comment, Will said, "I'll keep my eyes open for any Chinamen, Jack. But keep up what you're doing with the unarmed combat and keep us appraised. But the reason I dragged Colonel Johnston out here this evening was to discuss the coming campaign with you. Juan is due to head out on the first of June with his seven companies. We had hoped to start earlier but delays with expanding the quartermaster corps has required our timetable be adjusted."

Will continued, "We've stationed the two platoons of Company H at the first two depots, along with a few men from the quartermaster's corps to manage our supplies there. Additionally, we have a platoon of engineers building a military road between here and the second depot. We have two more depots to put out there, to the west. Tomorrow morning, Company I is scheduled to head out, to garrison the next two depots. The fly in the ointment is that we have no idea where we're going to position them. That's where your company comes in."

Hays asked, "Do we have anything operating west of the second depot?"

Will shook his head, "No. Your command needs to find suitable routes that lead to watering holes. Once you've found a good spot for the third depot, I want Company I marching toward it and the engineers extending the road. Next comes the fourth depot. Ideally you should try to establish it along the Pecos river. Once that's been established, you're still going to be two hundred miles from El Paso del Norte. That's two hundred miles through some of the most inhospitable parts of the Chihuahuan desert. Before Seguin gets out there with the main force, I want you to scout out a suitable route through the desert, with enough water for the horses. Captain, without water, Seguin's command will fail."

A bed of coals glowed in the hearth, an iron pot hung over them. Henrietta, the freedwoman who cooked and helped Becky with the household work, stood between the hearth and the Franklin stove, clenching a wooden spoon in her hands. The object of her ire stood inside the door, facing Will. Charlie sat at the dining table, with schoolwork spread across it, glancing between his father and his former slave, Joe. Next to the stove, sat Becky, in a rocking chair, her needles held in her hands, as they rested against her distended belly. Her pregnancy was well along.

The ex-slave stared at Will, with steady determination. "Marse William, sir, I come here tonight to ask you, why didn't I get hired to haul them supplies to your army out west? I ain't the only negro who asked for a contract, but I's the only negro who didn't get one."

Will looked around the room, avoiding Joe's eyes. He looked to his wife, who cast a look back at her knitting, then to Charlie. Abstractly, he saw the boy's pants were too short. Finally, he looked to Henrietta. The former slave wore a passive mask, as she tried to hide her feelings behind years of slavery into which she'd been born. Finding no answers, Will looked back at Joe. "Joe, I'm not your master. You've been a free man now for five years. Call me Mr. Travis or General. Hell, man, my friends call me Buck. But to answer your question, the contracts to supply the depots in the west are dangerous, man. I didn't give you a contract because I'm not going to do something that runs the risk of making Henrietta a widow."

Joe shook his head, stubbornly. "But marse, I mean, General, sir, I done made the decision to do this. If you done give me my freedom, but you're going to keep me from doing what I needs to do, I ain't got real freedom, sir. I need to do this for my wife." He stole a glance at Henrietta, who finally let the mask slip. Tears streamed down her face and she stepped across the room where she clung to Joe, crying, "Oh, my Joe, I don't know what I'd do without you. You're all I got."

Will was caught between conflicting views. At his core, he knew slavery was a great evil, dehumanizing both the slave and master. Freeing Joe back in 1836 had been the right thing to do. Even though he had transferred into William B. Travis' body, he had felt a moral sense of responsibility for Joe, despite the fact that he was not the William B. Travis who had trafficked in slavery. God alone knew what had happened to the spirit of the man he had replaced. On one hand, Joe was free to make the choices that would define his life, but on the other, Will felt a since of moral obligation toward the former slave. He would never admit that when the military contracts hauling supplies from the coast became available, he had placed his hand on the scale and saw to it Joe was one of contractors hired. But the coming campaign carried serious risks. Rumors of Comanche braves slipping across the Red River and stealing horses and cattle had started up and an unguarded supply wagon was vulnerable.

But on the other hand, Joe was right. Will had decided for him. What was freedom to the ex-slave if Will could make those decisions for him?

After a long, agonizing moment, Will nodded, and said, "I apologize, Joe. It wasn't my place to do that. If you want to apply again for a contract, I promise I won't get in the way."

Henrietta shook in Joe's arms, as Will heard her sobbing. Through her tears she whispered, "Oh, Joe, I don't want to lose you."

Becky lifted herself from her rocking chair, and wobbled over to stand beside Will, putting an arm around her husband, she said, "We'll be praying for Joe and all our brave men, Henrietta. And no matter what, you have a place here, with us."

Officially summer was still three weeks away, but nobody had bothered telling the weather that, Lt. Colonel Juan Seguin thought. As he stood next to his sorrel horse, he felt sweat beading on his forehead, even as the warm southern breeze ruffled his thick, black hair. He straightened his butternut-colored jacket again, as his wife and children waved at him as they crowded near the Alamo's gatehouse along with all the other wives, sweethearts, and children of the three hundred men assembled in formation in the Alamo plaza. A small platform had been erected in front of the Alamo's hospital and a narrow wooden podium stood upon it. Hanging from it were streamers of red, white, and blue. Behind the podium stood Texas' first elected president, David Crockett, who had traveled from Austin to speak to those assembled.

Seguin stood below the platform, studying the chief executive of the Republic. Crocket was in his mid-fifties; his brown hair had turned grey at the sides. His eyes crinkled, as though always ready for laughter. In place of the normal black suit jacket, Crockett had chosen to wear a finely embroidered buckskin hunting shirt. A coonskin cap rested on the podium. In all the years Seguin had known the president, he could count on a single hand the number of times he'd seen Crockett wearing the animal skin on his head. There was Davy Crockett, Lion of the West, who wore a coonskin cap then there was David Crockett, President of the Republic of Texas. Seguin had learned a long time ago which was myth, and which was real. When it suited the president's purpose, the two merged.

Crockett cleared his throat and looked across the sea of faces crowded into Alamo Plaza. "My fellow Texians, I reckon many of you remember when you and me stood on the bank of the Nueces River and whipped ol' Santa Anna that day. We shed our sacred blood and bought with it our freedom and liberty. Almighty Providence was with us and we captured that weasel of a dictator. When we negotiated with him in good faith, we expected Mexico to uphold their end of the bargain. In that spirit, we owe it to our wives and children to bequeath to them a legacy of a republic that is secure within our borders, recognized by all nations as a free and independent country. A country that stretches from the Red River in the north, east to the Sabine River, and south and west to the Rio Grande. You elected me to do a job and I would fail in that job, my brothers, if I did not do everything within my power to make it so!"

Seguin watched the president pause and look over the field of soldiers before the podium. "I would never ask a single soldier to go where I wasn't also willing to go. Unfortunately, congress has said they can't get by without me." Crockett cast a sly look at General Travis, who also sat on the platform. "I recall telling your general the same thing. I'm not so young any more that the idea of being hogtied and locked away in the basement of the Capitol appeals to me. Instead, my duty requires that I send each of you out not simply as a soldier of the Republic, but as guardians of our liberty and security. When this campaign is over, and you return home, it won't be just your wives, sweethearts, and children that greet you, but all of us will lift up a toast to you, our returning heroes." Crockett grabbed the coonskin cap and sketched a casual salute that took in the whole of the plaza and set the cap on his head.

The crowd in the plaza enthusiastically applauded their president. Seguin had heard worse speeches. He took the black, wide-brimmed hat and pulled it onto his head and swung into the saddle. "First Cavalry, mount up!"

Three hundred men answered by swinging into their saddles. A small band, to the side of the platform, enthusiastically burst into music. It struck up a lively tune, *Gary Owen*, recently imported from Ireland by immigrants, and taught to fellow Texian soldiers over copious amounts of whiskey.

Seguin gave the order and the companies wheeled to the right and formed up in columns of four as they rode out the Alamo's gate, heading into the west.

Chapter 2

Captain Jack Hays stared at the hard-packed road, heading west from the bank of the Concho River. The engineering platoon had extended the military road another ten miles into the West Texas wilderness. Another three hundred ninety miles to go, more or less, Hays cheerlessly chuckled at the thought.

But on the positive side, his Ranger company could have covered the distance in a week had they not slowed down to the pace of the infantry they accompanied. A few days after leaving San Antonio they had caught up with Company I, who were also marching to the west. Even with the infantry, they arrived in nine days. The easy portion of travel behind them, he turned in the saddle and saw his forty mounted Rangers ready to scout the best route for the army to take through the Chihuahuan desert. Behind them were the riflemen from Company I as well as a score of men from the quartermaster's corps. They would follow behind. They would garrison and supply the next two depots, provided Hays and his Rangers could find the right locations.

Hays shook his head slightly. *"I damned well better find the right spots."* Failure wasn't an option. He tamped down his doubts and turned forward, urging his horse to a canter, into the west.

Two weeks later, Hays cursed the dry heat of West Texas, as he leaned back, soaking in the shallow water of the lazy, Pecos River. He'd decided nothing took the bite out of the dry heat better than a swim. He sat up and swiped his hat from the flat rock next to the water's edge. It wasn't just the parched and arid landscape that was seared by the merciless sun, and he placed the hat on his head. The previous two weeks were productive. Both depots had been established along reliable water sources.

He was tempted to amend the thought as he lay in the sluggish, tepid water. Finally, in a moment of charity, Hays decided if any body of water could rise to the designation of a river in this part of the country, the trickle of water, known as the Pecos, flowing from the mountains of New Mexico to the Rio Grande deserved the unmerited title.

He got out and dried off and put his clothes and boots on and walked toward the camp. The handful of men from the quartermaster's corps had put the infantry to work turning it into Texas' westernmost outpost. Two lines of bleached white tents ran through the center of the camp. A half-dozen supply wagons were between the tents and the river.

A few soldiers were moving blocks of wet adobe from by the river to the camp, where they were left to dry, the sun acting as a natural kiln. There were too few trees in the area for the soldiers to use wood to construct buildings or erect a wall, but dirt and clay were available in as natural abundance as could be desired and the lieutenant in command of the infantry platoon had wasted no time in using the resources available.

Hays yelled back to the Rangers who were still soaking in the river, "Enjoy the breather, boys, that was the easy part. Tomorrow, we cross the Pecos and head for El Paso!" As he turned back toward his tent, a chorus of groans and catcalls from the river left little doubt the men felt the same way.

That night, the temperature was still warm, as Hays sat next to a cooking fire with his two lieutenants and the company's first sergeant. A small campaign-sized map was spread over his legs. "I've been looking over the map between here and El Paso, and damned if we have much to go on." The other men had become intimately familiar with the map over the previous weeks. El Paso was clearly marked, as was the long, looping Rio Grande River. But the river ran a couple of hundred miles to the south before curving back to its northwesterly route. Following the Rio Grande would add weeks to their travel time, as well as put their supply line dangerously close to Mexico.

With an audible sigh that brought smiles to the other men, Hays continued, "There's not much to it, we're just going to have to find a route."

The 1st lieutenant asked, ""What are the chances that we could angle southwest, towards the Rio Grande and then follow it up to El Paso, Captain?"

"We've been over that before, Ed. While it may ultimately be necessary if we can't find decent watering holes, my preference is to scour the desert and see if there's a more direct viable route. What we're going to do is split the two platoons up and send yours to the southwest. Somewhere to our west are the Limpia Mountains. I want your men to skirt the southern edge of the range, while me and Jed will take his platoon and try going around the north edge."

The last embers of the fire flickered briefly before going out. Hays stirred the coals with a stick and said, "It's late. Tomorrow will be here soon enough. We'll meet back here in ten days, hopefully one or both of our platoons will find a route with water."

The next morning, 1st Lieutenant Edward Brooks led his platoon across the river bed and veered away to the southwest. There were no trails to guide them. What trails they found belonged to those of creatures of the desert. They started and stopped so suddenly, Brooks couldn't help puzzling where they came from and where they went. The further away from the river they rode, the more dust their horses kicked up.

Dry arroyos, little more than bone-dry deep rivulets, crossed his path. They were created by storms and flash floods, as channels for floodwaters to flow back to the Pecos. Every attempt to follow one upstream resulted in fruitless backtracking, as each one invariably ended in the desert. After two days of blistering heat, the men and their horses were tired of the unforgiving Chihuahuan desert. Lieutenant Brook climbed down from his horse and pulled a map from his saddlebag. He penciled in the ending of the Limpia Mountains, as he saw them. His concentration was broken when a voice cried out.

"Indians!"

The pencil broke in his hand. One piece bounced off the saddle and landed in the reddish dirt. He swore and threw the other piece down then looked up. From the northwest a score of warriors casually rode toward them. "Steady boys. Let's see what we've got before we get twitchy. First Sergeant, to me!"

The company's first sergeant had accompanied Lt. Brooks' platoon, while Captain Hays had gone with the second platoon. The sergeant walked over, while holding his hat over his eyes as he tried to discern the warriors' features. His pale blond hair had gone to gray years earlier, Sergeant Maartin Jensen was approaching fifty. He had served in one army or another for the better part of thirty years, first with the Danish army during the Napoleonic Wars then in the United States dragoons, before he finally made his way to Texas, lured by the promise of free land. Sometime after arriving, he decided he'd rather stay in the army until forced into retirement or killed by a Mexican bullet or a Comanche arrow. He wasn't the best shot or the finest rider, but his ability to stay steady and calm when bullets started flying explained why Hays had selected him as senior non-commissioned officer of the Ranger company.

The sergeant retrieved his carbine from the saddle scabbard and said with a strong accent, "What are your orders, Lieutenant?"

Brooks wished he had a spyglass. Was he looking at Comanche, Apache, or some other tribe? He scanned his little command. Most of his Rangers were still mounted. "If you're already on foot, stay afoot, and grab your carbines. Fall in by Sergeant Jensen. Those on horse, to me." He swung back onto his mount and waited for the warriors to come closer.

Six men, who were afoot, joined Sergeant Jensen, with their carbines in hand, pointing in the general direction of the approaching Indians. Another dozen mounted men lined up to the right of Brooks, their hands resting on the butts of their new model revolvers, waiting.

When the Indians were less than a hundred yards away, the young Lieutenant saw they were wearing paint. "Hold fire, boys. Let's wait to see if they're up to any mischief."

From the center of the warriors, a single rider detached himself and with his left hand held before him, slowly rode toward the waiting Rangers. "Lieutenant, they're just boys."

Sure enough, even though they were around three hundred feet away, he could see that despite the fearsome face paint, they were all teenagers. It was impossible to be certain, but he guessed they were between fourteen and eighteen. "Hold steady, let's hear them out. It could be we're dealing with some young bucks wanting to test their mettle by ranging south of the Red River. If they're on their way to Mexico, I'd rather they keep right on going."

From the line of horsemen to Brooks' right, one of the Rangers quipped, "Apart from us and some prairie dogs, I'm damned if I know who they'd be raiding here."

"If you're going to talk in line, Reyes, why don't you join me as we go find out if any of them speak English or Spanish."

The two Rangers came to a stop halfway between the rest of the platoon and the young, mounted warriors. The lone rider approached from the Comanche. His horse was a majestic chestnut mustang. His face was painted white, with black stripes vertically overlaying the white paint. His long, black hair was braided down his back and his left hand remained outstretched. Despite the war paint, Brooks doubted the warrior was older than eighteen. In broken English, the warrior was the first to speak. "I, Naconah. I, we go to big river."

Knowing every eye was focused on him, Brooks chose his words with care, "Naconah, you are in Texas. The Comanche Treaty means you stay north of the Red River. Why are you here?"

With a serious expression on his face, the young warrior shook his head. "No. Treaty say we not raid in Texas. We," he paused, as he searched for the right words, "leave Texas alone. We go to big river." He pointed south, toward Mexico. Then he shifted and pointed to himself and then to Brooks. "Peace."

Brooks looked back toward his men. They waited vigilantly as he and Reyes stood next to the youthful Comanche warrior. After a lengthy minute in which he sized up the young Comanche he finally nodded. "Fair enough, Naconah. You're right. The treaty restricts you to no raiding in Texas."

The Comanche looked around at the parched Chihuahuan desert and said, "What to take? You hide something under rock?"

For a moment, a young Comanche warrior and the Ranger Lieutenant shared a smile at the absurdity of the situation. Finally, Brooks replied, "Leave our rocks alone, Naconah. There are plenty of Mexican rocks on the other side of the Rio Grande."

Before returning to his comrades, the young warrior let out a long breath of relief. There was something reassuring that the young warrior had been just as nervous as he. Even so, neither Brooks nor his men rested easy until the band of Comanche had disappeared to the south.

Over the next few days, Brooks' platoon pushed to the southwest, but found little water that would sustain more than a few dozen men, let alone the battalion of cavalry heading west with Colonel Seguin. On the fifth day, they turned around and retraced their route, hoping Captain Hays and the other platoon had better luck.

When Lt. Colonel Juan Seguin saw Captain Jack Hays at the final depot on the Pecos River on the 20th of June, he was delighted. The movement of the three hundred mounted soldiers had gone better than he had expected. Even the engineers building the military road were making good time and would soon arrive at the third depot. As he watched a physically exhausted Hays approach, a voice in the back of his mind echoed an expression he had heard Buck say, "You think everything is breaking your way, but just wait for it. The other shoe is about to fall."

The expression hadn't made any sense until the night he and Buck had been touring the coastal fort in Galveston. They had stayed at the newest hotel in town. It was the tallest building on the island with three floors. They had been sleeping when they had been woken up by the heavy thud of a shoe hitting the floor above their heads. After a few seconds the second shoe thudded to the floor. Buck had chuckled and explained the expression carried an expectation of waiting for something troublesome to happen. As Hays drew nearer and Seguin saw the pinched expression in the other officer's eyes, his delight fled, and he watched with apprehension for the other shoe to fall.

After ducking under the open tent flap, Hays drew himself up and casually saluted. He was late returning from his effort to find the best route across the desert from the Pecos River to El Paso, and he looked like hell. The younger officer's normally tidy beard was ragged and untrimmed. His eyes had dark circles under them and he looked like he had lost twenty pounds.

Seguin waved him into a camp chair. "Dear God, man, what the hell happened to you?"

Hays collapsed into the chair, which creaked in protest. He took his battered, black wide-brimmed hat from his head, as sand and dirt fell to the ground. Seguin passed his canteen over to the younger officer and Hays tipped it to his lips and gulped the water, as he sought to slake his thirst. He wiped his mouth with his sleeve and finally said, "Colonel, if I had me West Texas and Hell, I believe I'd rent this godforsaken land out and live in Hell."

Seguin raised his eyebrows. "Was it really that bad, Jack?"

"If I said it was worse, I might get close to the truth." Hays knocked some of the dust from his jacket before continuing. "Juan, I took one of my platoons west, looking for the most direct route to El Paso, and as God is my witness, there might be three watering holes within a hundred and fifty miles, if we're going to be charitable about what we call a watering hole."

Seguin glanced down at a map detailing what topographers had previously recorded of western Texas. The space between the Pecos River and El Paso was short on details. "I take it you marked them on your map?"

Hays rooted around in his jacket's interior pocket and produced a small map, where the watering holes had been marked. As Seguin added the locations to his own map, he measured the distances and finally grumbled, "We're going to need to have water casks for the infantry, next spring. That's too far to march infantry with so little water. But setting that aside, Jack, do you think we can take our battalion across that wasteland?"

"Would I want to? No. But can we do it? Yeah, I believe so. But we need to take every bit of water from here that we can haul. It's still going to take us a week to get to El Paso, and I'm blind about the last fifty miles. We turned around about three quarters of the way."

Seguin tersely nodded. "Then we had best get moving. We'll rest today and tomorrow. We'll ride out on the Twenty-second."

It took eight days rather than seven for Seguin's three hundred mounted men to cross the Chihuahuan desert. Seguin was with the lead company that arrived on the north bank of the Rio Grande on the last day of June 1841. Across the river, he could see the town of El Paso del Norte, where the Mexican flag fluttered in the warm, southern breeze. As the long, drawn out column filed down to the river, the horses and their riders spread along the eastern bank where the mounts were able to drink for the first time in nearly a day. As his own horse drank from the river, Seguin looked across at the bustling town of El Paso del Norte, founded by the Spanish in the mid-seventeenth century. It looked like a fine town, only slightly smaller than San Antonio. On his side of the Rio Grande were the few dozen adobe huts of the tiny village of Ysleta, populated by a couple of hundred people descended from the Pueblo tribe to the north.

There was no point in delaying things. He called an officer over to him and gave an order. A few minutes later, from the small mission chapel in Ysleta, a large Texas flag was raised. Seguin and his command had come to enforce the Treaty of Bexar.

He turned and looked back across the river at the Mexican flag, flying over the government building in the town's central plaza. He recalled how fondly his father had spoken of the flag in the years after the constitution of 1824 had been adopted. That dream had died, crushed under the boot heel of Santa Anna and his cronies as they destroyed the dream of a federal republic, replacing it with a central dictatorship. He thought, *"The flag may be the same but the government, sadly is not."*

He turned, grinning as the large Texas flag nearly dwarfed the small mission church over which it flew. For the past six years, the entire Seguin family had dedicated their lives and their fortunes for the success of the nation flying that flag. Where he had not been able to muster any emotional response when looking across the river, that lone star flag, rustling in the breeze, gave him a sense of pride and ownership.

Hays rode up, waving his arm at the town across the river. He and a few of his men had acted as advanced scouts, arriving the previous night. "We've scouted across the river, Colonel, and can confirm they may have a couple of hundred soldiers in town. Like as not, they're armed with those old British trade muskets old Santa Anna seems to favor. Give the order and we'll be across the Rio Grande in no time flat."

The breeze picked up, causing the Mexican flag on the other side of the river to unfurl, billowing in the wind. The sight riveted both men's eyes to the foreign flag. After a moment, Seguin shook his head. "Regrettably our orders only include the portion of El Paso on this side of the Rio Grande, Captain."

He tried to put on a smile as he waved toward the ramshackle village of Ysleta. "This part of El Paso is part of the Republic of Texas, and over there, is the Mexican part of El Paso. President Crockett was explicit that we are not to go any further than the boundary lines stipulated in the Treaty of Bexar."

As they turned and walked away from the river, Hays perked up, "Now that we're here, they can't help but notice our calling card." His eyes swiveled toward the large Texas flag flapping noisily as the wind picked up.

Chapter 3

The horses clambered up the steep trail which meandered alongside the east bank of the Rio Grande River, as the riders followed the trace northward. As Captain Hays led his Rangers north along the *Camino Real de Tierra Adentro*, the old road running from Santa Fe, south to Mexico City, pebbles and small rocks slid down from the route, splashing into the river below. Along the stretch of the trail, the pathway was only a few feet wide, forcing the men to lead their horses single file.

Jack Hays slid his eyes upward, a trickle of perspiration ran down his forehead. The hatband was soaked with sweat in the hundred-degree, July heat. Three days out from Ysleta, the terrain was rocky, as a narrow strip of fertile land quickly gave way to the rugged Las Sierras de los Mansos, a narrow mountain range, running north of Ysleta for thirty miles. His eyes returned to the map spread over the saddle horn, it looked like his force was still a week away from

Albuquerque. More sweat trickled down his face and he grumbled, "What the hell was Juan saying? It's a dry heat, he said. I know where he can shove this dry heat."

As the trail followed the contour of the river, it meandered into a long, narrow valley, where tall grass rustled in the hot southerly breeze. A few cottonwood trees grew along the river's bank. A piercing cry brought him back to the moment, thoughts of Seguin's dry heat forgotten. The two Rangers tasked with scouting ahead raced back toward him. "Captain, there's a bunch of Indians ahead, across the river!"

Around a wide bend in the river, on the opposite bank, a band of Indians rode into view. From his saddlebag, Hays grabbed a spyglass and brought the scene into focus. At a glance, he guessed there were more than a hundred men, women, and children. From the clothing they wore, they didn't look like Comanche, although it had been a few years since he had seen any Comanche against which to make comparison. At the head of the band, riding a mustang stallion was a swarthy, mustachioed man, wearing a sombrero and a serape. As he edged the mustang into the torpid river, the man waved at the Rangers. While the Indians waited on the Mexican side of the river, the man with the sombrero forded the Rio Grande, the water rising no higher than his stirrups at the midpoint

When he came ashore, Hays called to his men, "Let's see what we have here, boys. As you were."

The Rangers settled back in their saddles, warily eyeing the rider as he approached Hays. In the fashion of the plains Indians, he held his palm open, left hand extended, as a sign of peace. Underneath the multicolored serape, he wore a waist-length brown jacket and tan muslin shirt. His pants were the color of roasted coffee beans, as were his boots. He reined in before Hays and said, "Hello, *Señor Capitan*. I am Francisco Ruiz of San Antonio. I didn't expect to find Texas soldiers this far to the west, but you and your men are a happy sight."

By name and appearance, there was something vaguely familiar about Francisco Ruiz, but for the moment, it escaped Hays, so he waited for the other man to continue. "I was appointed by President Crockett to seek out my friends back there," Ruiz gestured across the river at the Indians. "If you would like, I have my commission in my saddlebag."

"That would be appreciated, *Señor* Ruiz."

As the Mexican reached into his saddlebag, Hays allowed his hand to drift toward the butt of his revolver. Ruiz's eyes stayed on Hays and his hand slowed as he reached into his nearest saddlebag. He smiled warmly as he brought out a letter wrapped in wax paper. He handed it over to Hays, who unwrapped the letter and saw President Crockett's unmistakable signature at the bottom of the lengthy epistle. As he read the letter, Hays learned the president had appointed Ruiz as Indian agent to the Mescalero tribe of the Apache people and had tasked him with offering the Mescalero a tract of land in west Texas.

Behind the letter he found a map of the western part of the Republic. In the bend of the Rio Grande River, between El Paso and the Pecos River, several thousand square miles were marked with the initials ALC penciled in.

Hays looked up from the map, "Senor Ruiz, what is an ALC? I'm not familiar with it."

Ruiz smiled apologetically, "You should thank the Cherokee for that, Capitan. President Crockett said to me and several associates of mine who routinely trade with the Lipan Apache south of San Antonio in the disputed territory, to provide the Apache a similar offer to what the Cherokee have built for themselves. With the aid of the Texas Land Office and bank, we bundled up a half-million-acre tract in the bend of the Rio Grande and have chartered a holding company, which owns the land. It's called the Apache Land Cooperative. More than a few of Flacco's people have expressed an interest and we hope to bring as many as fifteen hundred of the Mescalero to live on this land, if they're willing."

Hays thought the idea was crazy, but the president had a habit of crazy ideas. To some, the idea of a specially trained company of elite Rangers would be crazy, he reminded himself. Even so, this sounded risky. "Senor Ruiz, the Apache have not always been friendly to the interests of the settlers in Texas. Has something changed?"

Ruiz ruefully chuckled before replying, "Yeah, when Santana, the local tribal leader for the band over yonder, heard that Chief Bowles of the Cherokee had joined," he paused as he searched for the right word, "I think he said, Texas Tribe, he reached out to the government and asked if it were possible for the Apache to do the same."

This was news to Hays. He hadn't realized Crockett could play something like this as close to the vest as it appeared he had. He could think of several congressmen and senators who would pitch a conniption fit over the idea of seeking to build bridges with the Apache. He realized Ruiz was speaking, "This will give Texas a buffer along more than a hundred miles of the Rio Grande. We get something we want, and Santana and his people get something they want, which is security from the Comanche. Plus, as I understand it, General Travis will pay those who are interested in serving in the army or as scouts with the Rangers. I believe this is what the president would call a 'win-win' agreement."

Hays eyed Ruiz skeptically, but held his peace. He had learned that between General Travis' unorthodox training and President Crockett's unconventional means of governing, they took risks he would not have considered. It left him unsettled, not knowing where things with the Apache might end up, but it was clear this band was permitted to cross into Texas. He returned the letter and map to Ruiz, shook his hand, and wished him luck.

He and his Rangers allowed their horses to rest, grazing among the tall grass and getting their fill of water as Ruiz and his band forded the river. As they rode by, Hays watched as the warriors eyed him and his men, frequently with frank looks of appraisal. It was a bit unnerving to have them pass by so close, obviously taking the measure of his command. As the band climbed up the trail towards Ysleta, Hays shook his head in wonderment. Things in Texas were certainly changing.

The hard-packed dirt street ran parallel to the Rio Grande River, a quarter mile away. Squat, adobe houses lined one side of the road, while the other side was lined with shops. At the end of the road, a small building stood detached from the other businesses on the nearby street, a solitary reminder of better days under imperial Spain. Now with its eagle alertly perched atop a cactus, snake clutched in its talon, the Mexican flag billowed in the hot afternoon breeze. It flew over the Albuquerque customhouse. Several laden wagons were drawn up in front of the building, their teams of mules waiting for drivers to drive them forward. Several guards stood outside the building, as a customs inspector collected taxes from the teamsters.

Most of the town's residents were not Mexicans but were Pueblo, one of the tribes descended from the Anasazi. When three men, dressed in work clothes common to those of the men of the Pueblo, slipped into the town, making their way to a nearby cantina, their arrival went unnoticed. Captain Hays felt ridiculous, his exposed white skin was covered completely in dust and mud. He incredulously eyed his two companions, Corporal Estevan Gonzalez and Private Eduardo Perez, both of whom were dressed in the same stolen garments, neither of whom needed additional coating to hide their features. He was certain by their knowing smiles, they were taking pleasure in his own discomfort.

As the afternoon wore on, they sat in the cantina, ordering drinks, and keeping an eye on the customhouse, where they watched wagons come and go throughout the day. But by nightfall, they were no closer to learning how many soldiers and militia garrisoned the Presidio of Albuquerque than they had been at the beginning.

The next day, they found the main square and the presidio adjacent to it. Through the square moved most of the town's traffic, and the three men split up, still in their disguises, and observed the comings and goings of the presidio's soldiers. By the end of the day, when they met back at the disreputable cantina near the customhouse, Hays was convinced two companies of infantry were stationed in town. But on the periphery of Mexico, where the hand of the central government was seldom felt, the regulars were heavily augmented by militia. Hays was concerned the hundred-man garrison only told part of the tale.

As he plopped into the chair between Gonzalez and Perez, Hays was scratching at the dried mud on his arm when he said in a voice only the three of them would hear, "Damned if I won't be glad to get out of here, boys. What did y'all find out?"

Corporal Gonzalez said, "They've got near enough two companies, Captain. What's hard to estimate is the number of men in the militia. There's less than a thousand people in town, but how many more live in ranchos and farming villages in the surrounding area?"

As a mule brayed when a wagon rolled to a stop at the customhouse, Hays had an idea. "Boys, I think I know a way to find out ..."

Late that night, three figures snuck along the side of the road, hugging tightly to the store fronts, as they made their way toward the customhouse. The few clouds in the sky failed to cover the moon's luminescence, as the street was bathed in a watery silver glow. In front of the customhouse a sentry sat on a bench, his rifle leaning against the whitewashed adobe wall. Hays tapped Perez on the shoulder and pointed toward the sentry and motioned for him to circle around the building.

Despite the moonlight, the Tejano Ranger slunk into the shadows, and after a few minutes, reappeared inching along the customhouse's wall, only a few feet away from the sentry, with his Bowie knife in hand. Like a striking rattlesnake, he lunged the last few feet, and finding the sentry had fallen asleep, reversed the blade and used the knife's handle as a bludgeon, turning the sleeping sentry into an unconscious one.

Hays and Gonzalez sprinted across the ground between the closest store and the customhouse. Each knew their roles as a pile of supplies were collected from the back of a couple of wagons. Everything that could burn was laid against the customhouse's wooden door. They collected books and accounting ledgers, bolts of linen and cotton, and wooden boxes, piling them high. Once they were done, Hays took a jar of kerosene and sluiced it on the mound. He lit a match and tossed it on the pile. With a loud whoosh, the kerosene caught fire, as flames leapt into the air.

As Hays and his men ran out of town, the conflagration quickly reached the thatched roof, causing the flames to climb into the night sky.

Thirty minutes later, the three men joined a fourth Ranger, who had waited the past two days with their mounts a couple of miles from town. Winded from the run, as Hays climbed into the saddle, he turned to watch the result of his handiwork. From two miles away, he watched flames lick into the sky, as sparks and flaming cloth swirled into the superheated air over the burning building. The area around the customhouse was lit up by the roaring flames, and he saw all the wagons in the lot beside the government building were on fire. He wondered if they had been too successful, as he saw flaming embers blowing toward the other buildings on the edge of town.

A church bell had been clanging for several minutes, alerting the citizens of Albuquerque of the fire's imminent danger. Hays retrieved his spyglass and watched people racing around the edges of the inferno. It reminded him of a time as a boy, when he had taken a stick and disturbed an ant mound.

"Let's head back to the camp. Until they get that under control, I doubt they'll send anyone looking for us." Hays turned to the south and risked a short look back, hoping the people of Albuquerque could keep the fire from spreading. Destroying a government building was one thing, burning the town down would only sow seeds of discord against Texas.

When the sun came up, the town had been spared, while the customhouse was a gutted ruin. The denizens of Albuquerque had worked through the night and saved all the nearby buildings from catching fire. Hays was glad to see the town still stood, as he gazed through his spyglass at the town. It took another hour before he saw any sign of pursuit. By the time the sun was high in the morning sky, a large body of mounted trooper rode south. "We got what we came for, boys. It looks like they've got around two hundred between the regulars and the militia."

They returned to the Rangers' bivouac, south of town, and hastily broke camp. They rode south a short way before crossing over the Rio Grande, where the ground grew rocky. From there, they turned to the north and headed for Santa Fe.

Chapter 4

Next to the sturdy wooden door, the window in Will's office was open. His jacket hung on the back of his chair, his waistcoat was unbuttoned, and his sleeves were rolled up past his elbows. The hot, dry wind sweeping in from the Tamaulipan mezquital barely stirred the papers on his desk, as he dabbed the sweat from his brow. He glanced out the window, seeing the clear blue August sky and sighed, not a cloud in sight. Under his breath he muttered, "My kingdom for an air conditioner."

Despite the thick adobe walls, the temperature in the office must have been more than ninety degrees. *"You'd think after more than five years; a guy would get used to this heat."* He had gotten used to it, for the most part, but times like this when he was anxious for news from the west, his mind wandered, and the heat was a good target at which to direct his discontent. His mind needed a break from the reports and from the worry. He picked up a bill from the Schultz Mercantile Store in town. Becky and Henrietta did much of the household shopping there. As he perused it, he saw household staples such as baking powder, sugar, and coffee, as well as supplies for the baby, who was due within the next few weeks. Becky, a thrifty shopper, seldom bought anything for herself, and this bill was no different. She had, however, bought Charlie new clothes. He was nearly thirteen and had recently outgrown his old clothes.

Will eyed the total purchases for the previous month, did a mental conversion in his head as he tallied how much it would be in twenty-first century dollars and whistled through his teeth at the amount. He reached into a drawer and pulled out a ledger and wrote a check for the amount due and signed it. It was drawn on the Commerce Bank, which had recently opened a branch in San Antonio, in addition to its primary office in Galveston and another branch in Houston. He set the check aside, making a mental note to drop it off on his way home.

A shadow crossed in front of the window and a knock at the door drew his attention. "Come in."

The door swung inward and standing there was a tired and very dusty Captain Jack Hays. His once black wide-brimmed hat was stained a grayish brown, where the sweat stains competed with natural bleaching from the brutal West Texas sun, giving the headgear a disreputable appearance. As Will stared at the grungy officer, he briefly realized one benefit to the army's jackets being butternut in color was he couldn't tell where the tannish-brown color of the jacket ended, and the dusty grime began. Hays' normally neat beard was gone, replaced by a bushy, brown rat's nest of matted hair. As the young captain threw a sloppy salute, Will leapt from his chair, "Jack, it's damned good to see you. Get yourself in here and take a seat."

As Hays collapsed into the chair across from Will, the pouches under his eyes made the captain look far older and more weathered than his twenty-five years. He dragged his hat from his head, sending eddies of dust fluttering to the floor around his chair. Setting the hat on the chair's arm rest, he said, "General, it's good to see you, too. We've been on the trail for the past month, riding back from Santa Fe, as you had ordered."

A narrow credenza behind Will's chair contained several decanters of amber liquids, and Will turned and grabbed one and poured a large amount into a glass. He offered it to the other officer and watched as Hays downed the fiery whiskey in a couple of gulps. For a moment, his eyes crossed as he coughed. "Damn my eyes, General, but that hits the spot."

Will leaned back in his chair and waited for Hays to continue.

After setting the empty glass on the table, Hays said, "We arrived at El Paso on June thirtieth with Colonel Seguin and secured the village of Ysleta on this side of the Rio Grande. We raised high our flag then me and my boys went north to Albuquerque. We got there on the tenth of July and scouted out the town. They have two companies of regulars, around a hundred men or so, and probably another hundred militia, most of which are mounted. Our orders notwithstanding, General, I believe we could have captured the town and raised our flag over it."

Will acknowledged the comment with a silent nod, as he indicated Hays to continue.

"From there, we rode north to Santa Fe. It took us three days to get there. While Albuquerque may have close to a thousand folks living there, Santa Fe is an entirely different nut to crack. As best as I can tell, there must be over seven thousand people there. The Mexican governor, a nasty bastard by the name of Armijo, has at least five companies of regulars, and a much larger militia. All told, probably more than a thousand men."

Will grimaced when Hays mentioned the number of soldiers. "Are there any changes to the Mexican army that you could see, compared to five years ago?"

Hays' eyes had slid shut, until the sound of Will's voice jolted them open. "Ah, not that I could see, General. The soldiers we saw all carried those old Brown Bess muskets the Mexicans seem to favor."

Will was of a different mind than Hays. He thought there was world of difference between what the Mexican army would like to have versus what they actually had. This was evidenced by the rifled muskets their light infantry carried. "Did your men see any light infantry armed with the Baker rifle?"

Hays shook his head, no.

Will smiled at the good news. "You've seen both these towns up close, Jack. If we take our battalion of infantry and Seguin's cavalry, do you foresee a problem taking these towns and putting them under our flag?

Wearily, Hays replied, "No, General. Even if they had twice as many men, you'd sweep them away."

Will moved several stacks of papers from his desk, revealing a map covering the entire desktop. He studied his planned route between San Antonio and El Paso, making note of the engineers' progress with the military road. A penciled line was sketched from the Alamo to halfway between the third depot on the intermittently flowing San Pedro river and the fourth, on the Pecos. He shifted his finger over to the spot on the map marked El Paso and traced it along the Camino Real to Santa Fe. "If we leave in February, how long do you think it'll take us to get there?"

When Hays made no reply, Will turned, and saw he was sound asleep.

The open window let in a light breeze, but the officer barely felt it, as he gazed over the capital of Mexico in the valley below. The transplanted Frenchmen was glad his friend, Antonio, had returned to power. He had a magnetic personality, and the Centralists needed a strong hand, after the failure of the Bustamante administration of the past couple of years. Adrian Woll was certain Antonio Lopez de Santa Anna was the person to correct Mexico's faltering ship of state.

He turned away from the breathtaking view and saw his Excellency sitting at the head of a large table made from cherry wood. It was waxed and polished to a reflective shine. Most of the army's senior leadership was present in the room. General Urrea was deep in conversation with Vicente Filisola near a marble support pillar, while General Almonte sat next to his Excellency, quietly talking with *el presidente.*

The last of the officers arrived and Woll hastened to his seat. His Excellency glared at the latecomers, who at least had the good manners to appear embarrassed. Using a cane to support himself, Santa Anna stood. His one leg wasn't enough to support his weight. The wooden leg he had acquired in the brief, unfortunate war with France a few years before, necessitated the cane. "Thank you for coming, gentlemen. As you are all aware, my predecessor, Anastasio Bustamante failed and has left the government in shambles."

Woll was pleased to see the officers in the room giving his Excellency their full attention, as he continued, "He let the Yucatecan rebels declare a rump republic on the peninsula, and now, this latest insult from the *norteamericano* pirates in Texas. Who do they think they are, showing their pirate flag at El Paso del Norte?"

Many of the officers in the room shifted uncomfortably in their chairs. The news had arrived barely a week ago, when the *alcalde* of the town had written, requesting *soldados* to dislodge the Texian mounted troops from the northern side of the Rio Bravo del Norte.

"The time for compromising is over, gentlemen. We're not going to tolerate any more infringements against our territorial integrity. I've assigned my aide-de-camp, General Almonte, to put together a reorganization of the army. I am dismayed, between our permanent regiments and our active reserves, there are well over twenty thousand men in our army, yet, we haven't been able to field anything against Yucatan or Texas yet. That stops now!"

Every officer in the room was staring at his Excellency, Woll included. "While negotiations with the rebels in the Yucatan continue, and there remains a shred of opportunity for peaceful reunification, we're going to focus our efforts on punishing the *norteamericano* pirates. General Woll, my friend, I have decided to assign command of our Northern Army to you."

Woll perked up. There were close to four thousand soldiers in that formation. A sizable plum indeed. Santa Anna continued, "To Hell with trying to push a few hundred cavalry out of Nuevo Mexico. They have had the effrontery to build forts at the mouth of el Rio Bravo del Norte and at Laredo. I want you to put together a plan of attack that removes the fort at Laredo, captures San Antonio de Bexar, and pushes these pirates east of the Brazos."

Woll grinned like a schoolboy with his hand in the candy jar. An independent command, at last. "I shall prepare the plans at once, Excellency."

His Excellency smiled expansively. "When the plans have been completed, I will review them. I want your army ready to march at the beginning of the year."

Woll's mind was already at work on the details. The regiments had been allowed to atrophy under Bustamante. Recruits would need to be sent north, and supplies marshaled for the invasion. The new year was four months away, but there was much to be done. He picked up a pen, dipped it in an inkwell and began making notes.

The shutters on the window rattled as a gust slammed against the building. The mild Texas winter had fled before a bitter norther blowing across the plains from Canada. A small, wood-burning stove sat in the corner, radiating heat throughout the crowded room. Will sat behind the large desk, where a giant rectangular map of the Republic covered nearly every inch. Colonel Sidney Johnston sat opposite him and Major Almaron Dickinson sat to his left and Major Wyatt to his right. Behind them, crowded at the back of the room, were several captains, among whom was Jack Hays.

Johnston chewed on an unlit cigar, as he unfastened the buttons on his greatcoat. "Have you managed to get a full night's sleep yet, sir? I recall after my boy, Billy, was born, he would wake the whole house with his ruckus. My Henrietta, God rest her soul, would climb out of bed to feed, or change his diaper. That went on for months before he started sleeping through the night."

Will didn't bother stifling the yawn. "Yeah. Elizabeth has been sleeping through the night for the last couple of weeks. But before, Charlie came up to me and told me he wanted to join the army and march off to war so he could get some sleep."

After the officers stopped laughing, Johnston said, "General, over the past few months, we've increased the army by the newly authorized numbers, we now have fourteen companies of infantry, ten of which should be ready to march in three weeks. We have three regular companies of cavalry and nine of Rangers, including Captain Hay's special Ranger company and three batteries of artillery."

Will nodded. He and Johnston knew the composition of the army by heart. But hearing Johnston recite the numbers to the other officers helped Will to imagine the details in his mind. "In addition to the infantry and Captain Hays' Rangers, one battery of artillery will accompany the army to Santa Fe. They'll meet up with Seguin's three cavalry companies at Ysleta, and from there, it's on to Santa Fe."

Will calculated the math and liked the numbers. "We'll have seven hundred fifty infantry, around a hundred eighty cavalry and forty artillery. Add in our logistical support and that's roughly a thousand soldiers. Very good, Colonel. What does that leave us with here?"

Johnston reached into his coat pocket and retrieved a page full of notes, which he scanned before replying, "There'll be a company of regular infantry here at the Alamo, along with a battery of artillery. Two more companies are securing our supply line to Ysleta. Another company of infantry is stationed at Fort Moses Austin at Laredo, and another battery of artillery at Galveston. I'm not certain about Major Caldwell's current disposition of Rangers, but two of the Ranger companies Colonel Seguin used to capture Ysleta have been returned to Caldwell."

Will frowned at the thought of leaving barely a hundred soldiers at the Alamo. If Santa Anna tried anything it would leave San Antonio at a significant disadvantage. He dismissed the idea, given the level of chaos to which the Mexican government had sunk. "What about supplies? It does us no good to get out there with our army if we can't keep it supplied."

Johnston quirked a sardonic smile at Will and said, "At the moment, things are well in hand, sir. The military road between San Antonio and the far west has been extended over five hundred miles. Our engineers are less than a hundred miles from Ysleta now, and we expect them to complete that stretch of the road before we catch up to them. All four of our depots are adequately stocked with supplies and will be able to support the army as we move west."

Apart from the 'we' everything else was as expected. Will braced himself.

"Sir, my place, as colonel of infantry is at the head of our infantry. If I may speak boldly, General Travis, it's not appropriate for you, as commander of all Texian forces, to go off seven hundred miles across country on this expedition, especially when you have perfectly capable officers that you can send."

This was the same tired argument Sid had been pitching to him for the past week. Johnston argued that as Colonel of the Infantry battalion, he should command the field army. He also argued he was a very competent officer and had earned the opportunity. Will actually agreed with Johnston's opinion of himself. But he wasn't going to acknowledge this ongoing argument with Johnston mirrored an earlier one with President Crockett, who had traveled to San Antonio to see his newest grandchild a few weeks earlier. The two men had been sitting in the kitchen at his house, when the president asked him who would be leading the army to capture Santa Fe. When Will told Crockett that he intended to lead the army, his father-in-law asked him not to go and to send Johnston instead. Everything he had done over the past six years to build a capable army and the logistical support the army required was leading to the Santa Fe campaign. The truth of the matter was Will wanted to see his army in action and staying in San Antonio would deprive him of the opportunity.

When he asked the president if he were ordering him to not go, Crockett shook his head. "No, I won't stop you. I know all the effort you've put into this."

Will hadn't let the president stop him and he wasn't about to let Johnston succeed where Crockett had failed. "Colonel, I appreciate your concern, but I have complete confidence in your ability to manage things here until I return. You'll have the companies here and at Laredo, as well as the artillery. If there are any troubles that arise, you've also got the reserves of the San Antonio military district. I believe General McCulloch has done an excellent job equipping and arming the reserves hereabouts."

Johnston tried speaking, "General, I ..."

Will cut him off. "That's the end of the discussion, Colonel Johnston. You're staying, and that's final."

Chapter 5

12th March 1842

Clouds billowed across an overcast sky as Will stood next to one of the army's six-pounder field guns. As he held the telescoping spyglass in his hand, he thought about the last two months. *"My army, the Republic's army,"* he corrected himself, had crossed eight hundred miles of dusty South Texas prairie and Chihuahuan desert over the past fifty days. The military road from San Antonio had been completed to Ysleta. Even so, the last two hundred miles to the dusty west Texas outpost were difficult, with the army hauling wagons full of water from the Pecos to keep the troops and horses hydrated.

The situation between Ysleta and El Paso del Norte remained tense. President Crockett's orders expressly prohibited Texian incursion south and west of the Rio Grande, while the Mexican *alcalde* in El Paso either lacked the interest or the capability to challenge Texas' claim to the east and north of the river. When Will's army of a thousand men passed through Ysleta, it would not have surprised him to learn the rotund official, on the other side of the river, nearly set the presidio's chapel ablaze in his overzealous effort to light candles to the Blessed Virgin.

The *Camino Real de Tierra Adentro*, had once allowed traders to travel quickly between Mexico City and the extreme reaches of the Spanish Empire for more than two hundred years. But now the portion between Ysleta and Santa Fe had fallen into disrepair. *"No doubt active raids by both the Mescalero Apache and the Comanche haven't helped to keep the old road maintained,"* Will thought drily. In contrast to the newly constructed Military Road between San Antonio and Ysleta, traveling the *Camino Real* was slow going. From Ysleta, the army took nearly three weeks to reach Santa Fe. He had left a company of infantry to secure Albuquerque, although the Mexican garrison had fled to Santa Fe with the news of the Texian army's march.

Now, the army was deployed on the fields east of Santa Fe and the wind picked up and Will grabbed his black, wide-brimmed hat, saving it from blowing away, and looked to his right and left, where the six field pieces were lined up. The young artillery captain stood close at hand, ready to put his guns into action for the first time in combat. Nearly a hundred yards in front of him, six companies of the 1st Texas Infantry were deployed, using the new model tactics he had developed. They covered a front of more than four hundred yards.

Will grimly smiled as he raised the telescoping spyglass to his face and studied the Mexican line. At best guess, Governor Manuel Armijo had managed to collect together a battalion's worth of regulars. Will studied the center of the line. There were four hundred regular *soldados* holding the center of the Mexican line. Each *soldado* wore a dark blue jacket, with his cartridge box and bayonet hanging from crossed white-dyed leather straps across his chest. Most of the *soldados* wore bleached white cotton pants, although some wore blue that matched their jackets. Each regular wore a tall shako hat, reminiscent of the headgear worn during the Napoleonic wars a generation previous.

Two militia battalions were formed, one on either side of the regulars. Will guessed another thousand men had been mobilized. Most of the militia wore white uniforms, common among the active militia regiments which made a sizable portion of Mexico's army, although a few wore the same blue jackets of the regulars. Some even wore civilian jackets. As Will swept his spyglass across the front of the Mexican line, he saw a few members of the militia had brought their personal weapons, ranging from exquisite hunting rifles to ancient shotguns.

Armijo's commander had deployed his densely packed army across a front of three hundred yards. Several dozen mounted men were on either end of the Mexican line. In contrast, Lt. Colonel Seguin had deployed two of his cavalry companies on the left flank of the Texian line, while Hay's Rangers and the third company of cavalry secured the right flank.

Briefly, the clouds overhead opened and the weak, March sun shined down. A glint of gleaming brass brought Will's attention back to the center of the Mexican line, where he saw a couple of teams of oxen pulling two bronze guns. So little care had been taken with the old field pieces they had oxidized to an ugly green hue. *"Should I have the artillery open fire on their guns? It's an even guess that those old guns are more of risk to their gunners than to us."*

He shook his head. "On their own heads, be it."

The artillery captain said, "I'm sorry, sir, what did you say?"

Will glanced at the eager, young officer, "Nothing of importance, Captain. It looks like everyone's here for the party. Let the dancing commence. Suppress those two guns of theirs then focus your fire on the center of their line."

The young officer saluted and raced over to the nearest gun. He spoke to the gunnery sergeant, who made a small adjustment to the elevating screw. Then he used a vent pick to pierce the canvas bag of gunpowder before sticking a fuse into the vent. He took a linstock from another member of the gun crew and blew on the smoldering match. He looked back at the captain, waiting.

"Fire!"

He touched the match to the fuse and stepped back. A second later, the end of the barrel disappeared in a cloud of white gunpowder smoke, as the gun recoiled from the concussive blast. The round screamed downrange. It missed the two old guns, kicking up a dust cloud several hundred feet to the rear. The captain continued down the line of guns, encouraging them. The number two gun fired, sending the round crashing just beyond the Mexican line of battle. The number three gun's round overshot the Mexican guns, landing next to the oxen team behind them. The round was a solid shot. It careened across the ground. The oxen startled, were bucking in their harnesses, and trying to run away.

The two Mexican guns responded with their own counter-battery fire. The first round landed more than a hundred yards to the left of the Texas battery, skipping along until it casually rolled to a stop. The second round landed in front of the Texas infantry, where it careened into a crouching rifleman, turning him into a bloody pulp.

The round from the Texas battery's number four gun ricocheted off the ground in front of the Mexican line and knocked a gaping hole in the line of regulars. The next round, from number five gun smashed into one of the Mexican gun carriages, turning one of the wheels into deadly, flying splinters, and upending the old barrel.

The young captain was shouting to his men, "Load with shell, set the range for six hundred yards! Independent fire!" Battery C's well-trained men reloaded their guns, swapping the solid shot for explosive shells. Ninety seconds after the order was given, the guns resumed firing their deadly projectiles.

While the first Mexican gun crew were scattered on the ground, some writhing from the deadly splinters, others were still, dead where they fell, the second gun's crew was killed when a shell exploded directly overhead. Several other shells detonated over the line of Mexican infantry.

Will had refocused his spyglass on the Mexican line, and he saw the explosions were wreaking havoc on the enemy. He was tempted to order the guns to cease firing and send in his infantry. But as the shells rained shrapnel down on the unprotected *soldados*, he stayed his hand, and watched as the guns sent more exploding shells into and above the enemy line.

It started on the Mexican left flank. The battalion of militia had been wavering after the first shell exploded over the infantry, but after several shells had exploded overhead, killing and injuring dozens of *soldados*, men who had been huddling on the ground realized there was no cover to be found from the murder from above, began breaking from the line, running past officers who screamed at them to return. Some waved swords, slapping *soldados* on the backs with the flats of their blades, as they ran by.

The right flank broke only moments later. As the frightened men bolted from the ranks, one of the officers pulled a pistol from his belt and screamed at the men to stand and fight. But what was there to fight? The Texian soldiers stood nearly half a mile away while their artillery poured death down among them. One of the *soldados* dropped his old, rusty Brown Bess trade musket and tried running past the enraged officer, who raised his pistol and shot the man in the head, dropping him at the officer's feet. Another soldier watched his friend die at the hands of his officer. He raised his musket to his shoulder and fired. As the soldier fled back toward Santa Fe, he skirted past the bloodstained spot where his friend's blood soaked the same ground as the officer, who bled out beside him.

In only a few short moments, both militia battalions streamed back toward Santa Fe. All that remained on the field of battle, opposing the Texas army were the regular Mexican *soldados*. Their ranks had been thinned by the shells, and they had taken whatever cover they could find, but they had not broken. Beneath cottonwood and hackberry trees and behind scrub brush the regulars sheltered and waited.

Will's smile, watching the retreating militia, was cold, not touching his eyes. Scores of *soldados* had fallen under the artillery shells. Now was the time for the infantry to take control of the battlefield. He ordered the artillery to cease fire and he stepped to the front of the deployed soldiers. "Men of the 1st Regiment, let's drive the rest of the enemy from the field! Open order, advance!"

Across a front more than a thousand-feet wide, the army advanced. Each four-man rifle team moved seamlessly together, they were the building blocks of each advancing company. Two men led, the other two, following. The regulars of the Mexican army waited helplessly as they watched the undulating advance of the Texians. Their muskets were not effective much beyond a hundred yards, and there was nothing they could do but watch as the advancing formation came within a quarter mile.

With his sword drawn, Will walked across the dry and cracked ground a few feet behind the advancing infantry. When his men were three hundred yards away from the remnants of the Mexican line, their officers ordered the riflemen to stop. The soldiers of the 1st Infantry waited, their breech-loading rifles pointed downrange, toward the Mexicans. As Will stared across the field, he felt a moment's pang of sorrow. The men opposite his army didn't deserve the hell they were about to receive. He whistled through his teeth in consternation. It wasn't fair what was about to happen, but it didn't stop him from shouting, "Take aim," then a second later, "fire!"

Six companies, seventy-five men each. More than four hundred rifles fired as one. Even though the Mexican line was broken up and taking cover where it could be found, dozens of men fell, as bullets ripped into exposed flesh. In less than a minute, the average soldier had fired eight rounds from their Model 1842 Sabine breech-loading rifle. More than three thousand rounds had torn through the area inhabited by the Mexican regulars. They broke, fleeing back to Santa Fe as fast as they could run. Some shed their muskets and cartridge boxes, determined to run faster than their companions. They had never had the opportunity to fire their weapons at Will's Texians.

"Cease fire!"

Along the entire length of the Texian front, the soldiers screamed forth fearsome whoops and hollered at the top of their voices, as they watched the remnants of the Mexican line stream back toward the town. Many years before the transference, Will had heard a recording from the 1930s in which some septuagenarians had demonstrated the rebel yell. Chills swept up his spine as he heard the same noise echoing across the battlefield.

The battalion advanced, crossing the last few hundred yards to the slaughter that had been the Mexican line. The regulars, who had stayed the longest and endured the worst of the Texian assault had suffered heavy casualties. Many of the wounded lay where they had fallen, their comrades, made no effort to save them. Several score more were dead or wounded where the militia battalions had earlier stood. The officers and NCOs of the 1st Texas took firm control of their men as they swept through the devastated line. Will could never shake the memories of battles like San Jacinto or the Alamo or the Goliad Massacre from his mind, even though they happened a world away and lived only in his memories. As commander of the Texian army, he would be damned if he would allow a massacre on his watch.

Will found Major Wyatt and said, "Major, I want you to take two of the reserve companies and secure the field. Get Doctor Smith up here with his orderlies. He can attend to these wounded until we can get them to a hospital in town." No matter how talented he found the capable Dr. Ashbel Smith, nearly two hundred wounded Mexicans would overwhelm anyone. Once the town was firmly under his control, he would find every available doctor from Santa Fe to assist.

Several companies had continued through what had once been the Mexican line and were approaching Santa Fe. Will ran to catch up with them. As his heels slammed into the dry ground, he wished he had ridden his horse into battle, at least then he wouldn't have to run to catch up to his advancing soldiers. With his heart pounding in his chest, and gasping for air, he caught up with the lead company on the edge of town. The first couple of streets were completely deserted. Homes were shuttered, and storefronts had their windows boarded up. As Will scanned the scene, it was apparent the citizens of Santa Fe were significantly less sure of victory than Mexican Governor Manuel Armijo had been.

As rifle teams worked their way into town, heading toward the central plaza, the sound of gunfire started up again a few blocks away. Will joined with a few rifle teams as they carefully worked their way down a street, which led to Santa Fe's central plaza. He watched two men from one team sprint across the street, taking shelter in the recess of a door, while the other two riflemen covered them. Urban warfare was something he hadn't taken the time to consider when he wrote the training manual. As he watched his riflemen crouching in doorways, Will vowed to do something about the oversight. It was another area where he had not thought things through as thoroughly as he should have. As he joined the two soldiers on the opposite side of the road, he wondered what else he had missed. Despite two tours in Iraq before the transference, it felt as though he was constantly discovering something new that he should have considered. They had arrived at the edge of the plaza and he set the unsettling thoughts aside. There wasn't anything to be gained second-guessing himself in the middle of Santa Fe street.

He peered around the corner of the adobe building and saw the central plaza spread out before him. The presidio took up an entire side of the plaza, and he saw the Mexican flag flying over the long, barricaded building. Muzzles poked out the narrow slits for windows. Will swore as a musket ball chipped the adobe clay brick above his head. Involuntarily, he ducked, drawing chuckles from the riflemen behind him. A couple of rifle teams had already entered the plaza and were working their way across the open space, toward the presidio's main gate. Bullets careened off the ground, and one of the riflemen dropped his weapon and fell noiselessly to the ground, as a pool of blood soaked the ground beneath him.

The handful of riflemen moved while they reloaded their breechloaders. They fired back at the flashes of gunfire coming from the presidio, but after two more were hit, the remainder fell back and found shelter on the opposite side of the plaza.

When he saw another rifle team start across the plaza, Will decided the odds didn't favor a direct assault yet. "Enough of this," he said to the soldiers nearby. He called out, "Get your asses back here, boys!" When the advancing soldiers saw who ordered them to retreat, they fell back, taking up defensive positions in the buildings opposite the presidio.

Will reached into his tunic and pulled out a small notebook and scribbled a message. He tore it off and turned to the nearest soldier behind him, "Give this to Major Wyatt. We'll get one of our guns brought up here and make quick work for that gate yonder."

As the messenger scampered down the street in the direction from which the soldiers had come, the other riflemen found positions in the nearby buildings from which they returned fire on the Mexican *soldados* in the presidio.

Thirty minutes passed before one of the six-pounders was brought forward from the battlefield. The artillerists set the bronze gun up in the side road and angled the barrel toward the presidio's heavy wooden gate. The *soldados*, now surrounded, saw the field piece, and opened fire at the artillerists. A couple of men were knocked down, injured from the gunfire from the presidio and the riflemen returned fire, attempting to suppress the gunfire from the presidio.

Riflemen jumped in to assist the cannon's loaders. They finished loading a solid shot and aimed it at the presidio's gate. The gunner lit the fuse and stepped away from the gun and waited. An instant later, the round flew across the plaza, smashing into the wall beside the door, sending a jagged chunk of adobe crashing to the ground. As the riflemen tried to send enough aimed fire through the windows, the artillerists rushed to reload the gun. Less than a minute later, the gun fired again. The shot slammed against the gate, sending heavy splinters flying about.

While the artillerists raced to reload the gun, a white flag waved from one of the windows. The Battle of Santa Fe was over.

Before twilight several hundred men had been put under guard in the plaza. Nearly all the regulars and most of the militia had been accounted for. Next to the plaza, in the Church of San Francisco, Doctor Ashbel Smith had set up a hospital, after transferring the battlefield's injured to the sacred space. A few other doctors from town had volunteered with him to save as many of the wounded as their skills allowed. As the doctors worked into the evening, the cries of the wounded echoed across the plaza, adding to the despair among the vanquished Mexican *soldados*.

Inside the Palace of the Governors, the cries of the wounded from the nearby church reached Will's ears. The palace was within the presidio's walls and now Texian soldiers patrolled the halls where a few hours before governor Armijo's regulars had patrolled. Few residents of the town had yet to venture from their homes as Will's army had taken control of the town. One who had, stood before Will. Miguel Archuletta was the town's *alcalde*. He was dressed in the finery of a Spanish don, standing with hat in hand, waiting to be acknowledged. Correspondence was scattered across the large table, which until that morning had belonged to Governor Manuel Armijo.

Anger burned in Will's eyes, as he stared down the *alcalde*. "Where the hell is that great worthy, Governor Armijo? What he has left here demands an immediate answer, Mr. Archuletta."

Miguel Archuletta may have been the mayor of a provincial town on the edge of Mexican territory, but he was a sophisticated gentleman, educated at the best schools in Mexico City. He had not been addressed as "*Alcalde*, or *Señor* Archuletta. No, just the flat, *norteamericano* "mister." Even so, it didn't take an intelligent man to know that Will was furious.

"General Travis, I regret the, ah, worthy Governor Armijo was last seen riding west with a few mounted guards this morning."

Will swore. He looked down at the finely crafted, imported table and saw the documents he had scattered across the desk a little while before. While Will's Spanish had improved over the previous half dozen years, he relied upon Juan Seguin to translate the correspondence which had drawn his ire. The troubling letter was from the office of the President of Mexico. Will waved it under the nose of the *alcalde*.

"Santa Anna, God damn that one-legged, stinking bastard, ordered your superior to raise an army of a thousand men for the purpose of reclaiming Ysleta from us. When was he planning on carrying out these orders?"

The *alcalde* shrugged. "Mexico City is a long way away, General Travis. I do not know that Governor Armijo had any plans to fulfill *el presidente's* orders."

Will waved toward the Mexican official and a sentry guided him out of the governor's personal office. Colonel Juan Seguin sat at the table, rubbing his eyes after translating a small stack of papers.

"Juan, I don't understand how Santa Anna keeps getting power in Mexico City. That jackass has more lives than a cat."

Seguin's shrug nearly matched the *alcalde's* from a few minutes before. "He's charismatic, Buck. And I hear the women love watching him prance around Mexico City on his black horse."

Will glared at his friend and fellow officer. "His orders to Armijo don't bother me. What has me seeing red is the rest of this bullshit. He's ordered General Woll into Texas with four thousand men, Juan. Where the hell are we in all this? Sitting in God forsaken Santa Fe!"

Will shook with anger and helplessness, as he realized how serious a blunder he had made. The correspondence from Mexico City did more than simply provide orders for the capture of Ysleta. It provided the highlights of plans already underway to recapture Texas. He was seven hundred miles, as the crow flies, from San Antonio and the documents on the table revealed the Mexican Army of the North, under Adrian Woll was to invade Texas, commencing on 12 March 1842. Will closed his eyes, in defeat. This was the 12th of March.

Chapter 6

The doors to the courtyard were closed. The late winter wind blew frigid air down from the Rockies. Gusts rattled the glass window panes in their frames. The fireplace in the office of the governor crackled and warmed the room. The large, elegant table which had served Governor Armijo as his desk was covered with a large map of the western portion of Texas. Will was perched on the corner of the table. Major Peyton Wyatt, the 1st Infantry's executive officer sat in a highbacked chair next to him. Lt. Colonel Juan Seguin sat in an identical chair beside the major. Captain Hays and several other company commanders crowded into the office, too.

Will had slept poorly the previous night, and his temper simmered below the surface. The fact that Santa Anna had reacted to the previous year's enforcement of the Treaty of Bexar's boundary limits by sending an army north had surprised him. The political chaos in central Mexico was so destabilizing, he had thought it unlikely President Bustamante, Santa Anna's predecessor had the will to contest Texas' enforcement of the treaty. In a moment of honesty, he knew his anger was directed inward at being so far away from Texas' settlements with most of the army and losing anything to Santa Anna galled worse than he could have imagined.

When the last officer had come in and closed the door to the office, Will said, "Alright, gentlemen. We need to figure out how to get ourselves out of this this predicament." The other officers grew quiet, turning their attention to him, as he continued, "We're here to discuss options. As I see it, we have two from which to pick. Between us and San Antonio is seven hundred miles, as the crow flies. You all have read the correspondence from Mexico City, that the Alamo and the town are the Army of the North's primary objective. If we were to take off and go directly cross country, it will take us at least five weeks to relieve the town and fort."

He paused, watching the neutral expressions on his officers' faces, before continuing, "The other option is to retrace our steps. That will add nearly two hundred miles to the route. That would put us getting back to San Antonio around the end of April. Either option gives Santa Anna's army an intolerable amount of time to wreak havoc on our settlements." Will grimaced, not liking the taste of any of his words.

Major Wyatt picked up from where Will had stopped, "Alright, men, let's discuss the first option."

Captain Hays approached the table and stared at the map for a lengthy moment. "That would be one hellacious march, General, but I believe we could pull it off. That stretch across the Chihuahuan desert will be the most brutal part. But if we take all the food and provisions from Santa Fe we should be good for several weeks, I'd think." He drew a line with his finger between Santa Fe and the westernmost Ranger fort on the Red River. "Once we get to our frontier forts along the Comancheria, we could use them for supplies as we hurry back east."

Lt. Colonel Seguin snorted. "Captain, what in the hell do you intend to feed our mounts? It's the middle of March and you are proposing we hightail it back to San Antonio across the desert. Even if we could take enough feed and supplies to cross the desert, it would burden and slow us down, and I'm not convinced there's enough fodder in Santa Fe to get us across that stretch of Hell."

Seguin stood and walked over to the fireplace, where he warmed his hands for a moment. "Jack, I think what bothers me the most about going across country isn't so much your idea but what it means for what we have accomplished here. Imagine what these poor folks are going through, here. We've just captured their town from the governor's *soldados*. If we up and loot the town dry just to race back across country, it'll take a lifetime to build up goodwill with our newest citizens, and I worry if we do so, starvation would stalk the land hereabouts."

Listening to his officers debate the options let Will ignore his own anxiety and worry for the moment.

When Major Wyatt joined in the conversation, he listened to his second-in-command. "My heart wants to throw ourselves eastward by the most direct path, just like you, Captain Hays. I know if we could round up enough supply wagons we could move our entire force across the desert. But my mind must consider the logistical nightmare such a proposal would require." He looked back to Will. "General, I counsel caution. While we may be the largest component of Texas' army, we're not the only arrow in the quiver of Texas' defenses. Colonel Johnston and General McCulloch, I believe will mobilize our reserves and militia when they become aware of Santa Anna's attack. They may have no choice but to trade land for time, while they work to assemble the reserves, but within as little as a month, McCulloch can pull together between three and five thousand men. Even more than that, should President Crockett order Tom Rusk to mobilize the rest of the militia." The major paused, his soft drawling Virginian accent momentarily easing the tension in the room. "I believe we have the finest and best trained men in the Texas army. Hell, in the world, to speak candidly. I would caution against recklessly risking them in a headlong, emotional lurch across the Chihuahuan desert. That kind of behavior is best left for our enemies."

Will's nod was nearly imperceptible, but he realized he had been more interested in racing back to the Alamo without regard to the consequences. Seguin, who normally was the most likely to offer up reckless options, had reminded everyone in the room there were political considerations worth remembering, and Wyatt had offered up a prescient reminder that there were ample defensive forces back in the settled parts of the Republic. His lips twitched up as he thought about Hays' bold suggestion. As the commander for Texas' nascent special operations force, he provided a risky and audacious option.

Will chuckled, mirthlessly. "Our hearts definitely lead us to hasten to our Republic's defense. But you're right, Major, as much as I hate to admit it, we need to listen to the counsel of our heads instead of our hearts."

Having set aside the first option, Will had a few ideas about how they should proceed. Instead, he turned to Wyatt. "Major, what are you thinking?"

Wyatt stood and looked over the map. "I'm glad we've set aside the idea of heading off across the Chihuahuan desert, if for no other reason that while a crow can fly seven hundred miles, any route we would have taken would meander and add travel time. Add to that, as Colonel Seguin mentioned, doing so would likely destroy any goodwill with folks in Santa Fe, if we looted the town of available food and fodder, requiring a large garrison we couldn't afford.

"On the other hand, let's look at what it will take to get us back by our original line of march. We need only requisition enough food between Santa Fe and Albuquerque to get us back to Ysleta, it is likely they'd not miss it very much. If we pay for it, they'd likely miss it even less."

He pulled the map closer to him and set his finger on El Paso del Norte, on the southern bank of the Rio Grande, opposite from Ysleta. "There's a two hundred mile stretch of the Military Road between Ysleta and the nearest of our supply depots on the Pecos. What we can't take here in Santa Fe because of political considerations," he paused, smiling malevolently, "I think we can take from the Mexicans in El Paso. After all, Santa Anna's correspondence is a declaration of war against Texas. In response, I say, we raid it, plundering everything we'll need for the next few hundred miles."

Will studied the map and slowly nodded. "That makes sense, Major. If we march out within the next twenty-four hours, we could be knocking on the doors of El Paso before the first of April. What do we have in Ysleta currently?

"Just a company of Rangers, sir. The engineers who laid out the military road are likely somewhere between Ysleta and Albuquerque, repairing the Camino Real in between the two towns. Probably another twenty soldiers there."

Will glanced up at Seguin, seeking his reaction. "What do you think, Juan? Do you think this will work?"

The Tejano had earned a reputation for prickly notions of honor, especially when it came to how non-Anglos were treated in Texas. But he wore a thoughtful expression. After studying the map, he nodded. "Yes, sir. I think so. As far as I'm concerned, Mexican towns and settlements outside of the treaty boundaries are legitimate targets. I think we all agree, Santa Anna is at war with Texas. Had Mexico accepted our peace treaty back in '36, this wouldn't even be an issue. We can expect the Army of the North to capture Laredo and San Antonio, and even more if they are able. El Paso del Norte is simply our measured response to Santa Anna's depredations."

Hays asked, "When we capture the town, do we burn it to the ground?"

Seguin blanched. "Absolutely not. Doing something like that would give Santa Anna something to rally the Mexican people behind. Right now, he holds power because he controls or intimidates enough of the factions in Central Mexico. If we torch a city, that could stir more than a few factions and give Santa Anna more support. That would bode ill for Texas."

He stood and waved his hand over the map, "Jack, we can't do anything about Santa Anna calling us a bunch of *norteamericano* pirates. But we will not act like pirates, torching a town. I know we'll plunder it for food and fodder. We do that so that our army is supplied, not because we are capricious. After six years, most Tejanos have truly embraced the Republic. In that span of time, we've had one president. The Mexican government has changed hands like a hot potato. I can't speak for every Tejano, but I believe President Crockett has been a dear friend to every Texian whether his skin is white, brown, or red. All any of us want is a fair shake, and Texas provides each of us the best bet to receive it. When we capture El Paso, we will take all the food and provender we need, and we'll burn the military supplies we don't need, but we leave the people and their town alone, to the largest extent possible."

Hays looked ashamed for asking his question. Will decided it was time to end the meeting. They all had plenty to do if they were to leave within twenty-four hours. "We should all heed Colonel Seguin's wisdom, men. Make sure every soldier knows that there will be no individual looting, and any rapists will find themselves on the wrong side of military justice and a short rope."

Seguin held back after the other officers had hurried out. He smiled apologetically. "Jack's a little more aggressive than I think is good, Buck, but he means well."

Will stifled his own laughter, having thought the same thing only a few minutes earlier. "He's our bulldog, Juan. We've trained him and his men to hold nothing back and to be bold. I can't begrudge him for advocating a position both of us wish was possible."

Seguin's shoulders slumped. "Ain't that the sorry truth? I can't tell you how much I miss my Maria and the children. Knowing there's a hostile army coming north toward them, and I'm helpless to do anything to help. I'd be lying if I said it wasn't tearing me up inside."

Will sagged into the governor's soft, leather chair. "I can't get my mind off Becky, Charlie, and Elizabeth. No matter what kind of officer people may think of me, right now I feel like a horrible husband and father. Galivanting over here in Santa Fe, when my wife and kids need me the most."

The sun had not yet risen above the gently rolling hills to the east of Santa Fe, but the orange hues played across the early morning sky. The moist vapor cloud escaped his horse's mouth as the beast stamped its iron-shod hoof against the crystalline dew-covered brown grass. Birds waking up to another dawn were interrupted in their songs by the piercing sound of a bugle. Will decided if an army had to march, then the fourteenth day of March was as good a day as any. The lack of clouds in the sky, if it held, meant the morning chill should retreat as the sun rose into the sky, promising a pleasant day to be on the trail.

Despite every effort, he was still angry that after fighting and spilling blood, and capturing the town, they were forced to abandon their objective. He had argued with himself throughout the night to leave a portion of the battalion here, to defend their hard-won gain. The uncertainty of what they would find when they returned east was part of the reason for bringing the entire army back. The clincher though was when he asked himself how quickly Texas could resupply or support any troops left in Santa Fe, he didn't know. The fear of a stronger Mexico lopping off bits and pieces of the Texas army was something he couldn't shake, especially when he thought of the little outpost on the Rio Grande at Laredo. Fort Moses Austin was the first line of defense against a Mexican invasion of Texas. Knowing the soldiers at Laredo were at the mercy of an advancing army made him wary of creating a similar situation at Santa Fe.

The medical doctors in Santa Fe had taken over the hospital Dr. Smith had set up, and he and his orderlies were with the Texian soldiers, waiting for the order to march. Hundreds of newly minted Texian citizens turned out, on the edge of town, watching the thousand soldiers as they, too, waited for the order.

The sun finally peeked over the hills east of town, bathing the assembled people in a warm, yellow light. It sparkled off the rifle barrels and reflected off the bayonets. Will turned and looked at the people of Santa

Fe. Many of their faces smiled, glad to see the Texians leaving, others showed their uncertainty. The very presence of the Texian army was proof to many that Mexico was no longer able to protect its northernmost outposts. As the Texian army marched south, the citizens of Santa Fe were left with promissory notes for food and fodder they had requisitioned and a promise from the Texian general they would return soon. Will had also left a warning. If, when the Texian army returned, the city was under the Mexican flag, those responsible would be labeled as traitors, and given a traitor's punishment. It was a harsh warning for people who only days before had woken up as Mexicans and now found themselves under the Texas flag. Even though the order was his, Will thought the measure unjust.

The people of Santa Fe had been citizens of Mexico until Will's army had enforced the treaty of Bexar. They had thought of themselves as Mexican citizens and worse, as far as Will was concerned, would act as Mexican citizens in the absence of the Texian army. It left a sour taste in his mouth leaving such a harsh warning. But as he watched his soldiers marching south, his first duty was to Texas and the army. If his warning, no matter how harsh, acted as a deterrent to future rebellions, and saved the lives of his men, then it would be worth it.

He urged his horse to a gallop, as he rode by the marching riflemen, and couldn't shake the matter. Even after all these years stranded in the past, at his core, he was still Will Travers. He was a twenty-first century man. It bothered him more than he anticipated to leave the order behind that any attempt to reconnect with Mexico was a death sentence. By the time he reached the head of the column he wondered how much of the man who woke up in William B. Travis' body still remained.

Chapter 7

12th March 1842

The residents of the town had taken to calling their new village, 'Nuevo Laredo,' in honor of the town from which they had fled, when the Texian forces had claimed the northern side of the Rio Bravo del Norte. By March of 1842, nearly two dozen adobe brick houses surrounded the small plaza. Scaffolding ringed the low walls of the small church, under construction along the south side of the plaza.

On top of the wooden frame of the scaffold, a tall officer balanced himself on a wide wooden plank. His brown hair, receding from his forehead, except for the widow's peak, rustled in the cool, morning breeze. Adrian Woll had been in the service of Mexico for nearly a quarter of a century, but his gaunt, Gallic features still remained, although he noticed the waist of his pants needed to be let out, again and his facial features were rounder and fuller than they had been when he was a young man. At forty-seven years old, he sighed. Having survived more than a few brushes with death already, he knew he had already lost the battle with middle age.

"*Enough wool gathering. I can't turn back the clock.*" Woll hadn't climbed the scaffold to dwell on the past or his own mortality. He raised a telescoping spyglass and swept it across the other side of the river. Nestled in a bend of the Rio Bravo del Norte sat a squat, earthen fort. Built a few years earlier, grass now grew on its steep sides. Embrasures where artillery could be placed, were gaping holes cut into the earthen walls. But no guns were visible.

Woll had been present with his Excellency at the Battle of the Nueces six years before, only barely escaping capture. Born in France and having served in the defense of Paris when he was barely yet a man, then emigrating to the United States shortly thereafter, gave Woll a broader appreciation for the *norteamericanos* than most of Santa Anna's officers held. He had learned, when serving as an adjutant to General Winfield Scott, the Americans were individually as brave as any soldiers he could imagine, but they lacked discipline. No, he thought, it wasn't necessarily a fluke the men under Crockett and Travis had beaten the Mexican army before, but his army wasn't the same that had been defeated some half-dozen years earlier either.

Over the past week, he had sent men across the river, dressed as traders, but they had ferreted out the information he sought. A single company of infantry held the fort, perhaps as many as seventy soldiers. Against that, Woll's advanced column of twelve hundred men was approaching Nuevo Laredo from the south. His army's lead brigade, he was sure, would make quick work of the crude fortification. He was certain he could wipe the defenders out if they didn't surrender.

In the pocket of his navy-blue dress pants, Woll fingered a set of rosary beads and said a quick prayer to the Blessed Virgin it wouldn't be necessary to sacrifice the men of his army to reduce the fort. He was glad there were no cavalry within the fort's walls. Even south of the border, they had received reports of the Colt Paterson revolvers. He shuddered to think of the loss of life if he were forced to send in a charge against that kind of firepower.

Before the present campaign, he had studied the carbine the Texians had purchased from the United States. The 1833 Halls carbine was a mechanical wonder of precision engineering. Its parts were interchangeable. He had watched one of their gunsmiths in Mexico City disassemble two of the carbines and reassemble the weapons with parts from either gun. There was no difference in the weapons' performance. This spoke well of the United States' ability to mass produce the weapons. While there was much to like about the gun, he had been less impressed with the amount of gas which had leaked from the breech when the gun was fired. It had reduced the carbine's velocity and range. Before coming north to take command of the Army of the North, he had watched a *Cazadore* practice with the weapon. Despite the leakage, the skirmisher was able to hit his target at more than two hundred fifty yards each time.

Knowing the Texian soldiers in the fort would be using the same rifle, Woll had taken this into account and had devised a strategy against the carbine. He would neutralize it, of that he was certain.

Fort Moses Austin was a five-sided earthen fort. Nestled in a bend of the Rio Grande, two sides of the fort covered the river while the other three overlooked the irrigated fields, where farmers grew corn and other grains. A long, wooden platform ran the length of the fort's interior wall, facing the Rio Grande River. Riflemen could stand along the platform, covering the ford between Laredo and Mexico. Andrew Neill, captain of Company N of the 1st Texas Infantry, leaned against the top of the earthen embankment, studying the other side of the river. A spyglass rested atop the wall. It wasn't needed to see the regimental flags of the Army of the North. More than a thousand troops were parading into the tiny village on the river's southern edge.

His voice shook with emotion as he called down into the fort. "Sergeant Leal, I need you up here right away!"

A short, stocky Tejano, with sergeant chevrons on the sleeves of his butternut jacket, climbed the ladder to the platform, joining him in looking across the water. As the sergeant stared at the army, he muttered, "*Mierda*." He shook his head as he turned to the captain. "I don't think they'd bring that many men forward if they didn't intend to cross, Captain."

Captain Neill scowled at the army deploying across the river. As he spoke, the brogue of his native Scotland came through, "Yeah. Unfortunately for us, the only thing standing between that army and San Antonio is this wee fort."

The sergeant glared at the assembling force before replying. "We've got plenty of ammunition, Captain. They try attacking the fort, and they'll find the entry fee expensive."

"There's not going to be a we, Sergeant." Neill nodded toward a small corral. Several horses remained in the fort from the last visit of one of the Ranger companies. "I want you to take those horses and ride like Hell for San Antonio. Grab Private Jackson, if the Mexicans have slipped any cavalry across the river, two stand a better chance than one of getting through."

As the sergeant began to protest, Captain Neill leaned in close, "Listen to me, Lucas. If they cross the river, there's not a hell of a lot that we're going to be able to do to stop them from storming the fort. Major Dickinson must be warned, and I can't go. If there are Mexican cavalry swarming between here and there, you've got a better shot than most at getting through."

Neill watched, and saw the sergeant wanted to argue but eventually realized the truth of his words. The Tejano's eyes fell, and he said, "Thank you, Captain. Jackson and I will get through and warn the Alamo. I know you can slow them down, sir."

The Scotsman slapped the Tejano on the back and watched him climb down the ladder. He looked back across the river and said to himself, "And how the Hell am I supposed to do that?"

Twenty minutes later, Neill watched as the two men rode out the gate, each leading a remount, heading north. Not normally a devout man, Neill said a prayer that they would get through.

Sergeant Lucas Leal turned around in his saddle and looked at the low, squat fort a few hundred yards behind him and Private Jackson. A few men, standing on the earthen walls waved at them. He didn't want to wave back. It seemed a final act, as though saying goodbye for the last time. Some of the men he had served with for years.

Before he had ridden from the fort, he had been saddling up the horse when he felt a tapping on his shoulder. He had turned and saw Sergeant Julio Mejia. They had known each other for years, growing up together in San Antonio. When his friend spoke, his voice had been full of emotion, "Lucas, be careful out there, *hermano*. We've got these walls to protect us, and all you've got is a horse's ass between you and trouble."

Mejia handed him a hastily scribbled note, "If something should happen, please give my parents this letter, and tell them I love them."

Leal tried pushing the letter away, "Tell them yourself, Julio. Nothing's going to keep you from seeing them again."

Mejia turned, stuffed the letter into Leal's saddlebag. "*Pendejo*. Take the damn letter," he forced a smile onto his face, "just in case."

No, he wouldn't wave goodbye to his comrades. He would see them again. He sawed the reins around and dug his heels into the horse.

A few miles north of the river, they followed the road north toward San Antonio. They had not been on the road long when they spotted a small dust cloud to their front. Leal pulled on the reins and waited to see what would materialize from the brown, swirling dust. At first, he caught the glimmer of metal reflecting off the sun, then as the cloud grew closer, he saw mounted men carrying lances.

He swore in Spanish. No Texian soldiers carried lances. It appeared the Army of the North was attempting to seal off Laredo from the rest of the Republic. As the lancers spotted Leal and Jackson, they picked up their speed, racing to close the gap. Leal said a hasty prayer to the Virgin of Guadeloupe as he swung down from the saddle and pulled his rifle from the scabbard. Jackson copied his action, putting the horse between himself and the advancing lancers.

Leal levered the breech open and rammed the paper cartridge into it. He finished loading then stepped around the skittish mount, drawing a bead on the leading rider. He held his breath, steadying his nerves, and counted to three. Then he slowly squeezed the trigger. The recoil kicked back, but he held steady until he watched the rider slowly sag to the right and topple from the horse.

A few seconds later, Jackson fired. He had hurried his shot, hitting the mount instead of the rider. They watched the second horse crash to the ground, throwing the rider head over heels into the red dirt.

The third rider, seeing the results of two shots pulled up sharp, wheeled to the left, and raced toward the southeast, heading toward the river. Leal was about to let him go, when an image of the Mexican army swarming over the walls of the fort came to his mind. He raced to reload his rifle before the rider was out of range. He knelt on the road, using his elbow to steady the shot, and he aimed. He held his breath as he used both sights on the rifle to line up the shot, then he exhaled and fired.

The rider continued galloping away. Leal stood and shoved the rifle into the scabbard. "Two out of three ain't bad, Sarge," Jackson said.

Leal grabbed his mount's reins and swung into the saddle, and turned around and said, "Maybe. But three out of three is a sight better. Let's not wait for him to find any friends." Whether he wanted it or not, war had returned to South Texas.

Switching out their remounts, the two covered more than fifty miles on the first day. It took them until the morning of their fourth day to reach the Alamo, arriving on the 15th of March. Flying high over the Alamo's chapel was a large Texas flag, flapping in the morning breeze. The heavy wooden gates were open as was normal and an indifferent guard gave them a brief look as they entered the Alamo Plaza.

The officers' quarters were behind the fort's hospital, and Leal made his way through its long, empty corridor, exiting into the old convent yard. The stairs leading to the officers' quarters was guarded by an alert sentry. Upon learning of Leal's dangerous ride from the

Rio Grande, the guard hurried Leal into the narrow hallway lined with doors to the officers' quarters.

Leal knocked on Major Dickinson's door and waited. He heard small feet slapping on the wooden floor before the door swung open. Standing in the doorway was a young girl with dark curls. He recognized her as the major's eight-year-old daughter, Angelina. Major Dickinson and his family lived on the post, and his daughter was a perennial favorite of the fort's soldiers. She looked up and asked, "Are you here to see my daddy?"

For the first time in four days, the creases on his eyes crinkled and he smiled. He knelt on the floor, the pain of sitting in the saddle for so many hours sent sharp jolts of pain along his spine. "Yes, *mi bonita,* Angelina."

She left the door ajar as she ran back into the quarters. He heard her yelling, "Papa! There's a soldier at the door for you!"

A moment later, Major Almaron Dickinson came to the door, wiping shaving lather from his face with a rag. "Sergeant?" He took in Leal's dusty and haggard look with a single glance. "Which company are you with, man? Do you have word from the west?

Leal wearily shook his head. "No, sir. Captain Neill at Fort Moses Austin sent me. The Mexican army has invaded again. As me and Private Jackson were riding away, we were attacked by Mexican lancers on the road to San Antonio, while more than a thousand of the bastards were assembling on the other side of the river." He pulled a waterproof pouch from his jacket and handed over a hastily written note Neill had written before he and Jackson had left the fort. As the major opened the packet and read the letter, Leal leaned against the wall, as exhaustion threatened to overtake him.

Almaron Dickinson held the crumpled letter from Captain Neill in his hand. His wife, Susanna saw the shocked expression in his eyes and she came up and closed the door, where a few minutes earlier, Sergeant Leal had left. She asked, "Is it news from General Travis, dear? Is everything alright?"

He shook his head. "No. Not the General. But it's not alright either." He held the letter out to her and she blanched as she read the missive. She threw her arms around him and cried.

His wife's tears soaked into his jacket, but how could he blame her? The Alamo had a company of infantry and a battery of artillery in the fort. It held scarcely more than a hundred men, against an army of more than a thousand, most likely already marching north. He looked at the top of her hair, as she clung to him, then at the serious expression worn by his daughter, who hugged his leg. His youngest, William, played on the floor with blocks, too young to know the fear which had gripped his parents. The Major untangled himself from his wife and tried to sooth her. "I expect we have a few days before any Mexican army shows up, my love. Stay here with the children. I need to see Captain Anderson. We've a fort to defend."

Dickinson dashed from his quarters and found Captain Henderson, the only one of his battery commanders at the fort. He sent the captain to fetch the officer in command of the fort's infantry company to meet in the general's office above the hospital. In addition to Major Dickinson, Captains Henderson and Anderson arrived a few minutes later, followed by several junior lieutenants, who crowded along the walls as the major explained the situation.

"Since seizing power again last year, apparently Santa Anna has decided it wasn't enough to ignore his previous treaty with Texas. His Army of the North has apparently attacked us at Laredo and the assumption is they're marching north toward San Antonio, even now." Dickinson glanced out the window, as if expecting someone else to arrive, then shook his head in disappointment. "Of course, this had to happen while Colonel Johnston isn't here. Bob, when his he expected to return?"

He directed the last to a young infantry lieutenant, standing at the back of the room. The officer pulled a thin booklet from a pocket and leafed through the pages before responding, "Sir, unless things have changed, he and General McCulloch are leaving Galveston for the Trinity River. They're scheduled to tour the gun works there this week."

Dickinson sighed in disappointment. "We'll figure out a way to get word to him. Really makes me wish the telegraph network was further along." He scanned the back of the room, looking at the lower ranking officers before settling on the one to whom he had spoken. "Crockett, I want you to hightail it over to the Stagecoach Inn in town and have them put you on an express coach to Austin. Get word to the government about the invasion. Once that's done, take the stage to Houston then to the Trinity River. I want you to find Colonel Johnston and tell him yourself about the invasion."

The young officer protested, "Major, this ain't fair. I'll miss the fight here. You're doing this because my pa is the president."

Dickinson snorted in response. "Damned right I am, Lieutenant. I don't expect things to go to Hell here, but if they do, I'll be damned if I'm going to let the president's son get killed or captured."

"Major, sir! I protest!" the young officer raised his voice.

"Fine. I have noted your protest," Dickinson said, exasperatedly. "You can continue protesting all you want, as long as you do it at the Stagecoach Inn and you're on the stage when it leaves! Now, get moving!"

The office emptied of the other junior officers, as they followed young Crockett out the door. After closing the door, Dickinson sagged into General Travis' chair. "If we're lucky, we may have a bit more than a week before that Mexican army arrives, gentlemen, and it will be up to the three of us to put together the Alamo's defense."

Captain Anderson said, "We've got a little more than seventy soldiers in my company. But there's a couple of companies of reserve infantry in town. We might be able to muster up another hundred and fifty riflemen."

Hearing that lifted Dickinson's spirits. "By God, I like the sound of two hundred riflemen a whole lot better than seventy." He switched his attention to the other officer, "What about our artillery, Tom?"

Captain Henderson said, "The Bexareno Light Artillery is a company-sized unit in town, sir. I've trained a lot of their men on the Alamo's guns. The name's more pretentious than the men. There's around thirty-five men in the battery."

Dickinson found a nub of a pencil on Travis' desk and used the back of Neill's earlier letter to jot down the numbers. "Around two hundred twenty riflemen and seventy artillery. That's around three hundred or so. I'll get the orders issued. I want our reserves from town inside these walls before the sun goes down this evening."

Chapter 8

The grass-covered embankments facing the river were pitted and gouged where solid shot and explosive shells had slammed against the thick earthen walls of Fort Moses Austin. A few boards had been used to frame the embrasure through which he looked across the river. Captain Neill watched the Mexican field pieces, nearly six hundred yards away. The previous day they had thrown several hundred rounds at the fort from their positions south of the Rio Grande. Now, they were idle, waiting for the next chapter.

Sergeant Julio Mejia, the ranking non-commissioned officer since Sergeant Leal's departure the previous day, stood on the platform with the captain, looking through the same opening in the fort. After staring through the spyglass, the captain handed it over to his sergeant. "'Twas considerably nice of yon Mexican general to announce his war yesterday with his wee artillery barrage." Neill's soft lowlands Scots brogue was thick with emotion, knowing his little command had endured the first day without casualties.

Mejia squinted, looking through the spyglass, sweeping the device along the river. "Yes sir. But *Madre de Dios!* I wish they had stayed on their own damned side of the river."

He watched a long column of infantry a mile or more upriver of the fort, waiting for a couple of flat barges to haul the *soldados* across the river. Too deep to ford, except at the crossing between the two towns, the Mexican general had decided to build rafts and cross over upriver.

Neill laughed, a tinge of bitterness to it. "At the very least, they could have had the decency to cross at the ford, where they would have been inside the range of our rifles."

Below them, most of the other seventy men within the fort, sheltered along the interior walls, which faced the river. A half-dozen stood sentry duty, keeping a watchful eye on the Army of the North, as it crossed into Texas, too far out of range for the handful of men to contest the invasion.

In hindsight, spending the previous day attempting to compel the surrender of the fort with his artillery was likely a mistake. Too much powder and shot had been consumed that might have been better used later in the campaign. After more than a quarter century practicing the art of war, a victory won without casualties was much preferred to one in which his own army bleeds. Joining the advanced brigade on the northern side of the river, Adrian Woll stood under the canvas command tent observing the crossing. Each transit of the two boats unloaded another fifty men.

As he sat under the tent, he saw the brigade commander approaching, "Luis, will you join me for lunch? My cook is preparing a brace of chickens donated by the good people of Nuevo Laredo. In celebration of crossing the Rio Bravo, I'm opening a special bottle of wine from one of my favorite vintners in Bordeaux."

Brigadier General Luis Guzman sat on a camp stool opposite from Woll. "Thank you, Adrian. I would be obliged. A good wine might improve my mood." Woll watched his subordinate, who sipped the fine French wine while watching the flat bottom boats ferry his men across the Rio Bravo.

"They're not going to get into position any earlier by willing it to be so, Luis. We'll take the remainder of the day to position your brigade around the fort. Tomorrow morning, we'll give the *norteamericano* pirates the opportunity to surrender. If they refuse, then we've brought up some shells from Monterrey. One way or the other, we'll bring them to heel."

Guzman set the empty glass on the camp table between the two, and ruefully chuckled. "Was I that transparent? I'm eager to have this little stretch of the Rio Bravo behind us. San Antonio is the real objective."

Woll nodded knowingly. "And we'll get there in good time, my friend. Did you know I have been receiving regular reports from patriots still living among the Anglos and the Mexican traitors there and we are catching them with their pants around their ankles, Luis.

General Travis and all but one of his companies is out west. Let your mind dwell on that. When we get to San Antonio, we'll find but a single company of regulars to oppose our entire army."

After accepting another glassful of wine, Guzman said, "I have heard they are foolishly trying to capture Santa Fe. A bunch of bastard pirates have scant hope of seizing our jewel of the north."

Feeling the effects of the wine, Woll waved his glass before his subordinate. "Don't be too quick to gainsay these pirates. You weren't there when they defeated his Excellency six years ago. I was. General Travis is an able opponent. It wouldn't surprise me if we wind up trading towns with the Texians. The thing is, San Antonio is far more important to these so called Texians than Santa Fe is to Mexico."

The advanced brigade and a battery of artillery were across the river by twilight and the fort was barricaded off from the north. Wary of the Texian rifles, the three regimental commanders placed their loose cordon a half mile around the Texian fort.

The next morning dawned gray, a light drizzle falling. The men inside the fort took shelter under tent halves and waterproof tarps. Captain Neill had managed a few hours of sleep during the night, but any further thoughts of rest fled when he saw Sergeant Mejia crouching beside him. "I've been up on the parapet this morning, sir, and it's about what we saw last night. The Mexicans have us surrounded."

Neill scrambled from beneath the damp woolen blanket and hurried over to a ladder, which led to a narrow parapet facing north, into Texas. He saw the early morning campfires burning in the distance. Mejia followed and as the two looked to the north, he said, "A word with you, sir."

Neill buttoned his jacket up to the collar, trying to keep the damp chill at bay. "Is it about the men?"

Mejia turned away from the Mexican encampment and sagged against the wall. "Yeah. They're pretty unhappy to be trapped behind these walls. If it comes to a battle, they know we'll be overrun. There must be more than a thousand men on the other side of these walls. A battle will only have one outcome."

Neill shot him a disapproving look. "No doubt that's so. While there might only be two courses of action available to us, Sergeant, we're Texas' first line of defense. It's true, when whoever is in command of the Mexican army over there gives terms, we could take them and become prisoners. We'd be the first Texians captured by Mexico since Texas crushed Santa Anna's army back in '36. The other choice, is to sell our lives and bleed the Hell out of Woll's army."

As though in agreement with Neill's assessment, the weather remained overcast and gray even after the light rain passed. The Texians in the fort stayed below the walls, as a brisk north wind knifed through wet clothes. Neill looked heavenward, and thought the weather summed up his command's hopeless position as an outpost of his country's sovereignty.

The sky had been lightening for more than an hour when from the Mexican line an officer approached, in his red and green lancer uniform. Had the sun been shining, no doubt it would have gleamed off his polished buckle and buttons, Neill thought. Instead, as the officer approached, his black handlebar mustache drooped, and he appeared miserable, still wet from the earlier rain. A white flag was tied to his sword. He stopped around a hundred feet from the fort.

In passable English, he shouted, "You *norteamericanos*, you are invaders, interlopers in a land that does not belong to you. By order of Major General Adrian Woll, you are ordered to lay down your arms and surrender. If you do so, he guarantees your lives. You will be taken to Veracruz and repatriated to the United States. Failure to accept these conditions, and any survivors may find mercy in short supply."

Mejia's rifle rested on top of the earthen wall and he looked toward Neill. "Let me put a bullet between his cocky, Centralist eyes, Captain."

Neill wagged his finger in front of his sergeant, "We're not going to start killing anybody under a flag of truce, Sergeant," then he softened his voice, "as tempting as it may be."

He turned back toward the Mexican officer and called back, "Ten minutes! We'll give you an answer in ten."

Hearing that, the officer wheeled around and galloped back across the wet field to the Mexican encampment.

Neill climbed down into the center of the fort, he called for the soldiers to assemble around him. Every eye was fixed on him, waiting to hear what he had to say. "They want us to surrender, boys. I don't know much about this General Woll, but it could be that he's an honorable man. But we know what kind of man Santa Anna is, and he's the head honcho of Mexico again. We saw how he treated prisoners when he crushed the revolts in Mexico back in '36. Woll probably would attempt to honor any surrender today. But what about tomorrow? If I could be sure we could all march out of here and be free to go back to the States, I might be tempted to do it, even if it meant I'd never be able to hold my head high again."

The men surrounding him nodded in agreement. Despite the air of forlorn hopelessness, there was a palpable fear of what would be said of them if they left.

Neill's smile was sad and matched the desperateness they felt. "What's it to be, boys? Do we stand and fight or do we take General Woll up on his offer?"

From more than seventy throats there was a roar of agreement, "We fight!"

Neill led his men back onto the fort's parapets, where they stood protected by the earthen walls, waiting for destiny. Fifteen minutes after riding away, the officer rode back across the field. When he was three hundred feet away, Neill turned to Mejia, "Give him our answer, Sergeant."

The stocky Tejano sergeant cocked the rifle's hammer back and checked the percussion cap. The rifle was ready. He raised it to his shoulder, aimed and fired. The bullet kicked up dust only a few inches in front of the officer's mount. They watched as the horse, startled by the bullet smacking the ground, bucked and nearly threw the officer. An accomplished equestrian, he dropped his sword and used both hands to bring his mount back under his control. He patted the horse on the neck, as he glared at the walls of the fort. Sweeping down, he grabbed his sword from where it fell in the grass and untied the white flag from the weapon, letting the cloth flutter to the ground, as he trotted back to the Mexican encampment.

When the rider returned to the camp, the Army of the North stirred to life. Woll waited for his orderly to bring his horse to him, certain that from the fort, the bevy of activity must look like an ant mound that had been disturbed, soldiers rushing about. But out of the apparent chaos, the three regiments of the first brigade assembled. Each regiment had a company of *Cazadores*, or light infantry assigned to it. Woll ordered them deployed ahead of his infantry. They were there as a precaution. He couldn't imagine the soldiers sallying from the fort, but he'd learned not to take things like that to chance.

The soldiers of the first brigade were his men, and he wouldn't casually throw their lives away with a frontal assault across a half mile. Not when he had a battery of field artillery. Sitting in the saddle, Woll called to the artillery officer, "You may begin."

The officer saluted and returned to his guns. After a few minutes, Woll heard his cry, "*Fuego!*" The gun recoiled, and the shell flew across the distance. It exploded short of the fort. A couple more ranging shots were fired from the Mexican line and they, too fell short. Woll ordered his *Cazadores* forward, to screen the artillery, as they too moved closer to the fort.

99

Once the guns were moved forward a couple of hundred yards, they were reloaded, and they fired at the fort.

The first few rounds fired toward the fort had detonated short of the walls. Captain Neill watched the light infantry advance in a thin skirmish line while the field pieces were rolled forward by the gunners. As the enemy reloaded the guns, several riflemen sniped at the *Cazadores*. At more than five hundred yards, it was an extreme range.

As the gunners raced to reload their guns several hundred yards away, Neill cringed. He feared, these rounds wouldn't fall short of their target. The first shot screamed toward the fort. He ducked behind the earthen rampart, and felt the earth shake as the shell exploded against the embankment. The next couple of shells flew over the fort, plunging into the Rio Grande.

Another shell sent dirt skyward as it gouged a small hole into the earthen wall. Mejia joined him at the embrasure, "We gotta do something, Captain. They'll eventually get lucky and if they get lucky enough, we're done for."

Neill nodded agreement when another shell exploded above the embankment, sending a rain of iron fragments raining into the dirt. Mejia scampered down the ladder, returning a few minutes later, dragging one of the company's newer recruits. Neill noticed the newness of the soldier's uniform. The butternut jackets his soldiers wore, as they aged, tended to fade to brown. His black, wide-brimmed hat was unfaded.

When he and Mejia joined Neill, the young soldier lifted the brim of his hat, to get a better look at the enemy's guns. The soldier's strawberry-blonde hair and freckled face made him look younger than his years.

Neill pointed toward the artillery, "Do you think you can shoot any of those gunners, Smith?"

Private Jarvis Smith, a recent immigrant from Kentucky, leaned against the embrasure and studied the gunners servicing their field pieces in the distance. With an open smile on his face, he whistled. "Hot damn, Captain. That's a far piece."

Another shell exploded against the wall, closer than Neill would have liked, and dirt showered down on the three men. Neill pointed toward the guns, "All you can do is try."

He watched the young soldier as he leaned against the embrasure and aimed his rifle through the wide opening. He swept his hat from his head and sighted downrange. Then he picked up a handful of dirt and let it fall, gauging windspeed. He adjusted the aim, fixing a spot several feet above his target. Ready, he aimed, holding his breath. Slowly he exhaled then fired. Neill stared intently through the spyglass and jumped when he saw the bullet strike a ramrod one of the loaders was holding.

Smith frowned. "I thought I had him. Wind must have kicked up." He reloaded his rifle and went through the same ritual. This time he knocked the hat from the artillery captain's head, causing the officer to scurry behind the line of guns. On the fourth round, he dropped a gunner, shot through the head, who had been bending over the sights on the cannon, sending a reddish mist into the air. Neill and Mejia jumped up and down, praising the shot and pounding the young soldier on the back.

As he reloaded, Neill yelled, "Not bad, Private Smith. Show me it wasn't just luck!"

Three shots later, he dropped another gunner.

General Woll and his staff officers moved further back after the second gunner had been killed by the Texian sniper. Six hundred yards would have been an impossible shot for one of his own *Cazadores* with the English Baker rifles they carried. He could admire such skill. But that didn't stop him from ordering all his guns to focus on that one point on the wall, from where the rifle was fired.

Two more men died serving their guns before a shell detonated on top of the embrasure.

His ears were ringing when he picked himself up from the ground. Sergeant Mejia had been watching Private Smith shoot, when the world turned upside down and he found himself flung to the ground in the center of the fort. Mejia tried standing but his leg was numb. He looked down and saw a thin splinter sticking out from his thigh, dying his pants with his blood. He hobbled to his feet and put pressure on the injured leg. The numbness was fading, replaced by intense pain. But he was relieved he could still stand on it.

As his hearing returned, he heard people shouting and noticed several soldiers huddled in a circle nearby.

He limped over to them and saw what they were looking at. He frowned, shoulders sagging when he saw the broken body of Captain Neill, blood pooling around him, staining the ground on which he lay. One of the company's lieutenants was throwing up, next to the lower half of a body, all that remained of Private Smith.

Neill's second-in-command was Lieutenant Connors, a quiet unassuming officer who largely left the running of the first platoon to Sergeant Mejia. With Neill dead, Mejia knew the men needed to see the Lieutenant take firm command and restore order within the walls of the fort.

As he tottered over to the officer, the world seemed to come to an end, and he was violently thrown to the ground again. A shell exploded directly over the fort, throwing shrapnel across the fort's interior. Mejia fell hard on his injured leg. He screamed in agony as the splinter dragged across the ground, nearly causing him to lose consciousness. He swallowed several gulps of air, trying to push the pain and nausea away. His injured leg was soaked, and he grasped it, trying to find any more injuries.

He opened his eyes, and saw his leg was covered in red and gray matter. Lieutenant Connor lay at his feet, a fragment from the shell had clipped the top of his head, shearing it neatly off, as if cut by a surgeon's blade.

Enraged, Mejia screamed, "*Mierda!*" At least a dozen men had been hit, and those who were injured were writhing in agony.

Torn between rage and grief, he looked around the fort's interior. The officers were dead. He was the ranking non-commissioned officer. Could the men fight on? A few men were scrambling up ladders to the rifle platforms, but many were still shell-shocked from the explosion, and the wounded were bleeding, crying out in pain. Mejia staggered to his feet and saw less than half the men were in any condition to fight.

With every step toward the ladder, blood dripped from the splinter, still embedded in his leg. He moved slowly, as though in a fog, climbing each rung of the ladder, one at a time, his injured leg quivering with pain. When he reached the platform, he tied a white shirt around the barrel of a rifle and with tears streaming down his face, raised it into the air.

Across the south Texas plain the white banner fluttered in the breeze. General Woll turned to the artillery officer. "Cease firing, Captain."

Woll beckoned the cavalry officer who had earlier delivered his ultimatum. "Return to them, Captain. I'm feeling magnanimous. If they surrender immediately, I will offer them the same terms as before."

The officer warily stared at the General. "Sir, do you not worry that his Excellency, the president will countermand the orders?"

Woll snapped his fingers, "I am here, and he is in Mexico City. He can do nothing about my orders today." When the cavalry officer's scowl deepened, he clarified. "And if he changes the order later, I won't be able to do anything about it then."

Mollified, the officer took a white flag and carried it across the field, toward the fort.

One of the soldiers standing above, on one of the parapets called, "Sergeant, there's a rider approaching. He's under a flag of truce!"

Mejia came out of the captain's tent, carrying most of the fort's communication and dumped it in the camp fire. The breakfast fire had already been expanded when a few timbers from a small corral had been added to the blaze.

The pain was becoming unbearable in his leg as he eased himself down on a stool, using his rifle as a crutch. He looked at the deadly rifle in his hands, wishing he had been able to kill Santa Anna's soldiers. Instead, he and the rest of the survivors faced an uncertain future. He called one of the other men over to him and handed the weapon over. "Break the stock and throw the whole damned thing in the fire. Before that jumped up popinjay gets here from the Mexican camp, I want every rifle tossed in the fire."

He had no choice but to surrender, but he would be damned if he would let the company's breech-loading rifles fall into enemy hands.

When the officer arrived, Mejia was surprised to learn the terms of surrender were unchanged from earlier. He passed along he message he would lead his command from the fort, unarmed.

The entire first brigade was standing at attention, facing the fort, when General Woll saw around sixty men march out from the earthen defenses. Behind them, from the center of the earthen structure, flames licked into the sky, throwing ash and soot into the air. Their dirty uniforms, normally a particularly dingy shade of tan, were stained brown with grime. In contrast to the navy-blue informs of his own infantry, he found the Texians' uniforms drab and ugly, but they blended in well against the backdrop of the prairie.

As the little band of soldiers crossed the field, and approached the Mexican line, Woll noticed there were no officers. At the head of the column was a swarthy, short man with sergeant stripes.

The little column stopped short of the Mexican line and waited. The Colonel of the regiment in front of which the Texians had stopped, rode toward the column. Those Texians who were able, snapped to attention. The sergeant in command, snapped a salute, and in fluent Spanish said, "I am Sergeant Julio Mejia, Texas Infantry. As the ranking non-commissioned officer, I surrender my company and place me and my men at your mercy."

The next day, the 15th of March, as General Woll's army began the one hundred sixty mile march to San Antonio, Sergeant Mejia and his fellow Texians found themselves marching southward, into an uncertain future.

Chapter 9

Despite the chill of the north wind blowing from the Sangre de Cristos Mountains, Will was sweating as he sawed at his mount's reins. He pulled his hat off and used it to wipe the sweat from his brow. The horse responded to his rider by dropping his head and tearing a mouthful of dry grass. Clumps of snow dotted the ground over which his army was marching. He turned in the saddle and studied the weary soldiers who were traversing the same ground they had covered less than a month before. The column of infantry had been trudging along the road, which paralleled the meandering Rio Grande. The soldiers were dusty and tired. He gave the order for the command to take a short break.

The small army had barreled back down the Camino Real de Tierra Adentro over the past twelve days, breaking camp with the dawn, and marching fifty minutes every hour, for ten hours a day, with an hour's rest for lunch. Three miles each hour. Thirty miles a day, on the army's best day. But they had done it. Where his horse ate at the sparse foliage, the road forked. Straight ahead, another day's march was Ysleta. To the right, the road veered down the bank of the Rio Grande and forded the river. Another day's march down that route was El Paso del Norte.

A company of Rangers garrisoned Ysleta. Food supplies in the village were adequate for a few dozen men. Across the river, *El Paso del Norte* held several thousand souls. Will frowned as his eyes flickered between both routes. He weighed whether to head south, into Mexico or to continue along the road back to Ysleta. As he stared down the road, he heard someone clearing his throat and turned and saw Major Wyatt.

"Thinking about what happens if we go for *del Norte* and then later find out that Santa Anna hasn't invaded, sir?"

Standing still, the cold breeze quickly dried the sweat on his forehead and Will returned the hat to its rightful place. "The thought had crossed my mind. I know we discussed this before leaving Santa Fe. Even if Santa Anna doesn't throw a conniption fit with us taking everything he surrendered in the treaty of Bexar, if we go into Mexico and pillage that town, we've as much as declared war by any reasonable standard."

Will heard Wyatt chuckle. "You mean any other standard than the one Santa Anna uses? If you're of a mind to hear my thoughts, there's not enough food and supplies in Ysleta for a hundred men, much less a thousand. Then there's another two hundred miles back to the depot on the Pecos. Tell me, General, where do we get the food and fodder for our army if not *del Norte*?"

Wyatt's argument was the same he'd been wrestling with for the last day. Will grimaced. "Damn you, Payton. I've spent the last day trying to find a reason to avoid taking the army into Mexico and when push comes to shove, there's nothing else to be done. Give the order, we're going to take *El Paso del Norte*."

The column, which had been taking a ten-minute on-the-hour breather, was back on their feet, and swung south, leaving the level, graded road, and made their way across the shallows of the river, leaving the land claimed by Texas and entering Mexico.

Later, if not for the twilight, Will would have been able to see the white spire of the Mission of the Lady of Guadeloupe, as his soldiers made camp only a few miles to the northwest of *El Paso del Norte*. As the moon crawled into the night sky he was joined around a small campfire by Lt. Colonel Seguin and Major Wyatt. He watched the major poke a thin twig into the embers and pull it out, its end burning brightly, and use it to light a cigar.

When Wyatt settled back into a reclined position, puffing contentedly, Will said, "Part of me wants to send our boys into that town with their bayonets fixed. To Hell with whatever defenses the Mexicans may have erected."

Seguin nodded as he filled a cup of coffee from a pot which had been percolating in the red-hot coals. He took a sip gingerly before he replied. "My family's hacienda, south of San Antonio, lies on the most likely route the Mexican army would follow in an invasion. One thing I know for certain, Santa Anna won't forgive me or my family for what he sees as betrayal, and frankly, Buck, I worry about them."

Will's sigh was loud. "I know that feeling. I worry constantly about Becky and the kids in San Antonio, too. It would behoove us to tread lightly, if the situation allows. What I was thinking is that we should send an officer under a flag of truce into town and give them an opportunity to surrender."

After blowing a ragged smoke ring, Wyatt said, "That matches my thinking, General. I'd rather see a bloodless victory than one that sees the shedding of our boys' blood."

Will stared into the glowing embers, thinking about what the morrow would bring. Eventually, he broke the long period of silence. "Juan, I want you to ride into town tomorrow morning under a flag of truce and demand their surrender."

Hidden by the shadow of his hat, Will heard the Tejano's soft laughter. "Send the Mexican in. Is it because he can speak Spanish or because he's expendable?"

There was no edge to the voice. Will chuckled. "If you'd rather, I'll send Major Wyatt."

At that, the infantry major choked on the cigar smoke, and started coughing, as he eyed Will disapprovingly. Seguin reached over and pounded the other officer on the back until his coughing subsided. "*Dios mio*, Buck, but have you heard Peyton try to speak Spanish? He'd just as likely butcher it up and give our surrender."

The next morning, as a weak sun failed to pierce the fast-moving clouds, Juan Seguin prepared to ride into *El Paso del Norte*. His butternut jacket was brushed as clean as could be done while in the field. His black boots were buffed to a shine and his black slouch hat was worn at a jaunty angle as he grabbed the pommel and swung into the saddle.

He pulled his saber from its scabbard and tied a white linen shirt to the blade. As he prepared to head down the road leading into town, he saw General Travis approach. Behind the general were a dozen of Captain Hays' Rangers. "Colonel Seguin, your looks alone should drive terror into the hearts of your enemies."

Seguin warmly smiled. "Ah, flattery will get you nowhere, General. Any final instructions?"

His commander pointed toward the Rangers behind him. "While I'd prefer they think you're riding in alone, I think Maria will thank me if these boys keep an eye on you."

Seguin raised his eyebrows, as his lips turned upwards. "God help you if my wife finds out you're tossing me to the lions."

As Seguin rode into town, he saw the Rangers filtering into side streets until he alone continued toward the central plaza.

Once he had passed a half dozen places at which road blocks could have been erected, Seguin's curiosity was piqued. He had seen no *soldados*, and very few people moving about. And those who saw him riding along the road with his flag of truce fluttering in the breeze, disappeared just as quickly back into their houses. As he entered the central plaza of *El Paso del Norte*, a large church covered a quarter of the plaza, but the church's bell tower failed to catch his attention. On the opposite side of the plaza stood a two-story adobe building, above which flapped the Mexican flag. A dozen men carried muskets and shotguns and they stood in front of the building, watching Seguin warily.

He was more than halfway across the plaza, when from behind the armed men, a door swung wide and a tall man, dressed in the finery of a Spanish don stepped through it. He stepped down from the porch and the men parted to let him through. Seguin cantered up to the don and drew up the reins, bringing his horse to a stop. "I am Lt. Colonel Juan Seguin, commander of the cavalry of the Republic of Texas. Whom do I have the pleasure of addressing?"

The don, who appeared around thirty years of age removed his hat with a flourish and gave him a half bow. "Guadalupe Miranda, at your service, Colonel." His eyes flittered to the side and his calm demeanor slipped for the briefest of moments. "And here I thought you had come alone."

Seguin shifted in his saddle and craned his neck and saw two of Hays' Rangers kneeling in a doorway on the far side of the plaza, their rifles covering the armed men behind Miranda.

Seguin shrugged nonchalantly. "Just insurance, *Señor Alcalde*. It would appear to me that your city has been abandoned to the tender mercy of the Texian army by your Centralist overlords."

Miranda gave a sad shrug that could only mean it couldn't be helped.

Seguin ignored the helpless gesture. "My terms are simple. You will provide us forty tons of foodstuff and ten tons of fodder. Additionally, we'll require twenty wagons and their teams to haul the supplies. For your cooperation we'll leave our army outside of town."

Miranda's placid veneer cracked. "Forty tons! That's highway robbery, Colonel! You would take the food out of the mouths of our children."

Seguin frowned then casually shrugged. "The alternative is that we bring our soldiers into your humble town and take it ourselves. The choice is yours, *alcalde,*" he gestured to the south before continuing, "None of this would have been necessary had your central government not chosen this spring to try to conquer Texas. Again."

Miranda stood, staring hard up at Seguin, who glared back from atop his horse. After an interminable moment, Seguin prompted the *alcalde*, "Which will it be, *Señor*? Shall I bring in my soldiers or will you collect the required supplies?"

Miranda spat onto the ground and swore. "Damn you to Hell, Colonel Seguin. You've given me a Faustian bargain. You'll leave us hungry before the next harvest, but we'll collect the supplies and wagons. God alone knows what your soldiers would do to my town."

As the town of *El Paso del Norte* was plundered of most of its food, its denizens made their way into the plaza where they mutely stared at him and his well-armed Rangers. The injury made worse by the fact that it was Miranda's guards who collected the supplies from them at gunpoint. By nightfall, Seguin watched the twenty wagons rolling north, toward the nearest ford, leading toward Ysleta. He remained in the plaza, surrounded by the handful of Hays' Rangers.

When the last wagon creaked under the heavy load, rolling out of the plaza, Seguin turned to see Guadalupe Miranda standing on the porch of the government building. The *alcalde* had upheld his end of the bargain. The Tejano officer swept his hat from his head and gave the Mexican official a half bow. "On behalf of General Travis and the army of the Republic of Texas, I bid you adieu, *Señor Alcalde*."

Dismayed, Miranda's eyes flickered to the road down which the wagons had rolled. "Easy words, Colonel. The only consolation I take is that had you brought your army into town, many women and children would have been left homeless had you burned and looted, too. But these same women and children may go hungry now."

Seguin hardened his expression. "Take your petition to Santa Anna, sir. Were he honorable, your town would be untouched. When we catch up with him, there'll be Hell to pay."

Chapter 10

Colonel Sidney Johnston leaned against the low wooden table, watching the other man kneel on the manicured grass, aiming the rifle downrange. Johnston flicked his eyes toward the target, more than two hundred yards away. It was a crude drawing of Santa Anna, which had been drawn by one of the gunsmiths from Trinity Gun Works. A moment later, the gun fired, recoiling into the other man's shoulder. Despite a half-dozen rounds fired in quick succession, the acrid smoke was whisked away on a light breeze.

Johnston saw the faux Santa Anna's face ripple as the bullet smacked the target, joining a few other tightly grouped holes placed there only moments before. "What do you think of it, Ben?"

Benjamin McCulloch levered the breech open, letting tendrils of smoke vent out the open breech, before returning it to the table. "How long before some of these start making their way into my reserve regiments?"

As they walked toward the target, along with Andy Berry, the son of the gun works owner, Johnston said, "Providence and President Crockett alone can answer that. Let me rephrase that. The appropriation bill belongs to congress. We know they haven't a clue, so unless God can tell you the answer, I'm afraid you're out of luck."

Berry, walking behind the two officers, added, "Y'all keep sending payments and we'll keep on providing all the rifles we can make."

Johnston's glower at the young artisan was tinged with a sardonic smile. He couldn't help but like the young man, who was the irreverent tails to his father's dour heads. "Andy, how many of these have the gun works produced?"

Berry cocked his head to one side as he worked the math in his head. "Near enough fourteen hundred of the model 1842 Sabine rifle, Colonel."

Johnston smiled at the number. It was nearly the exact number he had calculated. "Tell you what, Ben, if congress doesn't abscond with our armament appropriation for the next year, we ought to be able to arm two of your reserve regiments by the year's end. Now that most of your reserve regiments use the Halls carbine, what do they think of it?"

"Compared to an old muzzle loading musket, they've taken to it, like the boys in the navy take to Galveston's ladies of the night when they're on shore leave."

Johnston interjected, "The sailors or the whores?"

McCulloch gave his counterpart in the regular army a dirty look for the interruption and proceeded to ignore the comment. "The downside to the carbine is that it lacks both the range and the punching power that the Sabine rifle has. But it's accurate enough at distances a musket can't even dream of hitting." As they neared the target, he turned to Berry, who was still a few paces behind, "How many of the Halls have y'all made?"

As Berry worked the math in his head, his lips quietly moved, until he spoke up. "Since getting the license from Harpers Ferry to manufacture the carbine in '39, we've manufactured around four thousand of them. Based on the number of them that have cycled through our shops for repairs, I'd guess that General Travis must have ordered upwards of three thousand of them from Harpers Ferry."

McCulloch unpinned the hand-drawn target and admired the tight grouping in the head of the ersatz Santa Anna and folded the target up. "I'll be keeping this one. Might be the closest I ever get to plugging that pompous jackass."

As they returned from the firing range to the complex of buildings which constituted the gun works, McCulloch asked, "Sid, what did you and General Travis do with those other Sabine rifles? You wouldn't have needed more than eight hundred to arm your infantry battalion."

After passing through the main building, which housed several forges, where workers were crafting firearms, they emerged back into the sweet-smelling air, in front of the gun works. Johnston flicked a few bits of coal dust from his uniform, which had acquired them as he walked through the building, before he replied. "More than a thousand were issued to the infantry. Another two hundred were assigned to the Marines. I think there's between one and two hundred that are at the Alamo waiting to be distributed to our soldiers guarding the military road to El Paso. Speaking of Marines, how many companies of reserve Marines have you been able to recruit?"

"We've managed to muster four reserve companies. Two on Galveston Island and two more in towns and villages surrounding Galveston Bay. If I can find the right officers, I'm pretty sure there are a couple of more companies of Marines we could muster."

As they bid good-day to Andy Berry and swung into the saddle, Johnston saw a cloud of dust racing down the road, toward the gun works. His hand edged toward the pistol at his belt as they watched a man racing toward them, galloping into the yard of the gun works. As the man pulled on the reins, dust swirling around him, Johnston recognized Lieutenant Robert Crockett. The young officer gave a perfunctory salute. "Colonel Johnston! The Mexican army has crossed the Rio Grande! They've invaded!"

The road between the Trinity Gun Works and Liberty, Texas was only a few miles. After borrowing a fresh mount from the Berrys for Lieutenant Crockett, the three officers hurried back to the town, where McCulloch, acting in his capacity as general of the reserve regiments, penned orders mobilizing both the reserve and militia units, and notifying them of the

Mexican invasion. From Liberty, they took the rest of the day riding to West Liberty, where they spoke with the local officers of the reserve companies, recruited among the workers of the Gulf Farms Corporation. After learning it could take as long as a couple of days to assemble the reserves, the two high-ranking officers decided to leave Lieutenant Crockett to aid the farmers in their mobilization. Johnston resisted the urge to race back to the Alamo. Major Dickinson would either hold them at bay or he wouldn't. Instead of racing back to the Alamo, the best bet was to build his army around the two companies of regular Marines on Galveston island. The fastest way to Galveston was by way of the railroad to Anahuac.

West Liberty was connected to Anahuac by a thirty-mile railroad, the first in Texas. The train depot also played host to the town's telegraph office, which went as far west as Columbus, and as far east as Beaumont. Before they embarked for Anahuac, Johnston and McCulloch sent mobilization orders racing along the telegraph lines across Southeast Texas.

22 March 1842

To: All reserve and militia officers

Mexico has invaded our Republic. San Antonio is the target. Assemble your companies and begin training. Further orders to follow.

Benjamin McCulloch, Brigadier General, Commander reserves.

Colonel Albert Sidney Johnston, Commander 1st Texas Infantry Regt.

The locomotive's wheels spun along the iron rails and thick black smoke belched from the painted smokestack as the unadorned passenger carriage lurched forward, pulled by the locomotive and coal car. Wheels squealed against iron rails as the train picked up speed, rocking along the tracks, as it left the company town of West Liberty behind. Johnston stared out the dirty windows, as coal dust tinged smoke slipped by. He had read in the *Telegraph and Texas Register,* Texas' widest circulating newspaper, about how the company which had built this railroad had nearly floundered when they had built the wood and iron bridge over the Trinity River. But after bringing in engineers from New York City, they had overcome the challenges and spanned the river. As he thought about this, he felt the train slow slightly as the tracks went up a slight incline, until it crossed over the river, rocking back and forth ever so slightly on the rails, until the train was once again on firm ground, racing at speeds nearing thirty miles per hour toward Anahuac.

The sun had fled the sky before the train pulled into the small port town later that evening. Steam vented from the train as it chugged to a stop. When Johnston and McCulloch climbed down from the passenger car, they were approached by a middle-aged man, wearing a blue, Texas Marine Corps jacket and brown civilian pants. "General McCulloch, we done heard about the invasion over the telegraph wire. I'm Wilberforce Atkinson, captain of Anahuac's reserve Marine company. About half my boys live in and around town here, and we're ready to answer the call, sir."

McCulloch was not one to stand on parade and responded to the salute with a casual wave. "Where's the other half of your company, Captain?"

"Around this part of the bay, sir. I've got a few of my boys out fetching the others. If you're of a mind to, we'll be ready to go with you or follow behind, as needed."

McCulloch casually nodded. "Are there any boats available tonight? Colonel Johnston and I are of a mind to get to Fort Travis on Galveston as soon as possible."

Atkinson pointed into the night toward the bay. "Other than a couple of fishing skiffs, no. There's a barge due in tomorrow morning early, to take a shipment of cotton back to Galveston. Like as not, that's your best bet, sir."

Throughout the night, the reserve Marines of Captain Atkinson's company filtered into town. When the sun had crested the eastern sky, most of the company's sixty men were assembled in the town square. A low, squat steam barge pulled alongside an empty dock before the sun was more than a handspan above the horizon. Several Marines had thrown a heavy wooden plank from the dock to the ship's deck, and before the barge's captain could protest, Johnston and McCulloch were boarding the barge with their horses.

The barge's captain, a grizzled, weather-beaten sailor appeared to be chewing at his salt-and-pepper beard before he managed to stutter, "What the hell is the meaning of this? Get those damned horses off my ship."

As the town's reserve company of Marines filed aboard, McCulloch strode over to the captain, resting his hand on the revolver on his belt, "I'll damned well tell you the meaning of this. You're going to get this tub moving and take us straight away to Galveston."

At an even six feet in height, the general of militia was nearly a head taller than the weathered sea captain. But the older man stood his ground, as the Marines crowded onto the deck. "Why should I do anything for you? It's not like we're at war with anyone."

McCulloch checked his impulse to lay the barge's captain out. He chewed back what he wanted to say, and with as much civility as he could muster, said, "Unfortunately, that's where you're wrong. Mexico has invaded. Unless you want me to order these fine Marines to throw you overboard, you'll untie this tub and get us back to Galveston, now!"

Ashen-faced, the old captain retreated away from the clearly angry McCulloch and ordered his men to slip the lines, and within a few minutes his barge was building a head of steam as it drifted back into the bay. A little while later, it was chugging toward the port of Galveston, trailing a thin black cloud of soot and ash.

The barge's underpowered steam engine chugged across the smooth waters of Galveston Bay, the bow slicing through the water, causing ripples to radiate away from the slow-moving boat. The sun was past midday when the cotton barge slipped into a berth on one of the busy Galveston docks.

In the shipping channel, a warship rode at anchor in the water. From the stern, the national flag fluttered in the breeze. As the marines filed down the gangplank onto the dock, McCulloch pointed toward the warship. "Looks bigger than our steam schooners, Sid. I take it that's our steam frigate from the Philadelphia Naval Yards?"

"Yeah, she's quite the ship. She's got twelve 42-pound carronades and a bow chaser that can throw a two hundred and twenty-five-pound shot or shell upwards of five miles."

For the first time since learning of the Mexican invasion the previous day, the two officers smiled, imagining the damage the guns would wreak upon the Mexican navy.

After the Marines had disembarked, both officers led their own mounts down the heavy plank connecting the barge to the long wooden dock. The crowd on the dock was a mixture of reserve Marines from Anahuac and sailors and dock hands unloading freight from another ship, berthed along the other side of the dock. As he led his horse through the milling mass, he saw another blue-coated Marine edging through the crowd making his way toward them. When the Marine with sergeant stripes on his sleeves slid up next to Johnston, his eyes fell on the eagles on his shoulder boards, then slid across to McCulloch, and the stars sewn on his collars. His eyes momentarily went wide as he came to attention and sharply saluted. "We wasn't expecting y'all, sirs. I was sent by Major West to secure this here barge. We just got word from the mainland about Mexico invading."

As they reached the hard-packed dirt road, which took the trade of the world and routed it to nearby warehouses, Johnston and McCulloch climbed onto their mounts. Johnston ran his hand along his horse's neck, calming the beast, who was still recovering from the few hours aboard the barge. "One moment, Sergeant." Johnston turned, and scanned the men on the dock then called out, "Captain Atkinson! Secure the barge, we may need it again shortly."

With that out of the way, he turned again to the sergeant and said, "Lead on."

After disentangling themselves from the crowds, they made good time as they headed east, along the road on the bay side of the island, arriving at Fort Travis in less than half an hour. As they came through the open gate, the fort was a bevy of activity. Before they could dismount, a tall, slender officer in a blue Marine Corps jacket came over to them. "Colonel Johnston, General McCulloch, I'm surprised to find you here. Word only reached us this morning of Mexico's invasion? How can we be of assistance?"

Although McCulloch was a general of reserves and militia, and Johnston only a mere regular army colonel, McCulloch deferred to the West Point graduate. Johnston asked the major, "Has the island's reserves and militia been called up yet?"

Major West nodded. "Yes, sir. The order has gone out. There are two reserve companies of Marines on the island and we should have them assembled before the end of the day. I know that there's also an army reserve artillery company assigned to the fort. I would expect they'll trickle in throughout the rest of the day, too."

McCulloch interrupted him. "What of reserve and militia infantry?"

West spread his arms and shrugged. "I'm not sure, General, sir. I believe there are a couple of your reserve companies on the island, but I'm not sure about the militia."

McCulloch cussed under his breath as they made their way over to West's small office. Johnston heard the reserve officer mention Thomas Rusk, the overall commander of Texas' unorganized militia units, and McCulloch's nominal superior. Johnson had heard McCulloch's acerbic opinion of Rusk on several occasions over the years, as McCulloch had worked to build a reserve command, separate from the militia.

While the criticism wasn't completely unfounded, most of the limited funds appropriated by congress for the reserves and militia found their way into McCulloch's meager budget.

While waiting for the reserve companies to assemble, the two officers took over West's office. As they passed the time, McCulloch's dark thoughts about Rusk shifted to the coming campaign, "Sid, when I spoke with General Rusk, on paper, Texas has more than ten thousand men in the militia, excluding the reserves. There are around thirty-two hundred men in the reserves."

Johnston leaned back in the hard-backed wooden chair. "I'm familiar with the numbers, Ben. What are you getting at?"

McCulloch was picking at a fingernail with a small penknife. "Until General Travis returns from Santa Fe, you're the ranking officer in the regular army, Sid. You know what a mess the militia is. Any army we put together to defeat the Mexican army will include our reserve regiments. I think you should command our field army and I'll start organizing our militia companies into something that might resemble a fighting force."

Johnston ruefully chuckled, "Better you than me, when it comes to getting Tom Rusk to do something with the militia. Trying to bring order out of that chaos is like wrestling with a pig. You both get dirty but only the pig enjoys it." Both men laughed at the mental image of a man and pig, that looked remarkably like Tom Rusk, wrestling. "Let's see what that's going to give me to work with."

McCulloch scrounged around in West's desk until he found a blank sheet of paper. "Let's start here at Galveston. Around the bay, there are a total of six reserve Marine companies. About three hundred and sixty men. You just need to gather the other three companies around the bay to have them all. Throw in two companies of regular Marines that garrison the forts. On paper, that's four hundred and eighty Marines. Then we have four battalions of reserve infantry, each with eight companies. That's another twenty-four hundred men. We also have six companies of reserve cavalry. Call it three hundred men there. We have five batteries of artillery, but three of them are heavy artillery assigned to the forts guarding Bolivar pass, here."

A ghost of a smile crossed Johnston's lips. "If we could assemble the entire force, that would give us nearly three thousand two hundred men to take to the relief of the Alamo."

Without intending to do so, McCulloch deflated Johnston's optimism. "If we can get there in time. Otherwise, it will be a hell of a useful tool to avenge it."

Johnston frowned at the militia general. "God help us if Santa Anna's army captures the Alamo. Let's hope Almaron can hold out until we arrive. I'd rather we be their saviors instead of their avengers."

Chapter 11

23rd March 1842

Rippling in the steady breeze, the Texas national flag flew from the rear of the cotton barge, which rode high in the water, alongside the dock. The old captain stood next to the helm, resting his gnarled hand on the wooden wheel. Johnston thought he looked mollified. *"Well he should, we're paying him enough."*

He glanced toward Major West, who stood next to the gangplank on the dock. The major was looking back toward the road that connected to the dock, wearing an approving smile, as he eyed the five companies of Marines assembled along the road. The two companies of regulars were smartly standing at attention, in their dark-blue jackets and light-blue trousers. Instead of the black wide-brimmed hats worn by the army, the Marines favored a wheel style forage cap.

Along with Captain Atkinson's company from Anahuac, the two reserve companies from Galveston were also drawn up on the road. While the reserves strived to match the uniformity of the regulars, there was still some variety in their clothing, including gray militia jackets and a smattering of butternut army jackets.

The regulars carried the new Model 1842 Sabine rifle. Most of the reserve Marines carried the older Halls breech-loading carbines. Johnston agreed with Major West's silent approval. The regulars stood at attention, holding their rifles with an ease that came from long practice with the new weapons. Johnston wondered how much difference he would find in the skill level between the regular Marines and their reserve counterparts. He glanced toward McCulloch, who was standing beside him. The general of reserves had poured his energy into turning shop keepers, laborers, and farmers into part-time soldiers. Johnston mentally shrugged. No matter their training, he'd work them hard over the coming weeks. With any luck, by the time they met the Mexicans in battle, he'd have them in shape.

There were less than three hundred men standing at attention, waiting for the command from General McCulloch to load up. He swung down from his horse, landing lightly on the wooden dock. "Colonel Johnston, the sooner started, the sooner we can get back onto the mainland."

The two officers led their mounts onto the ship, where a couple of sailors helped to secure the animals. As Major West started loading his men, McCulloch quietly said, "Do you think Galveston will be alright once the navy moves into the gulf?"

Johnston ran his fingers along the rough railing, "Apart from the artillery, there'll still be around a hundred men defending Galveston. Unless Santa Anna changes how he uses his navy, I think Galveston will weather this just fine. If you're worried, we can always send some of the militia to reinforce the forts."

Fully loaded, the barge rode low in the water. Its captain came up and said, "The last time we were riding this low was after the last cotton harvest. It's of no concern, I'll get us safe across the bay. Where do you want to put into?"

Johnston frowned in thought. "Can you get up Buffalo Bayou, Captain?"

Worry creased the seaman's wrinkled face. "I'd be risking my barge if she was half as full on that bayou. Lynch's ferry, on the other hand, should work."

"Then Lynch's ferry it is, Captain."

Most of the day was gone when the barge arrived at the ferry. A small dock extended into the wide, languidly flowing San Jacinto River. Normally, the ferry, which was the only regular service along the river, carried passengers and freight between Houston and Harrisburg to the east. The Marines offloaded at the small dock and Major West had them organized and marching west on the Harrisburg Road. Johnston and McCulloch were the last to disembark. Once on dry ground, the commander of the reserves offered his hand to the other officer, "I don't envy you, Sid. You've got more than two hundred miles between you and San Antonio. When I get to Liberty, I'll send orders by telegraph for reserve units to assemble west of Houston. The militia, I'll order to assemble at Liberty. It's on the rail line between West Liberty and Anahuac. I like my odds for being able to supply the militia there."

"Thanks, Ben. I hope and pray we can send Santa Anna's army packing without having to bring up the militia, but if we need to, at least we've got someone like you to organize them. I don't envy you about that. Getting the militia organized is going to be like riding herd on a bunch of cats, but if anyone can do it, it's you." With a salute to the colonel, McCulloch wheeled his horse around and cantered to the northeast.

Johnston watched until McCulloch disappeared around a heavy copse of trees. He nudged his horse around, toward the road down which the Marines had marched. Dust swirled into the air, clogging the road. Momentarily he was surprised at the amount of dust kicked up by a light battalion. He smiled sardonically. Before long, with any luck, there'd be a lot more men marching toward San Antonio. He'd make sure they'd kick up enough dust to choke Santa Anna. He dug his heels into his mount and galloped after the Marines.

The twenty miles to Houston was simply too far to march with most of the day already gone. They made camp less than an hour later, before they lost the last light of day.

The next morning, as the little column marched westward, word of the invasion had already reached the farmland through which they passed. Women and children came out from their homes alongside the dusty road and cheered the men as they marched along. Over the course of the day, scores of men, belonging to several reserve companies, streamed down the road behind them.

Fiery red splashed across the western sky as the burning orb slipped below the horizon. To his left, Buffalo Bayou lazily flowed. When the battalion of Marines marched through the bustling town of Houston more than an hour before, people had poured into the street to cheer the growing army marching behind Colonel Johnston. Over the past twenty miles, the five companies had been joined by a motley assortment of reserve and militia units, who marched behind the blue-jacketed regulars. More than four hundred men marched along Houston's main thoroughfare.

As he sat astride his mount, Johnston scanned the crowd, spilling over from the non-existent sidewalks. Amid the women and children, there were far too many men of military age for his taste. He would have to say something to McCulloch about this. If this crisis continued beyond a couple of months, every available man in Texas might be under arms. His analytical mind wondered what that would do to the farms and the mills and stores across the republic. Then his mind grew dark as he imagined men like James Collinsworth, staying on their plantations, while poorer men rallied around the flag to protect their property.

Despite his close friendship with General Travis, for years, he had found his friend's abolitionist ideas about manumission to be out of step with the reality of race relations in the American South, but the idea of rich men hiding behind him and the army offended his sense of honor and duty. Maybe there was more to Buck's grumbling than he had previously allowed, he mused.

Like a disturbed hornets' nest, since the news of the Mexican invasion, the town was abuzz with rumors. The Alamo had fallen, no the soldiers at Laredo had repulsed the invasion, the Comanche have stabbed them in the back and have raided below the Red River. No, General Travis and his army have returned from Santa Fe. He discounted the idle speculation of Houston's population. The surest way to find out what was happening was to get his army to San Antonio as soon as possible.

"Enough wool gathering," he muttered. He was glad to be beyond the town. No sooner had he wondered where the assembling troops were encamped, then the scent of burning wood gave away their position. He turned and looked at the Marines, who marched behind him in route step. He pulled back to where Major West traipsed beside his men, "Major, look lively. I believe we're approaching the assembly area."

The major shouted out a string of orders to the men, and they squared their shoulders, shifted their rifles, and their steps fell into unison and they marched proudly into the camp along the bayou.

The next morning, the 25th of March, he had a Marine bugler blow the call for an officers' assembly. Several hundred men, nearly all reserves, were already there. Finding out what arrangements the officers were making to keep their forces supplied was at the top of his priorities.

More than a dozen officers assembled under an expansive live oak tree. An older officer, with oak leaves

133

insignia on his shoulder boards was the first to speak, after Johnston introduced himself. "Colonel, I'm Lt. Colonel Erasmus Hodkins of the Third Infantry. We were under the impression that there would be supplies waiting for us here. When we got here, there wasn't damn all waiting on us. My boys don't have but another day or two worth of food. What's the plan to deal with this?"

A youthful looking captain nodded firmly. "I'm Captain Wallace Jackson, sir, of the Second Infantry. We're in about the same condition as Major Hodkins. If we don't have supplies within a few days, I don't know if I can keep my boys in the field."

The other officers voiced similar concerns. Johnson bit down on the sigh that threatened to escape his lips. "Alright. I understand. We need food to keep our army, here, in the field. We'll send back into Houston for supplies."

He tracked down Lieutenant Robert Crockett, who had arrived at the assembly area a few days earlier and gave him a handful of orders to take back to Houston. As the young officer galloped down the road, Johnston smiled at the younger Crockett's enthusiasm. He lacked his father's flair for the theatrical, but he was a conscientious officer, who would get supplies flowing from the east.

The dust from the horse still lingered in the air when a red stagecoach added another cloud of brown dust billowing along the road from Houston. The stagecoach rolled through the encampment until coming to a stop near the bayou. Before the driver could set the brake, the door to the coach swung open. Johnston closed the little notebook he used for scribbling orders and returned it to his jacket pocket and walked toward the coach, his curiosity piqued.

None other than David Crockett swung down from the doorway, landing lightly on his feet. Soldiers, seeing the president alight from the coach, came running, cheering their commander-in-chief. Johnston smiled and hurried over to the president. He came to attention and saluted. "President Crockett, you're a sight for sore eyes, sir. To what do we owe the pleasure of your visit?"

Crockett waved away the salute and shook his hand with the practice of a politician. His laughter was tinged with bitterness. "Colonel Johnston, it's good to see you again, although I allow I wish the circumstances were different. As to what brings me here, all our fair-weathered congress critters up and decided to suspend congress and skedaddle out of Austin when they heard about that Mexican army coming to San Antonio. Pack of cowards if you ask me. However, at the advice of several members of my cabinet, I have decided that until we have secured San Antonio from any threat from Mexico, that the executive branch will operate out of Houston."

The image of Texas' illustrious congressmen fleeing Austin brought a smile to Johnston's face. "That must have been a sight to see, your Excellency."

The president eyed the colonel disapprovingly. "Knock that palaver off, Colonel. Call me anything else but not 'your Excellency.' I won't stand on parade for such folderol."

They walked past the soldiers, who were smiling and shaking their president's hand. Johnston repressed his impatience as Crockett took his time pumping hands and glad-handing the soldiers as they made their way back to the old live oak tree, under which Johnston was conducting the army's business. As they took seats under the bare branches, Johnston said, "You're welcome to stay out here if you'd like while we organize our reserves. I'm working on getting supplies brought forward from Houston and may use this as our forward supply depot for when we move on San Antonio. Are you familiar with the town of Seguin?"

When Crockett nodded, he continued, "We'll move this army forward to Seguin then. That'll put us forty miles from San Antonio."

Crockett wore a thoughtful expression. "I suppose that's why I saw my son, Bob, riding hell-bent back to Houston when I arrived?

"Lieutenant Crockett should be able to get food and other supplies moving forward, Mr. President. He's shaping up to be a competent officer."

Crockett's laughter caused several soldiers to turn in their direction. "That makes a father's heart warm. When I was his age and serving in the militia, I'm not sure anyone would have accused me of being a competent officer. How many men are assembled here?"

Recalling the officers' meeting earlier, he replied, "We've got five companies of Marines, nearly three hundred men under Major West. We've got odds and ends from three of the reserve battalions, totaling nearly four hundred more men."

The president removed his jacket and laid it on the ground, under the tree and moved down from the chair until he was lying down, "You'll let me know if you need anything, Colonel? With the government's ass waving about in the air, I've got time enough on my hands."

With that, the president closed his eyes, leaving Johnston to continue preparing his weekend warriors for war.

Throughout the rest of the day additional men from the reserves arrived, individually and in small groups. Sometimes they were led into the encampment by officers, and just as often they came in alone, trying to catch up with their units. The highlight of the day, as far as Johnston was concerned was when the last reserve company of Marines arrived, assembled from the small towns on the west side of Galveston Bay.

Before the light had left the western sky, Major West had assembled all six companies of his Marines, giving both Johnston and the president the opportunity to review the three hundred fifty men of the Marine battalion. After checking another rifle, making sure it was ready for action, Johnston thrust it back into the waiting hands. Crockett, a step ahead of him, was back in campaign mode, praising the Marines' martial air. After passing in front of the entire line of Marines, they joined Major West as he dismissed the men to attend to their duties.

Spreading his arms wide, Crockett swept up both Johnston and Major West, patting them on their backs. "This is a fine start, gentlemen. Major, your men cut fine figures. I'm confident they'll make us proud. Colonel, the sooner you're able to get your army to

Seguin town, the sooner we'll be able to send that army limping back to Mexico. Seeing as the government is a little out of sorts right now, and I happen to be the commander-in-chief, I'm going to temporarily promote you to brigadier general of this here army."

Flushing from the news, Johnston stammered, "Thank you, sir. I'll endeavor to do my utmost. But speaking of generals, have you had any word from General Travis?"

"That's the ten-dollar question, Colonel, I mean, General. The last word that came back along the military road was that he had left Ysleta for Santa Fe, but that's a couple of weeks old. I'd imagine that he's probably still in Santa Fe, unless somehow or another he has learned of Santa Anna's invasion."

Seeing the army's campfires burning along Buffalo Bayou, Johnston's spirits were buoyed at the sight of so many fires. "We'll get moving as soon as possible and relieve the soldiers at the Alamo, sir."

Crockett gripped his shoulder, hard. "Please do, General. My daughter and her children are in San Antonio. I can't imagine losing them."

Chapter 12

Rain lashed the canvas sides of the long rows of A-frame tents. The ground was soaked, and water flowed into the Pecos. Will's boot heels sank into the saturated ground as he strode down the makeshift road between two long rows of tents, toward the river. He passed a few cooking fires sputtering under canvas awnings, as soldiers fought the elements to prepare hot food.

Water surged down the normally languid Pecos River, threatening to overflow its banks. With his boots sinking into the red clay mud, Will huddled under his poncho, as rivulets of water streamed off his hat, watching the water race down the too small channel of the Pecos.

His eyes shifted to the Pecos Depot on the opposite side of the river. A short wall encircled the depot. The men stationed there had constructed several adobe structures, where supplies were stocked. But the depot might as well have been a hundred miles away, at least until the river returned to its normally shallow, lethargic flow.

Will clenched his fist, angry at the delay. A squelching noise behind him made him turn around. Juan Seguin was attempting to dodge ever growing puddles. His cavalry boots were caked in mud. It reminded Will of kids playing hopscotch, leaping from one square to another. When he came up next to Will, Seguin glanced down at his boots and grimaced. "Damned rain. It's hard, staring across this accursed river, seeing the depot but not being able to reach it."

"Ain't that the sad, sorry truth. Any other time, and you can just about walk across it."

Seguin shrugged, water cascading from his poncho. "We'll keep our powder dry and when the rain abates, we'll get the army back across the Pecos and get them marching in short order. In the grand scheme of things, Buck, this isn't a setback. The Alamo and San Antonio are in Sid Johnson's hands. Even without this inconvenience," he paused, gesturing toward the incessant rain, "we can't get there in time."

Lucas Leal dangled his feet over the ledge of the new barracks, which spanned the southern wall of the Alamo. He spat down, watching as his spittle landed in the acequia outside the fort's walls. The sergeant from Fort Moses Austin was at loose ends. None of the officers had found time to assign any duties to him or to Private Jackson. Nor had they been assigned to any of the three infantry companies in the fort. He was sure events would soon catch up to him and he would have more than he cared when Woll's army finally arrived.

Twenty feet below, the ripples in the acequia disappeared and he shifted his eyes back to San Antonio. The past few days he had taken it upon himself to watch the comings and goings of the old town. He had served with Juan Seguin's cavalry six years before and was a Bexareno, a native of San Antonio. He felt protective of the town. It was where he had grown to manhood. Where he had kissed his first girl and had his heart broken. His father was buried in the cemetery there and no doubt when she passed on, his mother would join him.

Yet, it wasn't the same town that it had been in 1836. The town had grown. It was spilling over the San Antonio River. Despite the military's claim on the land around the Alamo, houses hugged the Alameda road as it crossed the river and went eastward. It was hard to fathom, but the town had nearly doubled in size since the end of the revolution. If it wasn't the largest town in the Republic it was certainly within spitting distance, Leal thought, as he spat again into the irrigation ditch below.

Well beyond the stubby bell tower of the Church of San Fernando, he thought he caught a glimpse of something reflecting in the March afternoon sun. He climbed up from his perch on the ledge and jogged over to one of the four 9-pound cannon emplaced on the heavily reinforced roof and climbed on top of the trunnion. He shielded his eyes from the glare of the sun and scanned the distance. There was a cloud of dust a few miles south of San Antonio, too much to be able to clearly see what was causing it. But there was only one thing coming from the south that would kick up so much dust.

Leal jumped from the cannon, landing next to Private Terry Jackson, who had taken his jacket and shirt off, and had fallen asleep on the roof. "Hey, *pendejo*, wake up! We got company!"

Jackson lifted his hat, exposing his face. "Eh?" He had been sleeping soundly.

"Get moving, jackass. The Mexicans are coming."

Jackson grabbed his shirt, and grumbled, "That's Jackson. The onlyest Mexican I know is you. And you're already here." As he fed an arm into the garment his eyes followed to where Leal was pointing. The cloud of dust was unmistakable, "Ah, hell."

Leal ignored the private as he walked over the side of the roof and looked down into the Alamo Plaza and shouted, "Captain, an unidentified force to the south!"

A few minutes later, a lanky officer climbed through the crow's-nest-like opening leading to the roof. He joined the two soldiers, as they stared to the south, and retrieved a spyglass from his tunic. It took him only a few seconds to find what he was looking for. He slammed the telescoping spyglass shut and raced back to the other side of the roof, where he called out, "Mexican cavalry force entering San Antonio!"

The door swung heavily on its hinges, as Charlie stood on the threshold of the house he'd called home for more than five years. He adjusted the strap of the backpack to keep the canvas from digging into his shoulder. A couple of blocks away, the bells of San Fernando Church rang out, alerting the denizens of the town to the Army of the North's impending arrival. He looked down the street, watching wagons lumber toward the central plaza, then back into the house, where he saw his stepmother, Becky, with tears spilling down her cheeks, helping Henrietta load food into a blue-and-white checkered blanket on the table.

The noise from the bells echoed in the room, causing baby Elizabeth to cry in her crib. He retreated from the door, leaving it ajar and knelt by his little sister, and made cooing noises as he tried to sooth the nine-month old. From behind him, he heard, "Charlie, please hand Liza to me. We need to get out of here. The Mexicans will be here any moment!"

He set the backpack on the wooden floor and picked up the fussy baby. As he settled Elizabeth against his chest she stopped crying. From the kitchen table, Henrietta swore below her breath as the blanket resisted her efforts to tie the corners into a makeshift bag, heavy with food. Charlie smiled at the mild profanity while Becky pretended she didn't hear the freedwoman. "Lordy mercy, Miss Becky, I'm hurrying. If I could just get this blamed blanket tied, we'd be halfway out of town."

Charlie wiped the smile from his face as he handed Elizabeth to Becky, "Hattie, I'll help with that."

He pulled at the corners, until he feared the blanket would rip. Then he tied them together, knotting the ends to keep them from coming undone. Henrietta hefted the load onto her back, "Showoff." But there was warmth in her voice as she groused.

Both women were out the door, heading toward the plaza as he swung the pack onto his back. He turned and took in the empty room. Over the mantle, above his father's desk was his prized rifle. It had been a gift from the Trinity Gun Works. It was the first Model 1842 Sabine rifle produced by the gun works. Charlie couldn't stand the idea of the finely crafted weapon falling into the uncaring hands of the enemy. He grabbed it and the brown, undyed leather belt with cartridge and cap boxes. The thirteen-year-old boy slung the belt onto his free shoulder and hurried after his family.

Bedlam reigned in the streets. Old men, women, and children streamed east, toward the Alemeda Street bridge. Burdened by his heavy pack and the weapon and accouterments, Charlie trudged behind the women. As they crossed the bridge over the San Antonio River, his stepmother stopped and watched the crowd surge past her. Nearly everyone went straight, towards Gonzales and Seguin Town. To the left, the road ran to the gates of the Alamo. The chapel's façade had been fixed several years before, giving the church a distinct bell shape. Atop the chapel's roof, the Texas flag waved briskly in the cool March afternoon breeze.

If Charlie had his druthers, he would turn to the left. He was of an age when the army seemed filled with glory and honor. He had stopped swinging wooden swords with his friends the year before, and now when he saw soldiers drilling on the fields outside the fort, his heart stirred, as he imagined himself, rifle leveled, advancing against Texas' foes. Boys younger than he had beaten drums for the Continental army less than seventy years before.

But he wasn't alone. No doubt his father expected him to look after Becky, Hattie, and Liza. He eyed Becky as she stayed rooted in place. Was she thinking about her place as an officer's wife? After an interminable amount of time, he shifted the backpack and said, "Becky, we going with the other civilians?" His voice cracked under the stress of the moment.

More time passed, as more folks moved across the bridge, heading east before she responded. "You should take Liza and go east with Hattie. Your father would want you and the baby to be safe from harm."

Charlie strode up next to his stepmother. Over the past year the boy had grown and was now slightly taller than Becky. When he turned to her, they were at eye level. "If one of us should wait for Pa, it should be me. It's too dangerous for you."

Becky dug her feet into the bridge's wooden planks, "No, Charlie. I won't go one more step away from my husband."

Exasperated, Charlie swore, "Dammit to Hell, Becky! Be reasonable." His voice cracked again.

If Charlie had been wise about the ways of women, he would have realized he had said the wrong thing, but to the barely adolescent boy, he had said what he thought needed saying. Rebecca Crockett Travis was, at that moment, anything but reasonable. Her eyes held fire in them, he thought she might slap him for the profanity. Instead, she stormed off the bridge and when she came to the fork in the road, she turned to the left.

As he watched her walk away, back straight, each angry step told him what she thought of his advice. He hefted the rifle and shouldered it, muttering several choice words he'd picked up from his father's soldiers, as he followed his stepmother. Henrietta followed the two of them, wringing her hands, "Lord Jesus, please don't let me be killed following these white folks."

Rebecca had already disappeared through the Alamo's gatehouse as Charlie walked up. A couple of soldiers stood on top of the building watching the town, to the west and nodded at him as he passed below them. When he entered the plaza, he saw his stepmother disappearing into the hospital building, no doubt heading toward the officers' quarters. He thought about following her, but the sight of soldiers rushing about the plaza, carrying powder bags and various types of ammunition for the fort's heavy guns, grabbed his attention. More soldiers were carrying heavy boxes full of paper cartridges to ladders where they were hefted onto the roofs, where riflemen would soon be taking up positions.

He thought about staying and watching but decided his pa would want him to make sure that Becky and Liza were situated in one of the tiny apartments set aside for the fort's officers. As he walked up the stairs to the narrow hallway, he heard a woman's voice, "Oh, heavens, Becky, what in the name of all that is holy made you come here?"

"Don't you start on me, too, Susanna. Charlie was being perfectly horrible about it, and dammit to Hell, I'll tell you what I told him!" Charlie's face colored, hearing his stepmother swearing, "I'm the daughter of David Crockett and the wife of William Travis. What kind of woman would I be if I hiked up my dress and ran away? I'll wait here for my husband, thank you very much!"

When Charlie stepped through the door of the Dickinson's apartment he saw the two women hugging. The major's wife said, "Bless you, dear heart! I think we love our men too much for our own good. I told Almaron the same thing."

Heavy footsteps sounded from the back room as Major Dickinson, his butternut jacket unbuttoned, came up behind his wife. "Here I went and told you that General Travis' wife would have the good sense to go east with the other civilians, and blast it, she comes into our own home and makes me out to be a liar."

While the words sounded jovial coming from the major, Charlie watched the officer's somber expression as he scooped up his wife in an embrace. As his wife's feet dangled above the floor, Dickinson planted a solid kiss on her lips. As he set her back on the floor he said, "I'll have Captain Henderson clear his things out of the rooms next to us and Mrs. Travis and her family and servant can stay there."

The chestnut stallion stamped its feet into the hard-packed dirt of the main plaza. General Adrian Woll let the animal have its way as he surveyed the scene before him. The church bells of San Fernando had long gone silent, the last of the Texians having scurried back to the safety of the Alamo's walls. His lancers, from the Santa Anna Regiment, had secured the town earlier in the day. The steady, rhythmic tramping of boots announced the arrival of the first company of infantry to enter Bexar. He turned and watched the company march into the plaza. Instead of the normal column of four men abreast, the company entered in platoon line formation. The rest of the battalion paraded behind the lead company, filling the plaza.

Woll swung down from the saddle and entered the church, where he climbed the narrow stairs of the bell tower. From there, he could clearly see the adobe walls of the Alamo, gleaming with a golden hue in the late afternoon sun. A large banner flew over the fort. The fort was certainly formidable.

For a moment, he closed his eyes and was transported back in time. Six years earlier he recalled Santa Anna describing the Alamo as barely worth the name of a frontier fort, with walls crumbling from disuse. Woll stared at the walls of the fort, across the San Antonio River and it was evident that the Texians had invested considerable resources into turning the old mission into a formidable fort, bristling with artillery.

Thursday, March 24 1842 was half-over once General Woll had been able to place the battery of field guns into position, which he had brought with his army's first brigade. They were established eight hundred yards to the south of the Alamo. The six guns were unlimbered, and their gun crews quickly and efficiently went to work, loading their guns with solid shot. Once the barrels were loaded, the battery's captain saluted Woll and gave him an expectant look.

Behind the artillery, an infantry battalion was encamped a few hundred yards back. There was no point in delaying things. Woll nodded and said, "It's time to take back what is Mexico's. Fire on the fort, Captain."

As he sat atop the roof of the southern barracks, Sergeant Leal's luck had continued to hold, and he and Private Jackson had managed to avoid being assigned to one of the infantry companies. He admired the work done to the heavily reinforced roof, where four 9-pounder guns were positioned behind sandbag emplacement along the roof's edge, facing south. In between each of the guns more sandbags were used to create low walls behind which rifle teams could fire upon any advancing enemy. Now, apart from a crew of gunners, only Leal and Jackson were on the roof, gazing southward at the Mexican artillery a half mile away.

Leal watched men scurrying around the field pieces then all six guns open fire on the fort. He resisted the urge to duck behind the sandbags and watched several of the shots land on the field south of the fort. One round struck the southern wall at the base, sending adobe dust flying into the air. But the wall was more than three feet thick where the cannonball had struck, and it gouged out only a few inches of adobe.

From within the walls of the fort, Leal recognized Captain Henderson's voice. "Let's send those bastards a warm welcome, boys!"

The Tejano moved back across the barracks roof and watched as the artillery captain directed several of his gunners to load the heavy 18-pounder, which sat in a bastion on the southwest corner of the fort. The heavy gun fired in response, throwing a heavy shell downrange toward the Mexican battery. One of the guns on top of the barracks also fired, sending its nine-pound shell downrange, too. The hefty shell overshot the Mexican artillery, exploding over a team of oxen, used to haul the one of the guns into position. The entire team collapsed. Most of the animals were grievously wounded, their shrill crying could be heard even within the walls of the fort and made Leal shudder as he imagined the gruesome wounds the innocent animals must have suffered.

The Mexican gunners were skilled at their work and sent six more rounds sailing toward the Alamo's walls only a minute after the first salvo. Over the course of the next ten minutes, the four guns above the southern barracks were manned and returned fire on the enemy emplacements. The artillery duel ended when one of the Mexican guns was struck by a solid shot from the gun closest to Leal, causing the wooden carriage to disintegrate in a shower of heavy splinters that cut most of that gun crew down. After that, teams of mules and oxen were brought forward, and the remaining guns were hitched to them and pulled back out of range of the Alamo's guns.

After the smoke drifted away, Sergeant Leal looked down at the wall and saw at least a dozen cannonballs resting along the base. The small chunks of adobe, gouged from the wall were scarcely noticeable.

The same evening, General Woll convened a small meeting with several of his ranking officers in the parsonage of the San Fernando Church. The general offered the officers wine as they settled into the utilitarian chairs. After taking a short sip and wishing for grapes fermented in the fields of France, he opened the conversation. "I had hoped that our guns would be more effective, but they hardly made an impression on the fort's walls. I can't say that I'm surprised. We have received periodic reports over the past few years that the *norteamericano* pirates have been expanding and improving the Alamo."

The ranking colonel asked, "What are our plans, General? Are we going to storm the fort?"

Woll shook his head. "No, not yet, Colonel Espinosa. We'll wait until the second and third brigades arrive over the next week. Once we have assembled our army, we'll have close to four thousand men here. With that, I'm confident that even with their superior rifles, we'll sweep over the fort and crush their resistance."

Colonel Espinosa nodded, "I agree, sir. We would overwhelm the Texians with the whole of our army, but would it not be just as sweet a victory if we could get the garrison to surrender?"

General Woll poured himself another glass of wine and took it in his hands as he rose to his feet and walked over to the window, looking out onto San Antonio's central plaza. After an interminable amount of time, he nodded. "Of course, Colonel. I will demand their surrender tomorrow."

Another younger officer, a major of cavalry, Ernesto Natividad asked, "Do you expect them to surrender, General? *El presidente* was very clear that we were to offer no quarter to these pirates who have taken up arms against Mexico."

Woll shrugged his shoulders, "I am here, and his Excellency is in Mexico City. If they surrender, I will honor whatever terms are necessary to avoid bleeding our own army. On the other hand, if they refuse and they force us to attack, then, yes, Major, we will put the defenders to the sword."

Chapter 13

From Major Almaron Dickinson, Commander of the Alamo

Bexar, 26 March 1842

To Colonel A.S. Johnston, the Congress of the Republic of Texas, the people of Texas and her allies abroad

We are besieged by a thousand and more of the Mexican Army of the North, under General Woll and have sustained a bombardment and have given an account of Texas arms for more than 24 hours and have not lost even a single soldier. The enemy has demanded our surrender and orders all Texians to leave our homes and property. We have responded by raising high the lone star banner of Texas over the Alamo. I am confident that the people of the Republic are advancing to our relief even now. I call on every Texian in the name of our liberty, patriotism, and everything that is dear to

the character of every Texian to come to our aid. The enemy is receiving reinforcements daily and will no doubt increase to three or four thousand within a week. Should our call fall on deaf ears, we shall sustain ourselves as long as possible and die like soldiers of the Republic who know what duty is owed to our honor and our country. Victory or Death.
Major Almaron Dickinson, Commanding

Brevet Brigadier General Sid Johnston sat astride his horse as he watched the soldiers and Marines traipse by. They cast long shadows as they marched into the west. The eastern sky was awash in red and orange fiery colors, as the sun climbed its way above the horizon, on a late March morning. The small cavalry battalion had led out before the sun had risen. He didn't think a cavalry screen was necessary yet, but he saw no reason to take any unnecessary chances. On paper, McCulloch's reserves had a battalion of six cavalry troops, but only parts of three had arrived in time to join the advance toward San Antonio. More than a hundred thirty men were assigned to the three troops, but only eighty were present.

He tried to be philosophical about the low turnout. It's not as though he had allowed much time for the reserve regiments to assemble. But as the 3rd Infantry marched by, he couldn't help but work the math in his head. The regiment's eight companies had six hundred men on paper, but only four companies were with the army, totaling a mere two hundred men.

Once the 3rd had marched by, he pulled his horse back into the road. Some of the problems were simply the logistical problem of assembling a reserve army that was scattered across more than a hundred thousand square miles. Several companies were organized in northeastern Texas. Johnston wasn't even sure those units had even received the mobilization orders yet. Things were moving too fast. In an ideal situation, which he knew this was not, he would have mobilized all the reserve components of the army and given them adequate time to assemble and drill before committing them to any sort of battle. He glared southward, biting his lip in frustration. Mexico had other plans, and now, he was forced to dance to the tune dictated by Santa Anna.

The steady steps behind him were a reminder that the rest of his little army was following along. He turned in the saddle and looked at the 2nd Infantry's banner, carried along by a color sergeant, as he led the regiment's two hundred thirty men. Behind the 2nd came the 5th infantry, with less than two hundred men. On paper, the three reserve infantry regiments represented more than eighteen hundred soldiers. In reality, only a few more than six hundred hurried westwards. The 4th infantry's companies were located so far to the north that it would be a couple of weeks before Johnson had any expectation of seeing them.

Bringing up the rear was a sight that made him sit in his saddle a little straighter, as his breath caught in his throat. Major West had assembled six companies of Marines. Their blue jackets contrasted sharply with the butternut uniforms most of the reserves wore. The three hundred sixty men of the provisional Marine battalion constituted Johnston's largest unit and brought his army's total to more than a thousand men.

When the last of the small army had marched by, Johnston wheeled his horse and raced down the long column toward the front. As the cold March breeze caused the tails of his overcoat to flap behind him, he hoped more of the reserves would be waiting at the town of Seguin. After leaving the army's camp on Buffalo Bayou, he had issued new orders for units to assemble at the small town named for the Seguin family, on the banks of the Guadalupe River. He hoped to pick up several hundred more reserve soldiers at Seguin, but no matter what, he was determined to advance on San Antonio as quickly as possible, even if all he had was the little army marching behind him.

29th March 1842

The wine bottle stood empty on the table in the parsonage's parlor. It served as a weight to keep the map from moving. The map had markers, which represented Woll's 1st brigade, cutting San Antonio from the besieged fort, and curving around to the south. "General, I think we need more men," Woll's aide-de-camp said, as he moved a marker across the map.

Outside the window, they could hear the traipsing sound of *soldados* marching by. The 2nd brigade had arrived in San Antonio, effectively doubling Woll's army. "Estevan, write up the orders for the battalions arriving today. I believe with a little stretching here and there, we'll have enough men to close off the Alamo from the outside. I'll not have their commander sending any more letters."

"Yes, General. Once the 3rd brigade arrives in a few days, you'll have more than thirty-five hundred infantry, more than enough to overrun the fort."

Woll smiled at his aide-de-camp, and walked over to the map, and took a handful of markers from a pile of green markers. He spread them to the south and to the west of the fort. "Indeed, Estevan. With the 3rd, we'll wipe these pirates from the face of the earth. Now, if you'll write up the orders for the 2nd brigade and leave them on my desk, I'll sign them when I return."

Seeing his aide-de-camp reaching for an ink well, General Woll left the parlor and walked out onto the parsonage's porch, where he could watch the *soldados* march past. The men were dirty, tired, and hungry. Between Laredo and San Antonio were nine days of miserable terrain, and once again, the army had outrun its woefully overstretched supply system. But San Antonio was full of supplies, having been abandoned by the *norteamericanos*, there was plenty to eat within the town.

There was a lengthy gap between two battalions marching along the road, and Woll's eyes fell on a boarded-up house owned by one of the more prominent Bexareno families. More than half of those who should have owed allegiance to Mexico had also fled. Something about that troubled the general. There was no getting around that the instability that had allowed Santa Anna to return to power the previous year had done nothing to build confidence in the

Centralist government outside of Mexico City. He glared at the empty house, before his Gallic temperament took over and he sighed. "Nothing to be done about the Tejanos who have left. That will wait for another day." He turned and went back inside. There were orders to sign.

Charlie watched Becky rocking Liza in a borrowed crib, as she and Susanna Dickinson sat the dinner table making small talk while knitting. Behind them, in what passed for a kitchen in the small officers' quarters, Henrietta was adding this and that to an iron skillet. He'd learned a long time ago that Henrietta's idea of "this and that" usually consisted of whatever vegetables she had managed to find. At the end of March, no doubt it meant something canned.

He slipped out the door, having heard enough about which officers' wives were not wearing the latest fashion from New Orleans. As he walked down the stairs, leading to the old convent yard, he muttered, "How can Becky stand to listen to her blather on and on?" As he passed the guard at the bottom of the stairs, he used a couple of swear words he'd often heard the soldiers use.

As the guard chuckled at his passing, he turned and opened a small door between the convent yard and the chapel. A few lanterns were hung on the walls of the old church, casting a dim light across the stone floor. Unlike the day a couple of years earlier when his pa and Becky were married in it, the chapel was full of supplies. Heavy sacks of corn and grain were stacked against one of the walls. On another were several crates of rifles and ammunition. Barrels of gunpowder for the cannons were stacked throughout the nave. At the front of the chapel, above the chancel, a heavy platform stood a dozen feet off the ground. A small battery of three guns were positioned there, facing eastward. A narrow staircase led up to the platform.

The last time he had come in, the gunners assigned to that battery had run him off when he had tried to explore that part of the chapel. There were no gunners up there now, and he strolled over to the stairs, and saw a couple of men from the quartermasters' corps working by the heavy wooden doors at the opposite end. They paid him no mind as he climbed up the stairs. The gun ports were closed, and the gun carriages were tied securely to the wall with heavy ropes. Charlie had watched the fort's artillerists drilling enough to know the ropes were used to catch the recoil. He recalled once, hearing Major Dickinson saying that an unsecured gun could ruin someone's day. Charlie smiled, recalling how his father had commented, "Almaron, damned if you don't have a way with understatements."

As if thinking of Major Dickinson would make him appear, Charlie heard the major talking as he walked toward the platform. "Captain Anderson, we should be prepared for any eventuality, including a breach of the walls, no matter how unlikely. I want the sacristy cleaned out. Those extra boxes of uniforms can be stacked under the parapet over there. If it should come to it, you're responsible for evacuating the women and children from the officers' quarters. You're to put them into the sacristy for protection."

Charlie, who had been crouching down beside one of the cannon, poked his head up and saw the major and Captain Anderson walking toward the door. The chapel's acoustics carried Dickinson's voice up to the parapet, "Take the negro teamsters and put them to building a barricade here across the nave with anything that won't blow up or explode." Charlie leaned forward, watching the major draw an imaginary line in the stone floor twenty feet from the double doors at the chapel's entrance.

As Dickinson reached the door, he turned and looked into the gloom, toward Charlie's platform. The boy ducked down, hoping he hadn't been seen. From below, he heard, "Have Henderson find me. I want him to reposition a few of our guns."

After the officers left, Charlie hurried down the stairs and scurried out the small side door. He didn't want to head back up to the officers' quarters. He wasn't ready to deal with listening to the major's wife rambling on, but he didn't want anyone to yell at him for being under foot, either.

He wandered past the guard at the foot of the stairs leading to the officers' quarters and strolled into the fort's hospital. It was a long building, with a row of beds on each wall. In the past, he would come here and find Dr. Smith. He enjoyed talking with the gregarious and eccentric surgeon. But Ashbel Smith was with his pa and the army out west. Charlie cast a long look around the vast room. It was currently empty. He plopped down on the foot of a bed and replayed in his mind the earlier discussion between Major Dickinson and the fort's infantry commander. Was the major really worried about the Mexican army swarming over the walls? He'd heard stories that Santa Anna had marched north six years before with a blood-red banner. Had the dictator won, even his pa said that Santa Anna had intended to take no prisoners.

He shuddered, as a chill ran down his spine. To an empty room, Charlie said, "I'll be damned if I'll let those bastards take me alive." It felt good to the thirteen-year-old to swear, even if only to an empty room; it helped to keep the fear at bay. He stood. He wasn't sure he felt better, there was still a cold feeling in the pit of his stomach. Now, though, at least he had a vow to sustain him, as he made his way back toward the officers' quarters. Maybe he could put up with Mrs. Dickinson's incessant nattering after all.

The muddy banks of the Guadalupe River had never looked sweeter to the footsore and tired men of Johnston's little army when they arrived in Seguin Town on the first of April. Johnston had hoped he would find more reservists and militia assembled there upon his arrival. He had done everything within his power to use his cavalry to spread word of the general mobilization as the army had hurried west.

Outside of the tiny hamlet, a militia battalion had arrived the previous day. As his own army made camp, he rode through the village and came upon the most bizarre military encampment he'd ever seen. Lean-tos were built next to A-frame tents, which were next to tee-pees and a host of other assorted shelters. Dozens of campfires were lit, as the men of the militia battalion cooked dinner, under a hazy cloud of smoke. A flag fluttered from a pole lashed to a large wall tent in the middle of the camp. The flag was red, with a half-dozen six-sided white stars in the formation of what Johnston recognized as the big dipper. Emblazoned across the top, in English, were the words, '1st Cherokee Rifles.' Johnston was opening and closing his mouth, as he took in the outlandish camp and the Cherokee war banner, when the tent flap was thrown back and Sam Houston strode out. When Houston saw him, he waved a casual salute. "Colonel Johnston, I'm pleased to deliver to you, the Cherokee nation's finest warriors."

Johnston ignored the incorrect rank. Even though he was a brevet brigadier general, he still wore the eagles on his shoulder boards. More sharply than he intended, Johnston returned the salute. A one-time general in the Texian army, Houston could have addressed by the former rank, but Johnston recalled he was also a disgraced former governor and a drunk. Etiquette failed him. He managed, "As God is my witness, Sam, it is good to see the Cherokee have answered the call to arms."

Houston smiled coyly at Johnston. "When I asked them to come to the aid of the men at the Alamo, the tribe took their oath to Texas seriously, Colonel."

Houston looked like he had more to say, when another figure exited the tent. Dressed in a butternut uniform, and sporting shoulder boards with silver oak leaves, denoting the rank of major, the second man came up beside Houston and saluted.

Houston nodded to the second officer, "You may have met my second-in-command, Stand Watie, from the Comanche peace conference a few years ago."

Watie said something quietly to Houston in Cherokee, to which Houston burst out laughing. He pounded the Cherokee officer on the back and waved at Johnston. "Major Watie will give you the grand tour, Colonel." With that, the former governor, general, and drunk closed the tent flap behind him.

Johnston allowed the Cherokee major to show him the encampment. The men of the 1st Cherokee Rifles wore everything from the butternut uniform of the regular army, to the gray militia jackets common throughout the American South, to a mixture of buckskin jackets, and black and brown civilian coats. They were armed as eclectically as they were uniformed. Johnston saw a few Halls carbines, plenty of muskets and hunting rifles, and knives and tomahawks. Despite the hodgepodge of weaponry, as he walked through the camp, there was an optimistic spirit among the nearly three hundred men from the Cherokee nation, and it rubbed off on the officer as he toured the camp.

When he left the Cherokee encampment and returned where his army was encamped on the other side of Seguin town, one thing he was sure of. He was glad the Cherokee had marched to war.

While Johnston's army, now bolstered to more than thirteen hundred, was being ferried across the Guadalupe River, thirty-five miles away, General Woll allowed his normally dour Gallic expression to slip, replaced with a feral smile, as he watched the 3rd brigade of the Army of the North parade through San Antonio's main plaza. All the chess pieces were now on the board and it was time to put the Texians into check.

Woll let the curtain fall and turned around and looked at the officers assembled in the parlor of the parsonage. The room was crowded. The three brigade commanders were present as were each of the regimental commanders. He cleared his throat, "Too many years have passed by since these Yankee pirates drove his Excellency from this land. Tomorrow morning, before the sun has risen, we shall be in the fort and the pirates shall be dead."

General Urrea, commander of the recently arrived 3rd brigade, took a long drink from the wineglass in his hand before he said, "General, our orders from his Excellency was to order these pirates to surrender at discretion. Why have you exceeded your authority by offering honorable surrender terms to these pirates and rebels?"

Woll glared at the brigadier general. The nerve of the man. Urrea had helped depose Santa Anna a few years earlier, and somehow, he had weaseled his way back into the dictator's favor. Woll wondered how long before the snake would send a detailed report of every perceived failure back to his Excellency in Mexico City. "Jose, my highest priority is the preservation of my army. If I can avoid bloodshed by obtaining an honorable surrender from Major Dickinson and his men, then I'm in a stronger position when I face the next group of Texians and they are all the weaker."

Urrea slammed the glass down on the table, cracking the stem. "His Excellency said to take no prisoners."

Woll glanced around the room. The other officers were clearly uncomfortable. *"Damn Urrea for the opportunist he is."* Finally, he cleared his throat and decided to ignore Urrea. "As I said, tomorrow before the sun rises, we shall make the pirates pay. They have refused every opportunity to surrender and be treated with the courtesy of prisoners of war, setting aside the fact that the government they serve is illegitimate. When we take the Alamo, his Excellency's command to take no quarter will be observed. Any man under arms against us will be summarily executed. Any women, children, or slaves should be spared as best as you and your officers are able."

A carafe of wine was passed around the room and glasses were refilled. "Each of you has your orders and know where your regiments will stage from tonight. Keep any construction of scaling ladders well back from the lines. No need to tip our hands until we go over the walls. We will launch our attack at five in the morning, when their sentries will be asleep or too tired to respond." He lifted his glass into the air, waiting patiently for the other officers to join him. "To victory, Mexico, and Santa Anna!"

Chapter 14

He decided spring had truly arrived as he swatted away something crawling on his face. He cracked open his eyes and looked at the stars in the night sky. The clouds overhead partially masked the quarter moon, reflecting a hazy yellow, washing out the stars closest to the moon. Sergeant Leal pulled his greatcoat up to his chin. It might be the 3rd of April, but the night still gave him a chill, and he wished he were asleep in one of the barracks. Try as he might, he couldn't fall back asleep, as his mind became cluttered with thoughts.

His and Private Jackson's days of idleness had come to an end a couple of days prior. Major Dickinson had assigned more than a dozen men from the quartermaster's corps and a few men from the engineering company to his command. Additionally, a half-dozen teamsters had been armed and added to his little mixed and matched force. The teamsters were freedmen, and armed negros didn't sit well with several of the soldiers under his command. Ever since the Revolution, Leal had served with Southerners and while he could not fault most of them when it came to bravery, he thought they had a blind spot when it came to the black men in their midst.

He sighed, as he tried to find a comfortable spot on the ground, it wasn't only the negro that these Southerners looked down upon. Despite proving his competency time and again, because his own skin was brown, and his English had a pronounced accent, some of those same men looked down on him. He shook his head. He'd deal with that, if he had to, when it surfaced in his new command. As the ranking NCO, he'd be damned if some insolent private would interfere with his own survival.

It was no use, he couldn't go back to sleep. He stood and slipped the greatcoat on and walked over to the large 18-pounder, emplaced on the south-west corner of the fort, and looked out into the inky darkness. A half mile away, he could see the campfires in the Mexican camp. As late as it was, they had mostly burned down to glowing embers. The longer he stared at the campfires he began to wonder if his mind was playing tricks on him. For a moment, he thought he saw shadows flitting in front of one of the fires that was burning brighter than the others. Intrigued, the Tejano sergeant turned and walked down the earthen ramp. Amid the gunners and riflemen sleeping on the ground, he tapped Terry Jackson on his bootheel until he heard a mumble from beneath a woolen blanket. Leal whispered, "Wake up, *pendejo*. I need your help."

Groggily, Jackson lifted his wide-brimmed hat, which had been covering his face. "I'd have to be a fool to let you ruin my sleep, Sarge. Why'd you wake me? I was dreaming of me and a beautiful *señorita*."

Leal grabbed the other soldier by the hand and helped him to his feet. "Leave my sister alone, Jackson. I don't want you dreaming about her. Remember, I hear what you talk about in your sleep." He led the private to the postern door in the gatehouse. From above, an alert voice harshly whispered, "What in the Hell are you fools doing by the gate?"

Leal turned and looked at the soldier standing on top of the gatehouse. He carried his rifle at the ready, pointing it in their direction.

Sergeant Leal waved at the guard. "Saw something outside the walls and wanted to check on it. Private Jackson here will keep an eye on the postern gate while I look into it."

The sentry shook his head, "Y'all know I ain't supposed to let anyone out the gate, Sergeant."

Leal swore under his breath and ground his teeth. How did he get stuck with the one guard who punctiliously followed the rules? "Alright, why don't you go fetch the sergeant of the watch and we can sort this out?"

He watched the sentry weigh his options before he finally said, "Alright. But both of you wait right there and don't you go anywhere."

As the sentry disappeared into the darkness, Leal glanced over at Jackson and said, "What are you waiting for, open the door." The two ran toward the postern gate, which was nothing more than a narrow door set into the large, thick wooden gates. With the private's help, he lifted the heavy, wooden bar and cracked open the door. Turning quickly to Jackson he said, "Keep this door open until I get back." He didn't wait to see Jackson's response as he crouched low and ran into the darkness.

Leal crept along the ground, heading south from the gate. Heavier clouds had covered the moon, making it difficult to see clearly more than thirty or forty feet in any direction. New grass was growing in the field, replacing the dormant grass of winter. He slid along as quietly as possible, thankful to not hear the dry, crunching sound of grass under his feet. He reckoned he covered close to eight hundred yards of flat prairie when he heard voices ahead. He ducked lower to the ground and as silently as possible inched his way forward until he saw the silhouettes of dozens of soldiers standing in a line of battle. He saw a pinprick of light from one of the shadowy *soldados* and moments later smelled the pungent odor of tobacco.

The sound of boots hitting the ground echoed in the still night air as he heard a slap and watched the burning coals from the cigarillo fly through the air, landing in grass heavy with the early morning dew. A harsh voice whispered in Spanish, "What the hell are you thinking, Juarez? Do you want the Yankees to know we're coming? When we get moving, grab that damned ladder and carry it. First one to get to the wall with a ladder earns ten pesos."

Leal resisted the urge to flee across the open ground. *"Okay, pendejo. Don't lose your cool. Steady as you go."* He thought as he slowly slithered through the grass, away from the deployed line of men. It seemed to take forever to crawl a hundred yards, but once he felt he'd put enough distance between him and the Mexican line, he stood, and ran back to the Alamo, crouched low, praying to the blessed Virgin that he remained unseen.

As the walls of the fort loomed out of the darkness, Leal slowed to a walk, scanning the top of the parapet, above the gates. Where was the guard? Had he returned to his post? Not seeing anyone, he picked up his speed as he dashed toward the postern gate. It looked as though the narrow door was cracked open. His mouth twisted into a grin. Jackson was waiting where he was supposed to. Before he could step through the postern gate, three rifle barrels protruded through the opening, aimed at his chest. "*Santa Maria*, Jackson, what the hell is going on?" he whispered.

Two beefy hands reached out and grabbed him by his jacket. Yanked off his feet, and dragged through the door, which closed behind him, Leal was thrown up against the wall. A tall, square-jawed sergeant pinned him against the wall and hoarsely said, "Alright you damned bean-eater, what in the blue blazes were you doing outside the wall?"

Despite his feet dangling inches from the ground, the other sergeant's rough handling pushed the normally easy-going Tejano over the edge. "That's Sergeant 'Bean-Eater' to you. Maybe I should put you outside the wall and let you welcome the Mexican army when they attack." Leal surprised himself with the authority of his low-pitched voice, as Jackson failed to stifle his laughter at the other sergeant's expense.

The large sergeant dropped him to the ground and pulled a smelly cigar from his mouth. He glared at Leal as he blew a fog of smoke into the Tejano's face. "What's that about Mexicans?"

Exasperated, Leal shook his head, "*Pendejo*," he muttered. He pointed back toward the closed gates, "The Mexican army is about to attack the fort. We can sit here and talk about it until they come over the wall, and you can ask them to confirm it. Or would you rather we notify Captain Anderson or Major Dickinson?"

As morning approached, clouds had rolled in, covering the moon and stars. He held his mount's reins in one hand, as he glanced into the heavens. The only thing missing was fog. He chuckled as he swung into the saddle. He fingered the rosary beads in his coat pocket and offered up a brief prayer to the Virgin Mother. Adrian Woll was a happy man. His well-trained army was completing its nighttime deployment around the Alamo with minimal noise.

He watched the shadowy figures of his *soldados* carrying ladders and taking up their preassigned positions in preparation of the pending attack. Things were progressing exactly as planned. Mentally he reviewed the coming attack. To have the best vantage point for watching the battle unfold, he had moved his headquarters from the parsonage of the San Fernando Church to the corner between the western and southern wings of his army, southwest of the Alamo. Two regiments from the 3rd brigade were to his right, ready to assault the Alamo's main gate along its southern wall.

He glowered, thinking of the insolence of General Urrea. The opportunist would happily plant a dagger in anyone's back if there was something he could gain from it, but when his men started forward, the vainglorious bastard would be leading them from the front. A ghost of a smile lit up his lips at the thought of a Texian sniper ending Woll's misery by putting a bullet in Urrea's head.

When he thought of his earlier prayer to the Virgin, he dismissed the thought. It wasn't Catholic to wish ill of a fellow officer, even one as nakedly opportunistic as Urrea. He turned his thoughts to what the men of the 3rd brigade would face once the assault was under way. Over half of the southern wall was twenty feet tall, where one of the Alamo's new barracks had been constructed. It was too tall for the scaling ladders his men would carry into battle. But a third of the wall was the gatehouse building, which was only about ten feet in height. That part of the wall extended another ten yards, and encompassed the bastion protecting the Texians' 18-pounder.

On the opposite end of the fort, two of the 2nd brigade's regiments would assault the northern wall. It had been rebuilt a few years earlier. Like on the south, a new barracks accounted for more than half of the wall and was also twenty feet high. The remainder of the northern wall was only twelve feet tall. It was there that the five hundred men of the 2nd brigade would focus. Thinking back to the idea of the battlefield being a chess board, Woll viewed the regiments assigned to these attacks as nothing more than pawns designed to draw the Texians' attention. He tried not to think about a thousand men as nothing more than mere pawns. In the end, though, they were nothing more than feints. But feints that if not protected against, would quickly bring the defenders to ruin.

No, Woll mused. The main attack would come from the west, from the direction of the San Antonio River. The three regiments of the 1st brigade would lead the assault. The last two regiments from the 2nd and 3rd brigades would serve as Woll's strategic reserve, behind the 1st.

East of the Alamo, a long acequia ran into San Antonio's reservoir. Between the acequia and the wall of the Alamo was a thicket of mesquite trees and thorn brushes. Woll wondered if the Texians cultivated the obstacle. It didn't matter, as far as Woll was concerned a group of old women could defend the eastern wall of the fort with slingshots. Nevertheless, a company of *cazadores* would take up position along the eastern acequia and bag any Texians attempting to flee in that direction.

Behind his assembled troops, Woll heard the faint sound of horses. That was the sound of the two hundred fifty men of the Santa Anna cavalry regiment heading to the northeast, between San Antonio and the other settlements. Any attempt by the Texians to relieve the garrison would run headlong into his capable and tough lancers.

Even though he subscribed to the philosophy that no plan survives contact with the enemy, Woll had taken care of all the things that he could control. Everything else was in the hand of the Blessed Virgin. He nodded to his aide-de-camp and said, "Estevan, it is time. Pass along the order to advance."

The beefy sergeant smoothed the front of Leal's jacket, and dropped his hands to his sides before saying, "That's probably a good idea." He turned to a smallish rifleman by his side. "Private Abramson, go and fetch Captain Anderson. Wake him if he's asleep." The smaller man turned on his heels and disappeared into the dark gloom in the direction of the officers' quarters.

Leal briefly entertained the thought of waiting there for the captain to arrive, but his curiosity about the Mexican army outside the fort was pitched too high to wait around, and he jerked his head toward the bastion where the 18-pounder was situated and walked up the ramp, as the other men followed. Atop the gun platform, it was impossible to see any distance into the darkness. The cloud cover that had moved in during the last hour, made seeing more than a few dozen steps into the night impossible. A few minutes later, Captain Anderson arrived, climbing the ramp, and joining the men standing around the gun, as they peered into the inky darkness. As he joined the half-dozen men he quietly asked, "What seems to be the matter at this ungodly hour, men?"

The large sergeant spoke up first. He pulled the cigar out of his mouth and used it as a pointer as he indicated toward Leal and said, "Sergeant Bean-Eater over there went out through the postern gate, against orders and said that the Mexicans are getting ready to attack, sir."

Leal let the snide remark slide, while Captain Anderson eyed the other sergeant with disapproval. Leal piped up, "Yes, sir. Me and Private Jackson here thought we saw something around their campfires, and so I went to check on it. When I got out about half a mile away, I saw the Mexicans standing in line, like they were ready to attack. And I saw more soldiers bringing up ladders. I'm certain they're preparing an assault."

Captain Anderson eyed both sergeants, doubt written across his face. Leal turned and looked out into the dark field south of the Alamo, and the captain's eyes followed. He stepped over to the wall and muttered. "Can't see a damned thing out past fifty yards." He looked back at Leal and added, "I'm not calling you a liar, Sergeant, it just seems unlikely that they'd sit on their asses for the past two weeks and only now decide to attack."

He shook his head. "But, there's one way to find out." He returned to the large, brass cannon and asked one of the gunners who had been roused by the men standing around his gun. "Is this thing loaded?"

Bleary eyed, the gunner nodded. "Yeah, it's got a charge of canister in it."

Ignoring the gunner's lack of respect for his rank, he stepped up to the back of the gun where he ran his finger along the top until he found the touch hole. He stretched his hand to Leal, "Let me have one of your cartridges, Sergeant."

The captain tore the paper open and poured the coarse gunpowder into the hole. He glanced around and reached out and grabbed the cigar out of the other sergeant's mouth. "Y'all might want to step aside." With that, he took a step back from the gun and leaned in, holding the smoldering cigar toward the gun and lit the powder on the touch hole. A split second later, the powder charge at the base of the tube ignited, shooting out flames from the end of the barrel. The canister exploded out the mouth of the gun, as the blast lit up the night and for a moment, turning night into day in the area in front of the gun. In that briefest of flashes, less than two hundred yards away, the line of advancing Mexican infantry was clearly visible. The element of surprise gone, the Mexican line yelled a terrifying battle cry and charged.

Chapter 15

Mist swirled around his feet, as he stood on the shore of a wide river. Somehow his mind knew it was the mighty Tennessee. Fog hugged it from one bank to the other, muffling the sounds of marching men and the jingling spurs as horses cantered by. Albert Sidney Johnston glanced down, perplexed to find his butternut uniform replaced by a gray jacket. He turned and saw a chestnut mare behind him, and an officer, also dressed in gray waiting on him. A long thin column of more gray-clad soldiers trailed along a road, which ran parallel to the river.

In the distance, he heard the deep booming sound of dozens of field pieces firing. Nearby, many more guns replied, shaking the ground beneath his feet.

He found the reins of the horse in his hands and turned and climbed into the saddle, but found the mist was rising and even the marching men only a few yards away were obscured. The officer next to him said, "General …"

"General! Sir, wake up! General Johnston, there's something wrong!" the insistent voice shook him awake. The heavy fog of sleep fled as the dream's images evaporated. He opened his eyes and saw a shadowy silhouette standing above him in the tent. The sergeant of the guard reached down and gently shook his shoulder, "Sir, are you awake?"

"I am now, Sergeant." The last of the dream was chased away as he thought he heard thunder in the distance. As he slung his stockinged feet onto the cold ground he asked, "What's the ruckus for, Sergeant?"

Stepping over to the tent's flap, the sergeant flung it open and pointed toward the southwest, toward San Antonio. "Just now, we started hearing what sounds to me like artillery coming from San Antonio. I could have sworn I saw of flash of light below the horizon."

He pulled on his boots and stepped out the tent and looked intently toward their destination. Heavy cloud cover made the night especially dark, and sure enough, there were a few flickers beyond the horizon. He shook his head, this was bad. He turned to the sergeant, "Thank you. Go and fetch all the battalion commanders, quickly!"

Following a quick meeting with his field grade officers, Johnston decided to abandon the camp and rush his army toward San Antonio. No more than fifteen minutes after being roused out of his own sleep, he sat astride his horse, glaring down at the men who he could see, after they had put on their boots, grabbed their rifles, and assembled by companies in line. Johnston glanced heavenward and muttered curses. Of all the nights to have heavy cloud cover, this was the worst. He tore his eyes back toward the soldiers. "Men! Soldiers and sons of Texas!" his voice boomed over the dark prairie, "We march to the sound of the guns! Do your duty this morning to your mothers, wives, and sisters, and to our children! You will march with valor and honor, against an enemy that would not only despoil our homes but drive us from this very land!"

As the order was given to switch from the long line into columns of four, the men under his command let loose with a defiant cheer. They hurried into the night, leaving most of their camp supplies on the prairie.

Before the flash from the cannon faded to black, Sergeant Leal watched the canister load explode from the barrel, sweeping toward the advancing line of *soldados*. Like a scythe reaping grain, Leal saw more than a dozen men cut low by the gun's discharge. Men who had been sleeping on the roofs of buildings set against the western wall, leapt to their feet when the powerful blast from the heavy 18-pounder shattered the stillness of the night and shook the ground.

Along with the other men on the bastion, Leal let out a loud shout. The battle for the Alamo had begun. He turned and saw Private Jackson running back up the ramp with both of their rifles and when he grabbed his from the private, he raced to load it. Out of the corner of his eye, he saw the gunners leap to action as one of them grabbed a rammer with a wet sponge and used it to clean the barrel out, damping any embers that could result in a premature detonation of the powder charge.

Leal fired into the blackness in the direction of the Mexican army. He could hear them, as they shouted war cries, but they were still several hundred feet away. Jackson and a couple of more riflemen added their own rifle fire along the lip of the bastion. Behind him, he heard the gunners rushing to get the heavy gun reloaded. Despite being suddenly woken up, they moved with an economy of motion that came from extensive practice and years of experience.

In his mind's eye, Leal imagined the Mexican *soldados* storming across the prairie, muskets at the ready. As though coloring in the mental image, from the dark fields, he heard thousands of voices screaming, "*Viva México*! *Viva* Santa Anna! *Viva* Woll!" The sound of their booted feet slammed against the ground, rapidly closing the distance with the fort.

A voice screamed from behind him, "Clear the way!" The 18-pounder was being rolled forward, into its firing position. Leal and Jackson scurried to the side, as the brass barrel eased forward. A ladder from the parapet led to the top of the gatehouse and the two darted up it, clearing the platform a scarce moment before the gun fired for a second time. The field before them lit up again, revealing the advancing enemy had more than cut the distance in half. Leal and Jackson added their rifle fire to those men already on the wall, firing into the darkness of the predawn.

Men poured out of their barracks, as they raced to their assigned places on the walls of the beleaguered fort. More of the fort's guns added their sound and fury to that of the 18-pounder.

The rough-hewn planks of the floor rattled Charlie awake. A moment of confusion made him wonder where he was until he heard Becky's voice, "Hush, Liza, Momma's here." His little sister, Elizabeth began caterwauling in earnest as the building shook with each successive blast from the fort's heavy guns. Adding to the noise of the fort's thundering artillery, was the rattling sound of gunfire.

The door to the room was thrown open, Susanna Dickinson's silhouette stood in the opening. Fear was engraved on her face as she cried, "They're attacking, Becky! We gotta get to the chapel, like Almaron told us!" She cradled her young son in her arms while her daughter, Emily clung tightly to her skirt.

Like the women, Charlie had slept in his clothes, and as Mrs. Dickinson fled down the stairs, he pulled off the blanket covering him and jumped up from the hard floor. Henrietta took Liza from Becky while his stepmother grabbed a few things she intended to use to distract the baby. She frantically looked around the room until her eyes fell on an engraved box they had brought from home, setting on a chest of drawers. "Charlie, please fetch me your pa's pistols."

The youth grabbed the box, which held the gift from Samuel Colt and handed it to her. "Hurry, Charlie!" she said as she and Henrietta started after Mrs. Dickinson.

The boy grabbed the brown leather belt that held his father's cartridge and percussion cap boxes and fastened it around his waist, tightening the belt to its last notch, to keep it from sliding down his slender frame. He grabbed his father's rifle in one hand and scooped down and grabbed his shoes with the other. He raced from the room and took the stairs two at a time hastening to catch up to the women.

The guard, normally stationed at the foot of the stairs leading to the officers' quarters, was gone from his customary post. Charlie scanned the old convent yard and saw a handful of gunners and riflemen heading over to a ramp which led to a platform with two guns facing eastward. A rifleman already stood there, peering into the predawn darkness. Through the small door, the boy heard his little sister crying from the transept and hurried toward the door, ignoring the defenders who ran past him to their stations.

He slammed the door shut, and as he had been instructed, threw a heavy wooden bar across the narrow opening. He turned and saw Becky and Liza had joined Mrs. Dickinson and several other women and children in the sacristy. Light flickered on their faces from lanterns along the wall, and the boy saw Becky open the box containing the brace of revolvers, while Henrietta sat beside her, cooing at Charlie's sister. Ignoring the gnawing fear in the pit of his stomach, Charlie gave a feral smile to his stepmother, as she started loading the revolvers.

The chapel's thick walls muffled the deep-throated booming of the fort's artillery and the rattling of gunfire. Charlie heard the sound of quiet voices coming from the nave and he walked over to the men who stood behind a barricade, which ran the width of the chapel. A half-dozen men in civilian clothes stood on ammunition boxes, peering over the barricade. More lanterns ran the length of the chapel and he saw the fear on the black faces of several of the teamsters, who had been trapped in the fort with the soldiers for the past two weeks. Watching the freedmen awkwardly holding their rifles, drew Charlie's thoughts to Joe, his pa's former slave and currently a teamster. Seeing the fear in their faces, he was glad that Joe was out west delivering supplies to one of the depots. Thinking of the west, his pa came to mind. He was certain his father would be brave if he were trapped here. He remembered a conversation he'd had with his pa before he had left to conquer Santa Fe. "Son, true courage isn't an absence of fear, but rather it is channeling that fear into action."

He took hold of his father's rifle and stepped up onto an ammo box, next to one of the negro teamsters. Glancing up, he could read the man's fear on his face. It was easy to recognize. He imagined he wore the same expression, too. He closed his eyes tight, willing the terror in his gut to not control him. After a long moment, he opened his eyes and forced a smile onto his face, as he reached over and patted the teamster on the arm. "My name's Charlie, what's yours?"

Standing on the corner of the southwest bastion, Captain Anderson was able to see the thick, solid line of Mexican infantry surge from the cloudy night's dark gloom. As the *soldados* reached the irrigation ditch encircling the fort, the first rank splashed into the knee-deep water. A mere fifty feet separated the advancing line from the fort's walls. Every cannon that could, had its elevation depressed, putting the mass of infantry within the guns' line of fire. Scores of riflemen were already on the wall, and more than a hundred raced across the plaza to join their compatriots.

Anderson screamed at the men along the wall to pour their fire into the ranks of advancing infantry. A word of caution from the artillery sergeant holding the linstock for the 18-pounder, was the only warning before the huge gun fired double-loaded canister rounds into the ranks of *soldados* crowding across the acequia. Dozens of men were swept from their feet, as eighty heavy, round balls slammed into the men wading through the ditch. They fell into the dirty, shallow water, only to be stepped upon and pushed down into the muddy bottom, where those who had not been dead already, died a hideous death by suffocation or drowning.

The devastating cannon blasts and accurate rifle fire wreaked an atrocious bill on the men of Urrea's 3rd brigade. The pressure along the southern wall eased as Urrea's men disengaged and retreated into the darkness of the predawn.

Anderson moved over to the west side of the bastion and saw several ladders had been placed against the wall. The problem, as he saw it, was the western wall had not been rebuilt like the fort's northern and southern walls. Although the clouds still obscured the moon and stars, the constant flashes of light and fires burning along the wall, illuminated the battle raging before his eyes. At least a hundred of his riflemen were on the wall, firing down into the milling mass of men at the foot of the fort. They fired as fast as their breechloaders would allow. The artillerists on the wall exposed themselves to the musket fire from below every time they rolled their cannon back into firing position and depressed their barrels so that the guns could fire into tightly packed *soldados*.

As men grabbed hold of ladders' rungs and tried to crawl over the wall, Anderson raced down the ramp, and shouted at every rifleman he could find and sent them rushing toward the western wall, where a fierce battle raged. He saw a group of men moving purposefully toward the wall, it was Major Dickinson leading several gun crews. Apparently, the dense forest of mesquite trees growing between the eastern wall and the acequia had deterred the Mexican army from attempting anything along that wall. He watched Dickinson and his men swarm up ramps and ladders, joining their fellow gunners as they rushed to fire and reload their guns.

As the attack on the gatehouse faltered, Sergeant Leal looked over at Jackson, whose face was covered in sweat and grime. For a moment, he felt guilt at not having rounded up the men from the quartermaster's corps and engineers assigned to his command. But as he looked at the dead and dying carpeting the ground before the gatehouse, he shrugged it off. Even so, duty called, and he grabbed Jackson by the collar and headed toward the chapel, where he figured most of his men would assemble.

He found nearly all of them in the nave of the chapel in front of the makeshift barricade. He saw the teamster's black faces on the other side of it, staring at him as he entered the chapel. He smiled at the image and thought they might be the only smart men among the whole lot of soldiers trapped in the fort.

He left the freedmen where they were. As far as he was concerned, they barely knew which end of the gun to load. He left a few men from the quartermaster's corps behind, responsible for doling out ammunition, and took the rest of the men back outside. There was a low wall between the chapel courtyard and the Alamo plaza which ran between the gatehouse and the hospital, about seventy feet, where he placed his men at evenly spaced intervals and waited. Across the plaza, along the western wall, the battle continued to rage. Most of the garrison was there, pushing over ladders nearly as often as they were raised.

He had lost track of time. It seemed as though the battle had been waging for hours. In the east, there was a hint of dawn on the horizon. Leal scanned the walls ringing the plaza and to his left, to the south, he saw dozens of riflemen atop the gatehouse and the 18-pounder's bastion firing at targets he couldn't see. To his front, the western wall was ablaze with cannon and rifle fire. To the northwest, at the corner of the fort, he saw the tops of several ladders poking above the wall, then *soldados* appearing at the top and clambering over the wall and landing in the corner of the plaza. A couple of rifle teams ran down from their firing platform on the northern wall and began slashing and stabbing at them, while the Mexicans reacted with their own bayoneted muskets and knives.

The eastern sky continued to lighten. More Mexicans joined their compatriots in the corner, clearing the wall to either side, as they overwhelmed the Texians who had met them only moments before. More than a dozen stormed up one of the northern ramps, where they cut and bayoneted the gunners who only seconds before had sent canister shots crashing into the milling soldiers still attempting to scale the wall.

Leal tapped Jackson on the shoulder and pointed toward the growing problem in the northwestern corner of the plaza. The two men raised their rifles and took a few seconds to aim and fire. Both men hit their targets; Leal's lips peeled back in a vicious grin as he levered the breech open and slid in another cartridge.

He no longer needed to rely on the fires burning along the western wall to see the deteriorating position of the defenders. He heard rifle fire from behind and Captain Anderson spun around and saw a few riflemen in butternut uniforms crouching behind the low wall in front of the chapel courtyard. They were firing at a growing number of Mexican *soldados* in the northwestern corner of the fort. A green, white, and red flag was being waved by a handful of *soldados* on one of the northern gun platforms.

Anderson realized several guns along the western wall had fallen silent, their gunners shot down by Mexican infantry, who had seized several sections of the long wall. Closest to him, near the 18-pounder, most of his regulars were still manning their section of the wall, but near the northwest corner, Mexican *soldados* were rapidly overwhelming his men. Recalling Major Dickinson's earlier arrival to shore up his batteries, Anderson scanned the wall, but the major was nowhere to be seen. With the crumbling defenses in front of him, he swore as he realized there was no option but to fall back. "Back, boys, Back! The wall's breached! Fall back to the courtyard!" As his men raced back to the relative security of the chapel courtyard, he turned on his heels and strode toward the low wall.

The captain came to the wall and saw a few butternut-clad riflemen standing atop the southern barracks. As dozens of his men knelt behind the wall, he called up to the men atop the barracks, "Hold your position there! Don't let anyone get ladders up to you, and by God, kill any of the bastards that try to use our cannons against us!"

He desperately hoped the reason the Mexicans hadn't tried to raise any ladders along the walls where the new barracks had been built was because they had no ladders tall enough to reach the top of those buildings. Anderson ground his teeth in frustration. What did it matter? More ladders were thrown up against the western wall and more *soldados* poured over the top.

The courtyard wall was only a couple of feet tall, split in the middle by a narrow walkway leading from the plaza to the chapel doors. Anderson passed through the narrow opening and directed the retreating men into spots along the wall, where they joined the men already kneeling. Once the places behind the wall were taken, the captain ordered the men to create a second line, standing behind those who were kneeling. As the last of the survivors from the western wall passed through to the chapel courtyard, he reckoned he had about a hundred men still with him. Additionally, there was a platoon's worth of men stationed on the rooftops of the new barracks buildings on both ends of the fort. As long as they held out, he would control the high ground. But time was running out.

With his sword in his hand he paced behind the line of riflemen. "That's it, men, aimed fire. Make every shot count!"

Chapter 16

From where he paced behind the line, Captain Anderson saw *soldados* swarming over the southwest bastion where the 18-pounder was positioned. Some had grabbed the trail handles and were lugging the heavy ordinance around. Using the sword in his hand as a pointer, he yelled, "Kill those bastards at the gun."

From the roof of the southern barracks, a smattering of gunfire began to drop the *soldados* around the large cannon. The captain whooped and raised his hat, cheering as the *soldados*, who only a moment before had been turning the gun around, now scrambled for cover. Apart from blasting a hole in the thick adobe walls from outside the fort, the only entrance to the southern barracks was through a door in the chapel courtyard. As long as his line held the courtyard wall, the men atop the barracks would have a commanding view of the plaza and walls.

With one threat neutralized for the time being, Anderson walked down the line, behind his men, "Keep it up, boys! They'll not drive us any further!" Acrid smoke hugged the ground before the wall, as his riflemen poured a devastating fire on the Mexicans assembling on the walls and in the northwestern portion of the plaza. A bullet crashed into a rifleman, standing directly in front of Anderson, with a wet, meaty smacking noise and the young man sank to the ground, crying out as he clutched at his shoulder. A nearby Tejano sergeant, who Anderson recognized as bringing word to the Alamo of the Mexican invasion from Laredo, helped him drag the badly injured rifleman from the line.

Although there was a doorway from the courtyard into the hospital, it was now guarded by a rifle team. The main hospital doors faced the open plaza, and Anderson worried the hospital would fall to the Mexicans as soon as they advanced from their positions. A couple of orderlies with green chevrons on their sleeves were evacuating the wounded, carrying them from the hospital's side door into the chapel. They left the injured soldier with one of the orderlies and turned to look at the firing line.

Anderson asked the Hispanic sergeant, "Leal, isn't it?"

The sergeant wiped the sweat from his face with his sleeve, "Yes, sir."

Anderson nodded toward the men on the firing line. "We're going to need more ammunition. Fetch a box from the chapel. We've got to be running low."

Sergeant Leal acknowledged the order with a single nod and turned, running toward the heavy, wooden doors of the chapel, where a couple of men from the quartermaster's corps stood with rifles. They stepped aside as he entered the chapel's dimly lit nave. The sound of wounded echoed from the thick walls, where they had been laid after the hospital's evacuation. Standing near a tall barricade, made from bags of grains, corn, and flour, a soldier with a quartermaster sergeant chevrons stood guard over several long ammunition boxes. Leal ran up to him, "I don't suppose you're planning on using all that yourself?"

Grimly chuckling, the other sergeant shook his head. "It's all yours. How's it going out there?

Leal's shoulders sagged. "We're still alive, some of us. But there are so many damned Mexicans coming over the walls."

The quartermaster sergeant helped him heft one of the boxes onto his shoulder and led him back to the doors, through which the medical orderlies were dragging more wounded. As Leal hurried back across the courtyard, musket balls kicked up dust near his feet. He swore as he reached the wall. The enemy's musket fire was increasing as their own sergeants and officers were joining the *soldados* along the wall.

After helping to pass the ammunition around to the riflemen kneeling and standing behind the low stone wall, he found Private Jackson kneeling against it. The private's actions were economical and fluid. He fired his rifle at a target, then levered the breech open and shoved a paper cartridge into the breechblock before levering it closed, slicing off the cartridge's excess paper. He fished a percussion cap from the box on his belt and slipped it onto the nipple and cocked the rifle's hammer, aimed, and fired. Each shot followed the preceding one by less than ten seconds.

To Jackson's right another rifleman was aiming at a target across the plaza, when he tumbled back, almost knocking Leal down. The sergeant was about to swear at the soldier when he saw the top half of his head had been messily clipped off by a musket ball. He grabbed the body by the shoulders and dragged it away from the line and slipped into the space beside Jackson and loaded his rifle and aimed at an officer on the western wall. Before pulling the trigger, he wondered how much longer the line would hold.

If there was a silver lining, Anderson thought, then it had to be that as the sun crested the eastern sky, it would be in the eyes of the rapidly increasing number of *soldados* opposite his line. A quick estimate put the number of Mexicans at several hundred, who were now blazing away, barely forty yards from his line. The training his men had gone through had turned them into fair marksmen, he thought, as a dandily uniformed officer near the abandoned 18-pounder tumbled off the bastion and disappeared. Officers and NCOs were always the preferred targets, but even so, the weight of musket fire was telling. Dozens of men were down behind the wall; some forever, and others crawled back toward the chapel doors.

From the western wall, the *soldados'* shouts and curses turned into a sustained battle cry. Anderson plunged his sword into the ground and drew his pistol. Hundreds of the enemy leapt from the wall or jumped off the roofs of the buildings there and ran as fast as they could across the forty yards of killing ground. Anderson didn't think his men could fire any faster, but the rising crescendo of gunfire belied his thinking, as dozens of the attackers dropped in their tracks. But there were far more men crossing the plaza than defending the courtyard wall.

Anderson pointed his Trinity Arms revolver at the nearest charging *soldado* and pulled the trigger. A hole appeared in his chest and he crumpled to the ground. Anderson pulled the hammer back again and again, firing at the men racing toward him, until the hammer landed on an empty chamber. The rush of Mexicans was upon them.

With all his might, he threw the empty weapon into the face of a rushing *soldado*. Despite the roaring sound of battle around him, he was sure he heard bones shattering as the *soldado* fell to his knees, screaming in pain. Behind him another *soldado* stepped forward, with his bayoneted musket and plunged toward him, driving the steel blade into Anderson's chest.

As he fired his rifle, Leal's vision became tunnel like, focusing on each target. But something broke his concentration and he became aware that the line of Mexicans was racing across the plaza. He levered the breech closed and capped the gun and hastily raised it to his shoulder, as the charging mass of men reached the wall. He pulled the trigger. Before red and gray mist exploded out the back of the nearest *soldado's* head, Leal thought he saw the man's eyebrows burning away as incinerated gunpowder flashed into his face.

Along the line, the enemy had closed with them, and bayonets flashed in the sunlight that peeked over the chapel walls. Leal climbed to his feet and grabbed Jackson by the collar. "Let's get back to the chapel, Terry. It's over here."

Turning to run, he felt the other man stumble against him, and saw him grab at his left shoulder. As he pulled the private away from the crumbling line, he saw blood flowing through Jackson's fingers, where he clutched at the wound. Casting a look around, Leal saw the Mexicans bayoneting anyone still at the wall, as they surged over it. Frantically, he pulled his friend toward the chapel by his good arm. They were the last two of only a score of men from the wall, to cross the threshold of the chapel before the heavy wooden doors were slammed close behind them and a massive oaken crossbar was dropped into place, sealing the chapel off from the rest of the fort.

He handed Jackson over the barricade then helped a medical orderly pass the remaining wounded across before he, too scrambled over the makeshift barrier. Although the light flickering from the lanterns was dim, he saw several gunners standing on the gun platform over the chancel at the front of the chapel. Someone had reversed the three guns, facing them toward the doors at the opposite end. The sergeant, fighting off the exhaustion which threatened to overwhelm him, chuckled mirthlessly, thinking about the deadly welcome the Mexican army would receive when they breached the chapel's doors.

Leal took a swig of the stale water from his canteen and tried to shake off the fatigue creeping into his bones. They weren't beaten yet. He stepped back from the barricade and looked at the men around him. There were around twenty men who had escaped the barricade with him. They were exhausted. Most sat behind the barricade, sitting on empty boxes. Some, like him, were slaking their thirst with water from their canteens. Several stared into the chapel's shadowy recesses, lost in their own thoughts. A few others were busy stuffing their cartridge boxes with more ammunition or otherwise preparing for the next thrust from the Mexicans outside the building.

Leal saw the quartermaster sergeant, standing at the far end of the barricade with a handful of other men from the quartermaster's corps. Their relatively clean uniforms contrasted sharply with those who had spent the last few hours fighting along the fort's walls. Next to them were a handful of engineers assigned to the Alamo's garrison. The last group were a band of teamsters stranded in the fort since the beginning of the siege. To a man, they were freedmen, hired by the army to haul supplies. The rifles in their hands were held inexpertly. Leal briefly wondered if anyone had taken the time to show the negros how to use the weapons they now held. He'd served alongside men from the American South long enough to know, the situation would need to be nigh on unwinnable before the typical Southern officer would have considered arming them.

Next to one of the teamsters, atop the last overturned box closest to the confessional, with his rifle resting on top of a burlap bag stood a youth, a boy of no more than thirteen or fourteen years. He was bareheaded, and his shock of red hair was an unruly mess. Leal's eyes traveled to the boy's rifle. It was the same as his, an 1842 Sabine breechloader. The rifle was well cared for, the barrel's bluing gleamed in the flickering light from the lanterns on the chapel wall. Around the corner, off the north transept, he heard several young children crying, as their mothers' voices nervously tried to sooth the unhappy toddlers.

Any thoughts coalescing around how to better protect the women and children fled from this mind, when he heard a loud boom, and the heavy chapel doors rattled on their hinges, as a battering ram slammed into them. The doors held. The walls of the chapel were four feet thick and expensive steel hinges holding the doors in place were bolted deep into the walls.

Minutes passed, the steady rhythmic pounding reverberated as the *soldados* attempted to breach the door. "To your posts, boys!" Leal shouted, trying to drown out the steady pounding against the doors. Those not already standing by the barricade, rifle pointing toward the doors, slowly climbed to their feet and joined the thin line of riflemen. When silence fell and the drumming against the door ceased, the sound of shooting continued unabated. Leal hoped the men on top of the barracks were selling their lives dearly.

Charlie gripped the rifle's wooden stock, as he nervously looked around him. The Tejano sergeant had taken up a position next to him, at the end of the makeshift defenses. He exuded confidence that fed the boy's own courage. As the sergeant stared over the wall of supplies, and spoke encouragingly to those along the line, Charlie eyed the Tejano's rifle. It was worn and well used. The steel barrel was filthy from hours of near constant use, and the light from the lanterns seemed to absorb into gunpowder caking the barrel. On Charlie's other side, stood a burly teamster, his ebon skin made the whites of his eyes stand out. He gripped the rifle in hands that shook with fear.

It was easy for the boy to recognize it, for terror's dark talons had dug into the boy's heart, too. Charlie swallowed, imagining it was the fear being swallowed rather than saliva. He reached over and placed his smaller hand atop the black teamster's much larger hand and quietly said, "You can do this, mister. I'm scared too, but my pa says that you aren't really brave if you're not scared. I reckon that you and me have gotta be two of the bravest men here because, I'm scared to death."

The ebon skinned teamster tried to swallow, but his throat was parched dry. After he took a swig from a borrowed canteen, he coughed before saying, "I reckon all of us must be mighty brave, then." He managed a weak smile at the boy as he gripped the rifle with more confidence.

The sound of gunfire outside the chapel walls continued, and the teamster closed his eyes. After a moment, his lips started moving. Charlie felt a moment of peace, as he heard the words slipping from the man's lips and a ghost of a smile tugged at the corners of his mouth, as he added his own unsteady voice to the teamster's prayer, "He leadeth me beside still waters. He restoreth my soul …"

Sergeant Leal didn't consider himself to be a devout Catholic. As far as he was concerned, life was too messy to fit neatly in the confines of the confessional. As he heard the boy's voice beside him, though, memories from his own hard childhood came unbidden; his mother prayed the same prayer during every hardship his family faced. If ever there was a moment of hopelessness, this was it. It felt right to add his voice, "Yea, though I walk through the valley of the shadow of death, I will fear no evil …"

Down the line of men, where only a second before, despair was palpable, others added their voices, "thy rod and thy staff they comfort me …"

Words not spoken in half a lifetime tumbled from Leal's lips. Beside him, the boy's tenorous voice strengthened, "Thou preparest a table before me in the presence of mine enemies …"

There was no knowing what was to come. In all likelihood, the chapel's doors would not hold for long, but at that moment, for the first time since waking several hours earlier, Leal felt a sense of peace. "Surely goodness and mercy shall follow me all the days of my life: and I will dwell in the house of the Lord forever."

The gunfire outside tapered off. Leal rechecked his weapon and sighted down the barrel, waiting. The heavy doors in front of them were stove in as a solid cannonball plowed into it. As debris slammed into the barricade, he dived for cover, grabbing the red-headed teenager by the collar, and pulling him down. Down the line, one of the teamsters hadn't ducked and was now writhing and crying on the ground, an immense splinter piercing his cheek. Dust and smoke swirled in the air around him, as Leal raised his head over the top of the barricade. One of the chapel's heavy doors was warped, hanging by a single hinge. The other door had been torn completely off its hinges and lay crookedly on the chapel's floor.

Rushing feet sounded across the courtyard. Leal knew what the sound heralded. He stepped back up on the empty overturned ammunition box and yelled, "Stand to! They're coming!" Musket flashes winked in the haze, as he felt the grain bag absorb a musket ball. From behind him, he heard a voice cry out, "Get down! Now!"

From above and behind, he heard a deep throated roar of one of the artillery pieces on the platform, above the chapel, as it fired a double shot of canister, which swept the entry clear of advancing *soldados*. He heard the men on the platform, swearing as they raced to reload the gun. Leal stepped up to the barricade and fired at the next *soldado* to step through. He didn't bother watching to see if he'd hit him, and mechanically reloaded.

Charlie joined the Tejano sergeant back on the line and squeezed the trigger as his father had taught him.

The rifle kicked, and bitter gun smoke filled the air. Every man standing behind the barricade fired into the surging mass of Mexican *soldados*, struggling through the breached doors. Dozens of men pouring through the entry, collapsed when the other two cannons on the platform blasted more than a hundred iron balls into the milling mass of *soldados*.

For a moment, Charlie wondered if the echoing booms had made him deaf, as silence descended before them. But it was an illusion. A ragged volley from the courtyard reverberated in his ears and peppered the front of the barricade. A few seconds later, a second volley lashed higher into and above the barrier. A few men tumbled from the line, their heads a bloody mess. Charlie couldn't tell if they were wounded or dead. Part of him thought it mattered if they lived or died, but like his father had taught him, he levered open the breech and slid a cartridge in and capped the nipple then aimed through the door and fired.

Leal lowered his rifle, smoke still curling from the barrel, as he looked over the barricade at the doorway. It was clogged with dead and dying three and four deep. Despite that, a flurry of musket balls flew through the entry, mostly slamming into the barricade, but also finding the soft flesh of a defender, maiming or killing indiscriminately. The shouts from the courtyard were indistinct, but when the musketry abated, Leal felt a sinking dread and jumped down from the ammunition box and crouched by the base of the barricade. "Oh, *mierda*!" he swore. A thunderclap from the courtyard shattered the morning, and for the second time, he grabbed the shirtsleeve of the youth, standing next to him, and pulled the boy down to the ground.

The shot struck the barricade dead center, and caused bags of corn, grain, and flour to collapse. Mixing with the haze of gunpowder, the flour swirled and eddied in the air. Enough found him and the boy to coat them both in a film of white. He struggled back to his feet and saw that more than a dozen men had been felled by the shot that destroyed the barricade's center.

As the rifle bucked in Charlie's hands, the butt slammed into his shoulder. He winced from the stock's bruising impact. He gritted his teeth through the pain and levered the gun open again. He reached into the cartridge box on his belt and felt a firm tug on his arm and he lost his balance. He landed hard on the flagstones and found himself staring at the barricade's backside when all hell broke loose. The center of the barricade collapsed in on itself, as men were scattered about like toy soldiers strewn around by a petulant child. A cloud of flour and cornmeal settled on the men, from the bags torn open when the cannonball slammed into the barricade.

Coughing, trying to keep flour out of his mouth, Charlie climbed to his feet. Beside him, next to the wall, the Tejano sergeant stood, ignoring the dust cloud, and called for the men to prepare for the next surge of Mexican *soldados*. To Charlie's other side, the burly, black teamster lay at the boy's feet, a large splinter embedded in his leg, blood pooling below it. His eyes were closed, and Charlie couldn't tell if he was dead or alive.

The horror of the moment threatened to overwhelm the boy, who had never in his wildest imagination envisioned such carnage. In his mind, he kept repeating his father's words, "Courage is turning fear into action." Slowly, the horror retreated, and he mentally closed the door to it as he stepped over a body and joined the Tejano sergeant and a dozen other men still on their feet. Whatever may come, he would cling to his father's words. Tears streaked down his face, creating rivulets in the flour caking it. He saw the hard look of determination in the eyes of the Tejano sergeant and looked on the faces of the rest of the men, who were formed up behind the ruins of the barricade. Some couldn't mask their fear, but others mirrored the sergeant's battle-hardened expression. Something stirred in Charlie's young heart. To a man, each stood resolutely, pointing their rifles toward the chapel doors. After wiping his nose with a grimy and torn shirtsleeve, the boy hefted his father's rifle in his hands and with every fiber of his being tried to match the stoic look on the sergeant's face.

"*Is this the end?*" Leal wondered. They had given an accounting of themselves that few could have matched. Was this all that was left? The ringing in his ears kept him from hearing much of anything. Whether the men atop the barracks yet lived was unknown. What he could see were the dozen men with him. One of the negro teamsters was still on his feet. Blood dripped down his cheek from a cut above his eye. But Leal approved the way he held his rifle. He was facing death, like a man.

Beside him, the red-haired boy stood, unharmed. Streaks of tears had tracked through the flour on his face, but Leal was struck by the grim look of determination on his youthful countenance. Had he a mirror, he would have recognized the expression. It was his own.

The ground shook beneath his feet, as a cannon on the outer wall fired. The rattle of musketry added to the cacophony outside the chapel's walls. Despite the ringing in his ears, the boy was close enough that he could hear him when he said, "They're on the walls, firing. It's coming our way!"

Leal growled, "Let's get ready, boys!" He raised his rifle to his shoulder. But like an ebbing tide, the roar of gunfire receded from the courtyard.

Charlie strained his ears, listening to the gunfire dying away outside the chapel and for the first time since being rousted out of bed during the predawn attack, he felt a flicker of hope. He took an unsteady step toward the barricade, along with the other defenders. Standing atop the collapsed center of the barricade, he looked out the doorway and saw whirling smoke and dust billowing across the courtyard. What he couldn't see were any *soldados*. What had begun as a tiny flicker of hope had grown into fire in his heart, burning bright. He carefully climbed through the debris, and around the bodies of the fallen, until he came to stand beside the doorway. He set one hand against the twisted door, held in place by a single hinge and held his father's rifle in the other, as he looked across the courtyard. Behind the Chapel, the sun had risen, but it remained an obscure, pale orb, partially concealed by the thick haze of smoke hanging over the fort's smoldering hulk.

Charlie stared agape at the courtyard, which was bathed in a hazy light. Between the doorway to the chapel and the low wall separating the courtyard from the Alamo plaza, the ground was carpeted with dead and dying men. The dirt was soaked red from the blood of the slain, who died either attempting to capture or defend the Alamo. More tears fell as he saw dozens of bodies wearing Texas butternut scattered amid scores more in Mexican blue and red.

He felt a presence beside him and turned and saw the sergeant, who placed a hand on his shoulder. "Everyone, stop here." Through the southern gatehouse, they spotted dozens of men streaming through, wearing the navy-blue uniforms of the Texian Marines. The men around Charlie burst into cheers as they saw the advancing Texian riflemen.

Charlie's legs felt wobbly. The sight of the Texians sweeping through the wreck of the fort filled him with an indescribable pride. He leaned against the swarthy sergeant, as his legs threatened to give way beneath him. When he saw the battle flag of the 3rd Infantry being carried by a color sergeant, he figured these were not his pa's force, but belonged to the reserves. At that moment, it didn't matter. He wiped his wet eyes on his sleeve. Maybe he was only thirteen, but he wouldn't let them see the tears on his face. A sharp banging broke his attention and he turned, raising his rifle and saw the warped door banging against the wall. He lowered his rifle and noticed the sun reflecting from the chapel's limestone façade. From there, he looked up and saw, waving in the morning breeze, the same flag that had flown defiantly for two weeks. The lone star, reflecting the light from the morning sun, was a dazzling white. It was centered in a field of royal blue that spanned a third of the flag. A brilliant white stripe above a crimson stripe filled the rest of the banner. The tears he wiped away earlier flowed again, but this time Charlie didn't care. That flag, his flag, waved defiantly in the breeze, unconquered and free.

Chapter 17

The horse sensed the rider's urgency, as he was guided up and down the line of marching infantry. He hated himself for doing it, but General Johnston urged his battalion commanders to march their men double time. One hundred sixty-five steps per minute quickly ate away at the distance between them and their goal, San Antonio. Even so, he ordered it, knowing those reservists who were less capable would be left behind, as they hastened to the sound of the guns.

He patted his mount as he pulled off the road, watching the men of the 1st Cherokee Rifles march by. Behind the men, a faint golden glow grew along the eastern horizon. The sun would rise within the hour, and he begrudged every minute spent marching. Not long before, the distant thunder of guns fell silent, but the dark western sky still flashed with an orange and red glow by whatever was transpiring at the Alamo. Beyond the grueling pace already set, he could order the army to increase their speed up to one hundred eighty paces per minute, but one glance at his men and the thought died unspoken. They had been marching at double time for the past hour, cutting the distance by half between their camp and the battle at the Alamo.

Johnston drummed his fingers on his thigh, impatiently. It was taking too much time, he thought. But it was plain to see these men were not trained to the same standards as were his own regulars and they were showing signs of fatigue. As men, in ones and twos began to fall out, unable to keep pace with their comrades, Johnston ordered the commander of the 3rd Infantry to detail an officer to bring up the rear at a normal pace with the army's stragglers.

Johnston trailed behind his column for a moment, watching a young lieutenant corral the winded men, and, after a brief breather, started them after the column at a more sedate speed. Satisfied that his army wouldn't fragment into more than a couple of parts, he urged his mount to a gallop until he saw Sam Houston, slouched on a horse, riding next to his command.

Houston shifted in his saddle as he caught sight of the army's commander. "Morning, Sid. Hell of a march, ain't it?"

Johnston slowed his mount, matching the former general's pace before replying, "You do have a way with an understatement, Sam. As God is my witness, I wish to hell we were already there. This invasion of theirs couldn't have happened at a worse time."

Houston shrugged laconically. In some ways Johnston wondered, was he misspending his life or was he just incredibly unlucky? He had squandered his opportunity as Governor of Tennessee more than a dozen years before, when his wife left him, and he crawled into a whisky bottle, then he had seen his own plans to become president of the republic of Texas slip through his hands, when David Crockett and William Travis garnered all the glory during the revolution. But if the rumors were true, Houston's luck was turning around, living with the Cherokee.

"What was that?" Johnston asked. The other officer had been talking.

Houston repeated, "Just saying, any time's a bad time, Sid. Although I'd like to think if this had happened when the army wasn't seven hundred miles away that we'd have whipped them the first day they tried to stick their noses into San Antonio."

Johnston's mood was dark, angry that he and the army were not already in San Antonio, but he bit his tongue before he could form a retort. It galled him to admit it, Houston was likely right. Rather than continue talking with the former general, he gouged his heels into his mount's flanks and gave the animal his head as he raced to the front of the column.

He yanked on the reins when he spied the cavalry scouts he'd sent out earlier, racing back toward the column. One of the men, his jacket covered in prairie dust, pulled up before Johnston and exclaimed, "General Johnston, sir! There's Mexican cavalry, less than a mile away, smack between us and San Antonio."

"Finally!" Johnston turned to Major West, whose battalion of Marines led the army. "Major, deploy your men into a battalion line of battle." The reserve battalions had received less training on small unit tactics than his regulars, and he thought it best to fall back on a simple battle line rather than a skirmish line. If the situation changed, he would adjust tactics.

Major West flashed a fierce grin, then turned and shouted, "Marines! By company, into line of battle!" The column of Marines, flowed smoothly from columns of four into a battle line, two men deep and more than a hundred fifty long.

As the other battalions approached, Johnston ordered the officer commanding the 2nd Infantry battalion to deploy to the Marine's right flank and the 5th and Cherokee Rifles to deploy to the Marine's left flank. The 3rd would follow behind, as a reserve.

Elated at the prospect of action, Johnston held his sword in one hand, and the reins in the other. He controlled the animal by guiding him with pressure from his knees. He came up next to the Marine major, "West! When you engage their cavalry, keep advancing while firing. Nothing's to stop us until we reach San Antonio."

Although the sun had not yet crested in the east, the sky was lightening, and Johnston could see his cavalry, falling back from the Mexican lancers. As they skedaddled from in front of their infantry's line, several were skewered from behind by the lancers. The sun was behind his line, and the men of Mexico's Santa Anna cavalry regiment were little more than silhouettes, but even a silhouette is a target, and the Texian line sighted in on the advancing lancers.

Mexican cavalry were typically recruited from among Mexico's well-to-do, and after putting down rebellions across Mexico over the past decade, had earned a reputation for bravery and élan. The regiment that bore the dictator's name was the unit by which other cavalry formations were judged. When they came under fire from the Texian rifleman, they wheeled their mounts and charged, racing to close the gap.

Shadows morphed into silhouettes, and silhouettes into men. The lancers saw the red, white, and blue flag flying over the center of the Marines' line, and they tore up the ground to reach it. At West's command, the Marines opened fire.

A rifle team crouched by the wall of the old Spanish Governor's Palace, rifles pointing across San Antonio's main plaza. Major West took a moment to rest against the adobe wall and catch his breath, as his men took up positions north of San Antonio's central plaza. They had swept around the town in an arc, while the rest of the army went directly to the Alamo's relief. They had run the last mile in an effort to be in position to attack the Mexican rear when the rest of the army attacked.

Across the plaza, atop the bell tower of the Church of San Fernando, West saw the national flag of Mexico flapping in the breeze. Apart from a few *soldados*, who appeared to be injured, the plaza appeared to be empty of enemy troops. He grabbed the corporal in charge of the closest rifle team, and pointed toward the flag, "Get that damned thing down from there, Corporal."

Gesturing at his teammates, the NCO started off across the plaza, joined by one of others, while the other two covered them. Leapfrogging across the plaza, they reached the doors of the church without incident.

A few minutes later, one of the marines appeared in the bell tower, where he cut the cord and lowered the Mexican flag. From his tunic, he pulled a small Texas flag, and hastily tied it to the cord and raised it over the church.

West allowed a faint smile to cross his tired features as he yelled to the other Marines. "Let's go, boys. We've got a flank to turn."

Johnston watched his men sweep through part of the Mexican army camp, north of the Alamo, less than half a mile from the fort's walls. Camp followers, who had followed the Army of the North from Mexico, scattered in noisy surprise when they realized the Texians were moving through the camp. Apart from the women and children, only a handful of wounded were in camp. Johnston had his men secure the camp and move on. He could hear the rattle of musketry coming from the Alamo and time was of the essence.

Once the northern wall of the Alamo had come into view, Johnston gasped in shock at the scene. Fires burned along the western wall, where he could see blue-uniformed Mexican *soldados* firing into the fort. Between his army and the fort, the ground was carpeted with dead and wounded Mexicans. Scores appeared to have been hit before ever reaching the north wall, where, a line of scaling ladders rested against the fort's northwest corner.

An echoing boom sounded from within the fort, as an artillery piece was fired. The fort hadn't fallen yet, and he and his men were still in time! Throwing caution to the wind, Johnston urged his horse forward, across the body-strewn prairie. He yanked his sword from its scabbard and pointed it toward the wall. The men of the 2nd and 3rd Infantry battalions heard his cry and raced after him, as he kicked his horse into a gallop. He reached the wall, and swung himself out of the saddle, as a dozen men raced by him, and hurled themselves up the undefended ladders.

Johnston heard the riflemen firing at targets within the fort as he grabbed the rungs and hurried to the top. The carnage on the field before the walls was nothing in comparison to the horror he saw upon reaching the top. One could step across the plaza on the backs of the dead and never touch the ground. He swung his feet over the wall and was lowered to the ground by a rifleman who had climbed the ladder behind him. But it was the hundreds of *soldados* on their feet, who had turned to see the Texians on the wall, that posed an immediate threat.

The length of the plaza from the north wall to the southern gatehouse was a little more than four hundred sixty feet, and as the Mexicans became aware, Johnston heard lead balls hitting the adobe wall behind him.

Riflemen threw themselves prone or hugged the fort's walls, making themselves smaller targets. The volume of fire from the north wall increased exponentially as more men crawled over it and added their aimed fire into the Mexican force at the far end of the plaza.

Kneeling beside an old building set into the western wall, Johnston watched a platoon-sized collection of men, who were lying prone, firing independently of each other. After firing a few rounds, they began working in tandem, under the command of a sergeant. Men, who had never before worked with each other, coalesced in ad hoc rifle teams, and began working their way toward their foes on the western side of the fort.

The dozens of ladders against the western wall were now carrying the men from the Cherokee Rifles over the wall, along its entire length, adding their weight to the growing pressure on the *soldados*.

Caught in a crossfire from both the north and west, the Mexican force broke, and streamed through the gates, heading south. Along the small wall separating the chapel's courtyard from the plaza, there had been more than a hundred *soldados* firing toward the chapel and with the rest of their force streaming away, they broke, and joined the retreat.

"At them, boys!" Johnston shouted. He joined his men, who were now racing across the field, firing at the backsides of the *soldados*, who were running away. Some threw their muskets away, running even faster.

Scattered gunfire came from the south a moment before blue-jacketed Marines under Major West began trickling through the southern gatehouse. The Alamo was once again in the hands of the Texians. Dozens of Mexicans stood around, their weapons thrown down and hands in the air. Riflemen and Marines rounded them up and herded them toward the fort's northwestern corner.

As he stepped around the bodies littering the plaza, Johnston saw mixed in among dead and wounded *soldados* in their blue and red uniforms, Texians in their butternut uniforms. There were plenty of each and he knew before the end of the day, that he would know the totals. As he accidentally stepped on a hand, he shuddered. Even a casual glance around the walls, told him the butcher's bill would be horrendous.

From the chapel, its doors damaged beyond any hope of repair, a dozen survivors emerged. Their uniforms were filthy, tattered and torn by the hell they'd endured over the past few hours. They approached the low stone barrier as Johnston stepped up to it and examined the haggard group.

They were led by a short Tejano; his jacket was caked in flour. The chevrons, normally black, were white with flour paste, and denoted he was a sergeant. Standing behind the sergeant was a youth. Bareheaded, the youth was as tall as the Tejano. He was jacketless. His shirt, once dyed blue, now was stained in equal parts black with grime, and white from flour. Beneath the coating of flour, a shock of red hair was visible.

As his eyes slipped toward the next survivor, the red hair registered, and he did a double-take of the boy. "Dear God in heaven! Is that you, Charlie?" Johnston stammered as he recognized the son of the army's commander.

With his father's rifle still clutched in his hand, the boy stepped forward, crying, "Colonel Johnston! Thank God y'all arrived." The boy's treble voice broke with emotion.

Any pretense of military formality forgotten, Johnston stepped forward and grabbed the boy's shoulders and stared at him intently. "By all that is holy, boy, what the hell are you doing here? Where's Becky? Please tell me that your family is safe."

Gulping hard, his emotions threatened to overwhelm him, Charlie managed a nod before he finally found his voice. "Yes, sir. They're in the chapel and safe."

The boy trembled as he spoke, and tears streaked down his face. Johnston pulled him into an embrace as he listened to the sobs that were muffled against his chest. Over the years, he'd watched Charlie turn from a slight little boy of seven into the gangly teenager he now comforted. As the boy's tears soaked Johnston's jacket, the general sent a silent prayer of thanks heavenward; the children and wife of not just his commander, but his friend, were safe. He tousled the flour-caked hair.

Chapter 18

30th March 1842

General Adrian Woll gasped and winced. A medical orderly held his arm tightly as the surgeon pulled the thread through the torn skin, where a bullet had gone through his upper arm. For what seemed the dozenth time, he thanked the Blessed Virgin the bullet hadn't hit an inch to the left. It would have shattered the bone. Had that happened, the surgeon would have been cutting the arm off, instead of suturing it. When the last stitch was in place, he wrapped clean linen around Woll's arm. With a final knot, securing the bandage, he said, "There you go, General. It'll be like new in a few weeks. If you'll excuse me, I have others to attend to."

Without waiting for permission, the overworked doctor turned his back on the general and was soon at work, trying to save a *soldado* with a bullet lodged in his shoulder. Woll flexed his fingers and grimaced as pain lanced up and down his arm. The tent was packed with injured men and smelled of feces and the metallic odor of blood. With his good left arm, he picked up the jacket from the ground and fled the tent. Once outside, he looked at the horizon, and saw the sun sinking in the western sky. Any hope for moving further away from San Antonio this day sank with the setting sun.

Under more favorable circumstances, Woll would have preferred to rest and regain his strength. His army was in tatters, and they needed rest. But time was of the essence. Less than a hundred yards north of the surgeon's tent, which had been hastily erected only an hour before, the Army of the North's 3rd brigade stood in line of battle, facing toward San Antonio. A few hundred yards beyond, the remnants of the army's *Cazadores* companies were deployed, less than ten miles separated his shattered army from San Antonio.

How had it come to this? Woll needed a few minutes to think and plan his next move. Feeling dizzy, he moved over to a supply wagon, and sat heavily down on the tail of the wagon bed and waited for the dizzy spell to pass. He closed his eyes and thought about where things had gone wrong this morning. The attack had gone as planned, more or less. The Texians were alert and repulsed a couple of attacks before his men had managed to force them from one corner of the fort's walls.

After his men had seized part of the wall, they quickly expanded their hold, and drove the remnants of the defenders from the outer wall. They fell back to a low wall in front of the old chapel, where they put up a strong defense for a while, until they were driven to within the thick walls of the chapel. It should have been only a matter of time before the defenders in the chapel fell.

Woll, in his location on the southwest corner of the Mexican starting position, had heard the sound of shooting in the town, then saw the army's camp followers streaming from the north and knew something was amiss. When he saw the blue-jacketed Texian Marines streaming toward his command post, racing down Alameda Street and seizing the wooden bridge over the San Antonio River, he commanded his orderlies and couriers to find any units not committed within the Alamo's walls and to pull back to the southern portion of their camp.

He had been climbing onto his own mount, when he'd been shot by a rifleman from the bridge, at a range of less than a hundred yards. He would have affected an organized withdrawal of most of his army, had it not been for the savage Indians who had accompanied the Texian relief column.

The first thing he'd seen splashing across the shallows of the San Antonio River was a blood-red flag with scattered stars on it, being carried by a screaming, savage Indian. He'd barely had time to read the words emblazoned on the flag, "1st Cherokee Rifles" before he had been forced to jerk on the reins and retreat toward General Urrea's reserve regiment, which was south of the Alamo.

After that, the retreat was a blur. Opening his eyes, he fished from his vest pocket the latest figures provided by his staff. The 1st brigade, under the command of General Guzman still fielded around six hundred fifty men. It was only half of their original strength. As his eyes read over the totals, he allowed doubt to creep into his thinking. *"Was it how quickly they broke when the Cherokee hit them in the rear that kept them from sustaining even more casualties, or are they broken and unable to fight?"*

He shook his head and hoped he wouldn't have to find out.

Gritting his teeth, as he used his injured right arm to shuffle the pages, he found the report on the 2nd brigade. The burden of any general is knowing that some portion of the men sent into battle will die. Unlike Santa Anna, Woll couldn't think of his *soldados* as little more than chickens. They were his men, and he knew when he ordered the 2nd brigade to assault the Alamo's western wall, they would take terrible casualties. No one was around to hear him say, "But over sixty percent! Holy Mother of God, so many dead."

The remnants of the 2nd brigade numbered no more than four hundred fifty. They had started the campaign in Nuevo Laredo with more than thirteen hundred. While they had suffered heavy casualties in the process of capturing the fort's western wall, it wasn't yet known how many had been taken prisoner within the walls of the Alamo when General Johnston's relief army had stormed over the Northern wall.

The next report was from General Urrea. The gods of war had shown him favor, and he yet lived. Woll harrumphed. Nothing else had broken his way this day, why should Urrea's survival surprise him? He chided himself for again wishing ill of his subordinate. He pushed aside his thoughts of Urrea and saw that the 3rd regiment of Urrea's 3rd brigade had sustained more than seventy percent casualties. They had caught the worst of the brunt of the Marines' attack and their sacrifice had allowed the rest of Woll's army to retreat. But overall, Urrea had husbanded the lives of his men, and escaped with the majority of the two regiments he'd used to assault the Alamo's southern wall. More than six hundred men had escaped. They had held their ranks until the survivors from the other two brigades had fled through their lines. Woll wanted to hate Urrea, for his naked ambition and opportunism, but the general had held his men together, when the rest of the army was in tatters, and the sacrifice of his 3rd regiment was the only reason Woll was able sit on the back of the wagon and review the army's miserable status. Without that sacrifice, the army would have been annihilated.

The last sheet of paper slipped through his fingers and landed in the dirt. He didn't need to see it. He cursed Colonel Moro, who had commanded the Santa Anna cavalry regiment for the lack of warning he'd received. He sucked in the cool, evening air, and reminded himself it wasn't right to speak ill of the dead. The report blowing away in the breeze said what he already knew. Moro's cavalry had been swept aside by Johnston's relief column and hammered to pieces by the breech-loading rifles they carried. Only one hundred thirty lancers had escaped from before Johnston's onslaught, and Woll added them to his tally.

The last branch of the army to consider were the artillery. One battery of four guns, 8-pounders, had been entrenched south of the fort, while the other, also four 8-pounders, had been positioned along the banks of the San Antonio river, west of the fort. He had taken care to position his guns outside of the range of the Texian riflemen, but he couldn't have anticipated how quickly Johnston's attack had rolled up his army . Not a single gun had been saved, but he was thankful nearly sixty of the artillerists had escaped with the army.

He thought back to the day after the earthen fort on the Rio Bravo had surrendered, back on the 13th of March. He had assembled nearly four thousand men and brought them north to besiege the walls of the Alamo. Now, according to his reports, only nineteen hundred men remained ready to fight, or so he hoped. He was only ten miles from San Antonio, and he prayed the Texians were too busy putting their house back in order to pursue him this day. He needed time to care for the four hundred wounded clogging the tents of his regimental and brigade surgeons.

As he thought of the eighteen hundred men, now dead, wounded, or prisoners of the Texians, he frowned. *"What was it General Wellington had said? The only thing worse than a battle won was a battle lost."*

Sidney Johnston carefully stepped across the plaza of the Alamo as the sun sank below the remains of the fort's western wall. Everything he'd ever learned at West Point and his natural inclination screamed he should be marching his army south in pursuit of General Woll and his army. He closed his eyes against the horror within the fort's walls, willing the images burned into his mind to let him be. What he wanted to do, and what he was able to do, were unfortunately, two different things.

There hadn't been time to find Rebecca Travis in the chapel before men started bringing him word that the Mexicans hadn't simply stormed the walls and driven off the defenders. No, it soon became evident the Mexican army had slaughtered the wounded along the outer walls, when they had seized them. Scores of mutilated bodies were found where they had fallen, dozens of bayonet wounds rendered some of the fallen unrecognizable.

Compounding Johnston's problem, was that as the Mexican attack fell apart and their army retreated, more than three hundred *soldados* had surrendered. More than five hundred more were wounded and were now filling up field hospitals set up outside the fort's walls and overflowing temporary hospitals in town.

But it had been a near-fought thing, Johnston conceded. He had nearly lost control of the army when the scope of the massacre had become known. He climbed the northern wall and looked over the field at where, less than an hour before, the ground had been carpeted with the dead. In the distance, to the east, a bonfire burned, turning the dead of the Mexican invasion to ash. Between the Alamo and the river, he spied a thin line of Marines guarding prisoners. His fingers turned white as he gripped the wall, realizing how close the army had come to anarchy following the battle. "Thank God for Major West."

As the remnants of the Mexican army retreated to the south, the captured *soldados* were rounded up and pushed into the northwestern corner of the plaza. As his reservists became aware of the massacre of most of the fort's defenders, his men approached the *soldados* and started screaming for their blood. A few rocks were thrown at the unarmed men and they crowded against the walls, trying to get away from the encroaching enraged Texians.

Even now, as he looked over the prisoners, now guarded outside the Alamo's walls, Johnston wasn't sure what had kept his men from opening fire during those tense moments. Moments after a fist-sized rock had knocked a *soldado* from his feet, there was the sound of rushing feet as Major West barreled through the milling men, his two companies of regulars on his heels. Once the Marines created a barrier between the reservists and the demoralized prisoners, the rocks stopped, but the din of shouts continued unabated.

He thought back to what he had been forced to do. There was a battery of guns along the northern wall, and he had raced up the ramp, and climbed atop one of them, where he could see over the heads of the men in the plaza. Even now his throat was still raw from how loud he had been forced to shout. "Men of Texas! We haven't come and relieved our valiant brothers here at the Alamo, only to turn ourselves into the very thing we abhor! If any among you attempts to murder these men before you, who have surrendered, you are no better than they were when they killed the wounded and defenseless."

He could see the murder in the eyes of his men, even after he had harangued them. The iron control Major West exercised over his regulars was something

Johnston would never forget, then the officers finally came to their senses and began establishing order, pushing their men away from the prisoners. He would make sure his report to General Travis praised the major. Unless he misread the tea leaves, war was on their doorsteps, and officers like West would be needed.

He turned away from the camp, and strode back down the ramp, and as he walked across the plaza, toward the office over the hospital, he pulled out the totals Major West had collected for him earlier. He shook his head as he reread the notes. The Alamo defenders had lost two hundred twenty-seven men dead. Only fifty-nine were wounded. He crumpled the note as he felt a hot tear slide down his cheek. Many of these men had served under him, when he had commanded the 1st Infantry. They were men he had known. Some, like Almaron Dickinson, he had counted as friends.

He climbed the stairs and closed the door to the office. He needed to be alone, as more tears slid down his face into his mustache. He pulled a glass from a desk drawer and from behind the desk took a bottle full of an amber liquid of uncertain provenance and filled the glass. He hoisted it in his hand and turned toward the eastern wall, toward the military cemetery in the distance, where Dickinson had been buried and where several hundred more would be interred on the morrow. He slammed the shot back and gasped after the liquor hit his stomach. It was vile stuff, probably brewed somewhere in the Republic. General Travis had always gone on about buying from domestic producers when possible. As Johnston's eyes crossed, he thought domestic alcohol production had a very long way to go.

His toast complete, he collapsed into General Travis' chair. The crumpled piece of paper with the casualty report sat balled up on the desk. More than two hundred killed. Not even during all the battles of the revolution had this many Texians been killed. As the warmth of the alcohol spread beyond his gut, he let his mind drift to his own relief force. Only twenty of his men had died when they had lifted the siege and sent General Woll and his army limping away. Against that, he knew he had won a devastating victory against Adrian Woll.

More than five hundred Mexicans had been killed. Their bodies would light up the night sky. Travis wouldn't like it. He was soft when it came to how the dead should be treated. "I'm here and he's not. If they hadn't massacred our boys, maybe I'd feel different," he muttered to himself. At least he'd kept a lid on things today, and the prisoners hadn't been killed out of hand. In addition to the three hundred prisoners, more than five hundred Mexican *soldados* filled the hospitals and were under the care of the Texian surgeons and doctors from San Antonio.

No matter how impressive the victory, it didn't lessen the pain and loss he felt in his heart for the dead he had once commanded. As the alcohol worked its medicinal properties on the general, he leaned back in the chair and for a moment imagined Major Dickinson and the other defenders answering to a heavenly roll call this night.

The kerosene lamp had gone out, and the office was dark when Johnston awoke. He lit a candle and stood, stretching his muscles after falling asleep in the chair. He felt far older than his thirty-nine years as he heard his joints popping.

He stepped over to the door and opened it. The sounds of wounded men in the hospital below drifted up, but the cool breeze felt good, so he left it open and returned to the desk, after refilling the kerosene lamp and relighting it. A glance at his pocket watch showed it was just past midnight. He pulled a few sheets of paper from a drawer and inked a pen and began writing orders.

His supplies had been left where the army had camped the previous night. Additionally, he had eight hundred prisoners to watch, and that included feeding them and taking care of their injuries. As his pen scratched across the page, he detached West's Marines to watch the prisoners and secure the town. As he set the order aside, mentally he subtracted them from his available forces. Next, he wrote instructions for the 3rd Texas to return to their previous camp with enough wagons to retrieve the army's supplies. He subtracted them from his available forces, too. That left him with less than five hundred reservists and Houston's Cherokees.

He set the pen down and rubbed his eyes. He resisted the urge to shudder when he allowed his thoughts to play over the numbers. He couldn't fault the bravery of Houston's Cherokees. They had done a

227

commendable job during the morning's attack on the Mexican command, but after Woll's army was in headlong retreat, Houston had lost control of his men, as they looted the Mexican encampment. With no one to see him, Johnston heaved a heavy sigh as his shoulders slumped. Better that they had been looting the camp instead of inside the fort when things came dangerously close to another massacre.

He jumped when there was a knock on the open door. Major West stood in the doorway. "I guess it's early enough to say, good morning, General. The cleanup of the bodies has been finished. We'll be putting the Mexican prisoners to work in the morning digging graves in the cemetery. Any other orders before I find a quiet place to get a few hours' sleep?"

Johnston smiled ruefully at being startled by the major, before looking down at the orders he'd written. He scribbled the last note and addressed each one to the battalion commander for which they were intended then handed them to West.

"If you'll see to it these get to their intended, I would appreciate it."

He'd decided, the rest of the army, composed of the 2nd and 5th Infantry regiments and the Cherokee battalion would march out at dawn and stage a demonstration of strength ten miles south of San Antonio. If Woll's army hadn't fled any further, they would hopefully encourage him to return to Mexico. He didn't want another battle, if he could avoid it.

The sun was climbing above the tree line of mesquites and hackberries. A couple of lancers had ridden in only few minutes earlier with word that a few battalions of Texians were on the march from San Antonio. The idea of standing and trying to fight never crossed his mind. Even after a full night's rest, the stink of defeat hung heavy over his much-reduced army.

With the aid of an orderly, Woll climbed into the saddle. He wore his blue- and red-trimmed jacket like a cape. His right arm hung before him in a sling. Apart from a few scouts, who were further north, the remnants of the Santa Anna cavalry regiment were deployed to the north of the encampment, keeping an eye on the road to San Antonio.

The badly mauled 2nd brigade was already on the road, heading south. The 1st brigade was assembled just south of camp, waiting for the wagons loaded with wounded that would accompany them in their retreat south.

The *soldados* of the 1st brigade, turned from their line, and went into a long column of four men abreast and started south, as the wagons creaked and groaned under their heavy load, behind them. Several hundred walking wounded trudged after the wagons. Those unable to walk were carried in litters. Woll was determined to leave no more wounded behind. He winced when he thought of what the Texians would do to the prisoners already captured.

Once the Alamo's defenders had refused his last demand to surrender, he felt no compunction in following his Excellency's orders that no prisoners be taken. But now, he worried how the Texians would react to the order. In the chaos of the retreat, he presumed hundreds of his men had been captured. After the last of the walking wounded were on the road to the south, Woll coolly nodded to General Urrea. With quietly spoken orders, the three regiments of the 3rd brigade, brought up the rear of the army.

The lancers followed behind Urrea's brigade. If the Texians attempted to pursue, Woll hoped there was enough fight left in his rear guard to knock them back.

To one side of the encampment were the hastily dug graves of several dozen men who had succumbed to their injuries during the night. Woll gulped down the bile in his throat. He hated to leave them on the South Texas prairie, without the decency of burial on consecrated ground. It's not something a good Catholic would normally do and being forced into it didn't sit well with him. He shoved the thought aside as he urged his horse to a gallop, catching up with his lancers. He couldn't help but wonder how long it would be before another army from Mexico would finally force Texas back into the fold.

Chapter 19

3rd April 1842

His jacket lay under his head, propping it up, and keeping it off the dirt floor. He stared at the whitewash which coated the adobe walls of the small church. Sergeant Julio Mejia couldn't ignore the itching in his injured leg anymore and he sat up, to get a better look at it. His pants had faded to brown, and the left leg of his trousers had been cut away above where the splinter had torn open his skin. He touched where the wound was healing, and it only twinged a bit. Without proper medical care, it was doing better than expected. While he wasn't normally a religious man, he had sent a few prayers heavenward to Santo Gregorio, the patron saint of soldiers, that his leg not become infected.

Others had not been as fortunate, and the tiny cemetery outside the walls of the church had added a few new graves since the Texians had been imprisoned there for the past couple of weeks. A blue-jacketed *soldado* stood guard inside the door, his bayoneted musket held resolutely in his hands. His cautious eyes scanned the sanctuary, eyeing the sixty other men packed into the room.

The little town of Reynosa was on General Woll's supply line, and after he had surrendered Fort Moses Austin to the overwhelming might of the Army of the North, Sergeant Mejia's company had been marched to the tiny, dusty hamlet, ostensibly to be sent on to Veracruz, where they would be kept until, as they had been told, Mexico had reclaimed Texas. Then they would be repatriated to the United States.

Even though the town was on Woll's supply line, the food Mejia and the other prisoners were given was a meager meal of rice and beans each day. As he limped around the men on the floor, checking on several of them, it was clear they were tired and hungry. *"Damn the Mexican army. Give us just enough to survive, but not enough to be satisfied."* Then he turned his eyes on the rail-thin guard at the door and couldn't decide if he and his men were being deliberately starved or the lack of food was a systematic problem with the Mexican army's supply lines. He suspected the Mexicans were learning that it was a long way from their heavily populated states in central Mexico to the frontier and keeping the army supplied was more difficult than anticipated.

Mejia found himself at one of the windows. It was stain glass, depicting the Sermon on the Mount. Beyond the window was freedom, but a quick glance at the guard showed he was staring intently at Mejia. In addition to the alert guard, from without, he heard the voices of more guards patrolling around the church's exterior. He gave up the thought and returned to where he had been lying.

Lieutenant Javier Morales tilted his canteen to his lips and gulped down the tepid water. He was bone-tired, having been on the road between Tampico and Reynosa for what seemed like forever. Twelve days was a long time. But apart from the occasional farmer hauling food to market, he had seen hardly any traffic. Before leaving Tampico, he'd been assured the road was safe between the two towns, patrolled regularly by the state government of Tamaulipas. After more than three hundred miles, he was willing to concede the road was safe. Not because the Tamaulipan militia kept it that way, but simply because there was nothing worth taking.

After too many fourteen-hour days in the saddle it wasn't possible to find a comfortable position, no matter how often he shifted around. He'd long ago decided this road was a pain in the ass. His laughter at his wit would have been louder, save for the hard truth. When he came around a bend in the road, his fatigue fell away as he spotted the town of Reynosa in the distance. "At last. Not long now and I'll get off this nag and sleep in a soft bed tonight."

A little while later he rode across the plaza to a small adobe brick building, opposite from the town's only church. The guards patrolling around the largest building in town drew his attention. No doubt the objects of the reason he had spent nearly two weeks on the back of that flea-bitten horse were ensconced within.

He grabbed the saddlebags and walked through the building's open door and found himself in a tiny office that under normal times housed the office of the town's *alcalde*. Since the beginning of the most recent campaign into the rebel province of Texas, the office was where Morales' equally junior counterpart, Lieutenant Estevan Alameda conducted business for the understrength company charged with guarding the supply depot and prisoners. Against one corner of the room was crammed a small desk, and opposite from it was a narrow cot. There was less than a couple of feet between the sparse furnishings. On the cot, Morales found the other officer, lying down with a white handkerchief covering his face. Every few seconds the small piece of cloth fluttered up as Alameda snored.

Morales began to set the saddlebags on the desk, but then thinking better of it, he plopped them heavily on his fellow officer's chest. Lieutenant Alameda snorted and coughed before reflexively brushing the leather bags onto the floor. The dust-covered Morales stood over the startled Alameda, laughing. "Wake up, old boy!"

The other officer rolled off the cot and stood, crowding Morales' space, as he rubbed the sleep from his eyes. "What the hell was that about, Javier?"

Morales scooped the saddlebags from the floor and deposited them on the desk. "You should have seen the look on your face, Estevan. You'd have thought that the devil had come to collect your poor soul."

Alameda managed a severe glare in the direction of his friend and fellow officer. They had grown close while cadets at the *Colegio Militar* at Chapultepec. Ultimately, he couldn't stay mad and he sat back down on the cot and began pulling his boots on. "What's the news from Tampico?"

Morales unfastened the leather straps on the saddlebag then dumped a few letters on the desk. He plucked one from the small pile and handed over the sealed envelope. "If you're still the commander of the Reynosa garrison, such as it is, this one's for you."

Alameda chuckled. "This is one hell of a garrison, Javier. Me and forty soldiers. It's good that our northern neighbors are otherwise busy being properly educated by General Woll, lest they cast their hungry eyes our way." He pulled a penknife from his pocket and broke the wax seal and perused the letter's contents.

The letter slipped from his fingers and drifted to the ground, landing on Morales' boot. His friend picked up the letter and handed it back to him. He then looked into Lieutenant Alameda's face and saw its pallor. Alameda pursed his lips and shook his head.

Perplexed, Morales asked, "What'd it say?"

Alameda wordlessly handed the letter to his friend and sat heavily on the cot while the courier read the letter.

From the office of his Excellency Antonio López de Santa Anna
To the Commander, Garrison at Reynosa

You are hereby ordered to execute general order number 77, signed by this office on the 9th of January 1842. Any pirates caught under the rebel flag of the North Americans is to be summarily executed, by order of the office of the presidency.
Antonio López de Santa Anna

Morales gently set the letter down on the desk. Alameda frowned as his color returning to his cheeks. But he struggled with his words, still dumbfounded by the letter's contents. "Who? How did they find out so quickly about the prisoners, Javier?"

The other officer shrugged. "I doubt that his Excellency actually knows you have them here, Estevan. Yours is the third letter I have delivered since leaving Tampico, and I have another just like it for whomever is holding Laredo. I think his Excellency is simply being thorough."

Alameda trembled, his hands shaking as he began to consider what needed to be done to carry out the fateful orders. He struggled to put on a brave face for his friend. His voice tremored as he said, "I don't suppose I could carry that last letter for you to Laredo, eh, Javier?"

An unpleasant duty behind him, the other young lieutenant slapped him on the back, "Not for anything you've got, Estevan."

The next morning, the church doors were thrown open, slamming against the walls, waking Sergeant Mejia as the noise echoed in the church's close confines. He climbed to his feet as he watched the young Mexican army officer, in command of the Reynosa garrison, walk through the doors, accompanied by a squad of *soldados*. In heavily accented English, he said, "You all have fifteen minutes to prepare. I've been ordered to send you on to Tampico, and from there to Veracruz." The officer turned sharply about and strode out the church, leaving the squad behind.

Mejia eyed the *soldados* warily, uncertain what to make of the announcement. Perhaps General Woll had finally gotten around to getting them ready to ship to the United States. If that were true, what did it mean was happening in Texas? Had the French General in the pay of Mexico defeated Johnston's men at the Alamo? With so many unknowns rattling around in his mind, Mejia grabbed the one positive thought. It would be good to see the sun overhead. Holding on to that thought, he turned to helping his men prepare to leave the church's cramped quarters.

As the emaciated Texians emerged from the church, they squinted as the April morning sunlight filled the town's plaza, where they were forced to line up. The town's entire garrison was assembled in the plaza, surrounding the prisoners.

The young lieutenant sat on a chestnut mare, wearing a stern countenance, as the men were lined up in a column of twos. As they were herded out of the plaza and onto a road leading south, the *soldados* from the Reynosa garrison marched on both sides of the prisoners. Bayonet-tipped muskets were slung over their shoulders, as they set a demanding pace. The road south was nothing more than a hard-packed wagon trail, and the Texians struggled to keep up with their guards.

As best as he was able, Sergeant Mejia tried to encourage his fellow soldiers to maintain the grueling pace. He worried his men would be dead on their feet when they arrived at wherever the Mexicans intended to stay for the night. That thought led to another. The *soldados* escorting them carried no backpacks. If they were sending him and his men to Tampico, why were they not carrying packs?

After a little more than an hour's march, the column stopped. He helped the soldier who'd been beside him to the ground. The other man was still recovering from his wounds. Mejia looked around and found the young officer at the back of the column, deep in conversation with an older sergeant. He felt a sense of alarm growing within. He had expected the *soldados* to push them along the road with few breaks. When the young officer finished talking to his NCO, instead of relaxing, the *soldados* became tenser. Every warning bell in Mejia's head was sounding off, when the guards to the prisoners' left crossed over the road, joining their compatriots to the right of Mejia's men.

With little warning, the entire force of *soldados* came together in a single line and raised their bayoneted muskets to their shoulders.

Too late, everything fell into place. How could he have been so stupid? Mejia screamed out, "Run, boys! They're going to kill us!"

As the exhausted Texians reacted to his warning, forty muskets fired into the mass of men at point-blank range. Mejia involuntarily ducked when he felt a bullet zoom by his head. He crouched down and saw most of his company fall to the ground, dead or wounded. The *soldados*, bayonets fixed to their weapons, leveled their muskets, and started in among his men. To the open side of the road, Mejia sprinted, trying to ignore the stitch of pain in his leg, but each time his left foot pounded into the soil, he winced. He dodged a prickly pear cactus and stepped around a thorn bush. He chanced a look behind and saw the *soldados* bayoneting men on the road. A couple other Texians, to his right and left were, like him, trying to flee into the desert.

Thinking there was strength in numbers, Mejia angled to his left, with the idea of connecting with his nearest compatriot in a few hundred yards. Behind him, he heard a scattering of musket shots and saw a bullet kick up dust a few feet to his front. But the man he was veering toward stumbled and fell, a red mist exploded from where the bullet slammed into his back.

Too breathless to swear at the *soldados* behind him, Mejia renewed his focus on putting one foot in front of the other as fast as he could flee the danger behind him.

Five minutes or ten, he wasn't sure, but with his heart thundering in his chest, Mejia slowed to a walk for a few seconds then stopped. His left leg spasmed in pain. Even though largely healed, the running had taken a toll on his leg. He turned and looked behind him. There was no one he could see in pursuit. He figured he must have put at least a mile between him and the massacre back on the road. Thinking about all his companions lying dead on that dusty road brought tears unbidden to his eyes. They ran into his beard. Those men back there had been his responsibility and he had failed them. It would have been better for them to have died at their post back on the Rio Grande than to die at the hand of Mexican treachery.

The tears continued, even as his breathing returned to normal. He had to escape and tell people back in Texas what had happened, he owed it to his companions. His best guess was that the river was only a few miles away. He had to hurry. Surely the garrison commander knew that if he made good his escape, word of the massacre would travel far. With each step north, he knew that even the river wouldn't provide the safety he needed.

The haze of gunpowder was gone before Lieutenant Estevan Alameda dismounted, a gentle southerly breeze seemed eager to rid the air of the acrid smell of smoke. But the cloying smell of blood lingered, resisting the wind's effort to cleanse the air.

A Texian, with a bullet hole in his chest, stared with vacant eyes at him as he stepped amid the carnage along the road. Alameda jerked away from those accusing eyes, as his stomach threatened to disgorge his breakfast. This was the first time he'd witnessed death since graduating from the *Colegio Militar*. This was as far removed from the glorious and heroic images of war as he could imagine. He swallowed, trying to keep the contents in his stomach down. He had grown up imagining war was glorious cavalry charges, sweeping Mexico's enemies aside and riding to victory, trampling over the enemy's flag. But there was no glory in watching helpless men being slaughtered. Especially those who had honorably surrendered. No, there was no glory in this.

His men cleared the dead from the road, dragging them into the ditch. His ranking non-commissioned officer, Eduardo Hernandez appeared from the other side of the road, carrying a couple of ragged brown jackets. He cast a look at the bodies along the roadside. As a veteran of Santa Anna's earlier campaigns, crushing rebellions across northern Mexico, he took it in stride. He'd seen this before. In place of a salute, he offered the jackets to the young lieutenant, "Sir, we've accounted for all the rebels except one. We killed two who attempted to escape, but I'm pretty sure, their sergeant, the Tejano, escaped."

Alameda was sick. His eyes kept returning to the long line of bodies beside the road. This wasn't war. But he held his tongue, certain his sergeant wouldn't understand. Instead, he pointed toward the dead bodies, "Perhaps we should send a few men back into town and fetch some of the men to help us bury them."

Sergeant Hernandez eyed him circumspectly. "It's your call, sir. But if I may, perhaps I should have the boys drag them further into the field. They can build a pyre and burn the bodies. I'm sure that we'll capture our missing Tejano, but the fewer folks who know of today's actions, the better it might go, if General Woll isn't successful."

The lieutenant wanted to scream. It wasn't enough that they had murdered these men, now it was necessary to burn the evidence and find and silence the one who escaped. He shook his head, this certainly wasn't what he signed up for. He turned his back on the sergeant and swung in the saddle. "As you say, Sergeant Hernandez. Assign the corporals to oversee the absolution of our sin here and take a couple of men with you and find that Tejano. Don't let him get away."

Chapter 20

6th of April 1842

Water dripped from his threadbare, faded jacket as he crouched behind a cypress tree. He was soaked, water puddling at his feet, but at least he was on the northern bank of the Rio Grande. His last half hour on the Mexican side of the river, he felt as though he was not alone. Now, as he gazed back across the river, he thought he saw flashes of red and blue moving among the Montezuma cypress growing along the southern bank. Sergeant Julio Mejia remained hidden behind the large native tree when he saw a *soldado* approach the shoreline.

It was the sergeant from the Reynosa garrison. He walked along the bank of the water, eyes riveted to the ground, evidently looking for where Mejia had entered the river. While he walked along the edge of the river, a couple more men appeared alongside, and joined him

243

in his search for any evidence Mejia may have left as to where he crossed the river.

The Tejano cast a fleeting look at a large branch lying on the shoreline less than a dozen yards away. It had only washed up a little while earlier, after Mejia had pushed it into the water up river and used it to swim across. It was possible, if the Mexicans continued on their current path for a few hundred more yards, they would find where he'd dragged the large cypress branch into the water. As they moved away, he rose from his hiding place and began following the river, heading east, toward his goal more than sixty miles away, Fort Brown, on the mouth of the Rio Grande.

He hurried his pace as much as he dared, as the sun began to set behind him. With no food, and only the questionable water source of the river to quench his thirst, it was best to keep moving as late into the evening as possible. He stepped around a copse of mesquite trees and looked behind him. There was every possibility he was being followed. He stepped up his pace and kept walking long after the sun had fled the sky.

A boot slid through the grass only a few feet away from where Mejia was lying down behind a fallen oak tree. He'd passed through nearly sixty miles of the Rio Grande Valley. Surely the Texian fort was only a mile or two away, and here he was, trapped behind the fallen trunk, listening to the footfalls getting closer.

He briefly closed his eyes, wondering how he had wound up here. It was around sunrise on the second day after the massacre when he determined he wasn't the only one moving eastward along the shoreline of the river. On several occasions he had turned, looking behind him and saw a flash of metal, and a glimpse of a blue and red uniform.

The weeks in the church-turned-prison had sapped his strength, but he had forced himself to press onward. Everything since his escape would be in vain if he were caught. He owed it to the murdered men of his company, to make it back to Texas and tell people what had happened.

The boot stopped. It was close by. He could smell the stench of sweat on the woolen jacket worn by whomever was on the opposite side of the tree trunk.

Mejia willed himself to be still, taking the smallest breaths as possible, as he attempted to listen to the slightest change. The boots shifted, and grass rustled, but if it was the Mexican sergeant opposite him, he wasn't moving away enough for him to risk a deeper breath. As his eyes were closed, in his mind, he saw his men lying dead in that dusty road. Their eyes stared at him, accusing.

He had replayed the massacre in his mind repeatedly as he had hurried toward Fort Brown. He should have noticed the Mexicans were without their packs, that it was an execution into which he and his men had been led. Tears came unbidden. It seemed like every time he closed his eyes, the men from Company N accused him, blaming him for their murders.

The leather soles resumed sliding across the grass, as they circled around the small clearing, on the side of which lay the fallen oak tree. It had to be the cagey sergeant. Maybe the other *soldados* had been sent back to report on their progress. Mejia could only speculate. But he was sure, the one still following him was the persistent non-commissioned officer.

The images in Mejia's head fled back into the recesses of his mind when he opened his eyes again. This cat and mouse game had to end. He pressed his body more closely against the tree trunk, willing himself to be invisible. His eyes were open, looking into the blue sky, but all he could see were the accusing eyes of his former comrades. Their blood called out to him, as he hid from his pursuer. The boots had gone silent, but it didn't matter. He couldn't take the voices in his head crying for vengeance any longer.

He sat up and saw over the trunk. It was the Mexican sergeant. His back was turned, at the other side of the clearing. It looked like the man was relieving himself. His musket was propped against a tree within arm's length of where he stood.

Noiselessly, the Tejano rose to his feet, and stepped over the log. The other man was, for the moment, oblivious to Mejia's presence behind him.

The voices in his head grew louder, drowning every thought in their rage. He screamed. It was primal, carrying the burden of every man he'd seen murdered, he lunged at the Mexican sergeant.

The other man was half-turned, when Mejia crashed into him, driving him into the wet ground before him. Mejia landed on top of him and hammered him with his fists.

The Mexican sergeant reflexively brought his hands up, blocking some of the blows. Others smashed into his lip, his nose, and eyes. His musket had fallen away when they had crashed to the ground, but he still carried a knife at his belt.

The Tejano's fists pounded into the other man's face, as hands fell away, making it easier to land each powerful blow with a meaty thwack. He wasn't sure what alerted him, but something in the way the Mexican shifted, made him roll back as a wicked blade sliced the air where he'd been just a second before.

The man in the blue and red jacket clambered to his feet, waving the pig-sticker toward Mejia, who backpedaled until his knees bumped against the fallen oak tree.

The Mexican spat in the grass as he crouched low and approached. Mejia edged to his right, along the tree trunk, hoping to maneuver around his wary opponent. But with every sidestep, the Mexican sergeant matched it with his own adjustment.

Separated by no more distance than the height of a man, Mejia watched him heft the blade, as though testing the balance. The Mexican at last broke the silence, "Your situation is hopeless. Surrender and I'll take you back to Reynosa."

Mejia couldn't believe what he'd heard. "I've seen your mercy, *puta*."

With a snarl, the Mexican sprang forward, driving the knife toward Mejia. The Tejano sprang onto the tree trunk and lashed out with his foot, catching the other man in the face.

The Tejano saw the knife sail past his eyes, as he watched the other man collapse to his knees in surprised pain, blood flowing from his broken nose.

Mejia pounced onto the Mexican, knocking him onto his back. He pummeled the Mexican's face until his knuckles bled. The other man swatted at his hands and tried to dislodge him.

His hands hurt and still the other man attempted to stop the beating. Finally, Mejia wrapped his bloody hands around the Mexican's throat and as though his life depended upon it, squeezed with all his might, until long after the other man stopped struggling and went limp.

He staggered to his feet and found the knife in the grass and slipped it into his belt. He hadn't seen any other *soldados* with the sergeant, and hopefully no one else was following, but he still felt better carrying the knife.

Less than half a mile later, he crossed a well-worn trail leading to the river. In the distance he saw an earthen fort, similar in construction to Fort Moses Austin. Above the rampart flew the Texas flag. Despite his earlier victory over his pursuer, he couldn't resist a furtive glimpse behind him. A glimmer of a smile crossed his lips. The only one in pursuit was dead. He straightened his jacket and stepped onto the trail leading to the fort. He hoped he cut a soldierly figure as he walked toward the earthen embankment. The last thing he wanted was to be mistaken for a Mexican *soldado*.

When he was within shouting distance, he saw a blue-jacketed rifleman standing behind the wall, near a wooden gate. The gun was already pointed in his direction when he stopped and waved at the sentry. After a too long wait, Mejia's nerves were worn, but the guard waved for him to come closer. Under his breath, he muttered, "I hope he's not trying to line up a shot."

When no more than fifty feet separated him from the fort, the sentry shouted, "That's far enough there, old boy!" Mejia stopped and assessed the man holding the gun on him. The guard was dressed in the uniform of a Texian Marine. With a thick Irish accent, he continued, "What's one of General Travis' men doin' here? You're a wee bit too far from home, if I'm not mistaken."

With his hands open before him, Mejia shrugged and replied, "I'd rather not be here at all, but I was part of Captain Neill's garrison at Fort Moses Austin. I'm all that's left of it."

The guard eyed him for another long moment then said, "You'll be needin' to wait there." He turned and shouted into the fort and a moment later the ramparts were lined with more marines, their rifles now trained on Mejia. A young officer came up next to the guard and Mejia watched the two conversed. The officer pointed toward him and asked, "Who did you say you served under?"

Mejia repeated, "Captain Neill was our commander." He felt the knife at his waist and was tempted to let his frustration get the better of him. But he left his hands at his side, realizing the officer was only doing his duty, protecting the post.

After that, the Lieutenant waved him to approach the gate. As Mejia advanced, he heard a wooden bar sliding out of place and the gate swung outward. There was a short, open corridor between the gate and the fort's interior, and several Marines stood along the wall, with their weapons at the ready. His temper was already frayed, and he exclaimed, "Can't tell the difference between a loyal Texian and a Mexican?"

The guard, still standing above, piped up, "Faith, man, when I was in the old country, I couldn't tell me own lads from the bloody lobsterbacks. Seems the same could be said of you."

The first response to come to mind, Mejia dismissed, after all, there were rifles pointed at him. "I might be disposed to tell you what I think of that, if you all would be kind enough to stop pointing those damned things at me."

The lieutenant motioned for the Marines to lower their rifles. As they complied, an involuntary sigh of relief escaped Mejia's lips. When the officer climbed down and stood before him, he said, "I'm from Fort Moses Austin. The fort fell when the Mexican army crossed into Texas at Laredo."

The young officer was genuinely shocked. "What the hell? When did this happen? We've heard nothing of it."

"The fort fell when Captain Neill was killed on the fourteenth of March."

The lieutenant paced back and forth, visibly upset. "What happened after that," he eyed the dirty chevrons on Mejia's sleeves, "ah, Sergeant?"

For the past three days, all Mejia had been able to do was survive, only one step ahead of his pursuers. Now, what had happened on that dirt road south of Reynosa came back to him in all its horror and his eyes welled up with tears as he recounted the barbaric execution of the remainder of his company. When he'd finished, the Marines standing around, listening were visibly angry. Several were shouting that they should burn down the sleepy farming village of Matamoros, on the other side of the Rio Grande.

Mejia looked at the lieutenant, attempting to gage which way the wind would blow. He saw a man of no more than twenty-five years, who by virtue of a congressional appointment, commanded the thirty men assigned to garrison the little fort at the mouth of the Rio Grande. The way he continued pacing told Mejia all he needed to know, the officer clearly agreed with the sentiment. But he stopped and took stock of his men and saw they were itching to give a little payback.

He waved his hands until the men grew quiet. There were feral gleams in their eyes. All they needed was his permission. But when he spoke, he said, "Calm down, Marines! We're not going to repay evil for evil, here." He turned around, looking at each of his men, until his eyes fell on one of the older Marines. "Tell me, Parson, what does the good book say about that?"

The Marine who had fallen under the lieutenant's gaze was easily the oldest man in the fort, his gray hair stuck out from under his hat. He returned the officer's gaze with a glare of his own. "Lieutenant, I hate that name. I ain't been a man of the cloth since the Comanche killed my wife and children."

The young officer's only response was a withering glare of his own. It lasted until the older soldier growled, "Fine. In the apostle Peter's first letter, we're not to be rendering evil for evil, but to repay evil with goodness. But, Hell's bells, Lieutenant, I ain't affixing to go heaping blessings on those bastards across the river."

The officer waved away the last comment. "Shut it, Parson. I believe we would dishonor our oaths to the Republic if we took it upon ourselves to go across the river and kill a passel of Mexican dirt farmers. They are innocent of any crimes committed by the Mexican *soldados* who killed the sergeant's company."

Mejia swiveled his head around and saw the men were disappointed, but it didn't keep the Lieutenant from forging on. "I'll tell you what we're going to do. We're going to get Sergeant ..."

He paused, until Mejia said, "Mejia."

"Sergeant Mejia onboard the packet ship at the mouth of the river and get him back to the government as quickly as possible."

The young officer had been true to his word. Mejia was shocked at how quickly things happened after the lieutenant had decided on a course of action. Mejia had been bundled onto a packet boat before the end of the day, and the next morning, with the tide, the packet boat had raised anchor and hoisted sail.

The 9th of April found Sergeant Mejia sitting in a rowboat in Copano Bay, being rowed ashore in the tiny town of Copano. After the boat deposited him on a rickety dock, he decided the town wasn't much to look at. On a busy day, there might be a couple of hundred souls in town. The buildings were a ramshackle lot. Those closest to the bay were mostly warehouses. Wagons rolled in and out of town, carrying loads to and from the warehouses. Despite the town's small size, plenty of goods flowed from several ships riding low at anchor, into the warehouses, and from there, to towns across South Texas, including San Antonio.

In his jacket, which he had cleaned and patched while on the packet boat, he carried a letter from the Lieutenant at Fort Brown. It instructed any citizen of the Republic of Texas to provide Sergeant Mejia every assistance necessary.

It had garnered him a ride on a military supply wagon, carrying gunpowder and boxes of artillery shells from the United States, to the garrison at the Alamo. As the wagon rolled along the gulf road, Mejia had warned the driver of the wagon, a freedman, that there was a risk the Mexican army could still be in possession of San Antonio and the Alamo.

The driver tilted his head back and laughed until tears ran down his ebon skin. "Like as not, that might be true. But it's also true that I'm black and you're Mexican. If they's there, I don't figure they'll do much to us."

Mejia sat back on the bench, biting his tongue. The memory of Reynosa was fresh on his mind. He still carried the knife he'd taken from that Mexican sergeant. It hung at his belt. "I'll not let myself get caught a second time."

Eleven days and more than a hundred thirty miles later, on the 20th of April, the wagon crested a low rise, and in the distance, Mejia and the driver saw the town of San Antonio, spread across the prairie before them. There were no burned buildings on the edge of town. He said a prayer to the Blessed Virgin that the town was still in the hands of the Texians.

The driver cracked his whip over the heads of the mules hauling the wagon and it lurched forward, eating away the remaining distance. Along the road, they saw a couple of tents alongside the road, and several soldiers in butternut waved at the wagon, flagging it to stop at the checkpoint. Seeing the Texian soldiers approaching, Mejia realized that he'd been holding his breath for too long. He exhaled in relief. He was home.

Chapter 21

Spring was in full bloom on the South Texas prairie. Bluebonnets and Indian Paintbrushes carpeted the ground in a riot of blues, purples, reds, and yellows. A dry creek bed ran alongside the military road. The men of the 1st Texas Infantry moved with purpose down the hard-packed dirt road, as the distinct hump over the chapel became visible on the horizon. They were nearly home.

The past six weeks had been the longest in Will's life, since leaving Santa Fe behind. He felt a profound relief, looking at the walls of the old mission-turned-fort, even if only through the spyglass' telescoping lens. He trained the lens on the flag waving proudly atop the chapel, and realized he'd been holding his breath until he brought the red, white, and blue of the Texas flag into focus.

He slipped the spyglass into its case and wheeled his mount back onto the road where he took in the sight of the seven hundred fifty men of the 1st Texas marching in route step along the road. They were dusty, and their uniforms were caked with the grime of the road. He was proud of his regulars. They had marched over eight hundred miles in only forty-two days. Seguin's four companies of cavalry included Hay's Ranger company, and they were riding on the column's flanks. Bringing up the rear of the column were the six horse-drawn field pieces, rumbling over the road on their caissons.

As they drew closer to the walls of the Alamo, the men walked a little straighter and they switched from route step to a cadenced march. From within the column someone began to sing a song written along the way back from Santa Fe, and the entire little army joined in.

There's a Yellow Rose of Texas I'm going there to see,
No other soldier knows her, no soldier only me!
She cried so when I left her, it like to broke my heart.
And when I go to find her, we never more will part.
She's the sweetest little rosebud, this soldier ever knew,
Her eyes were bright as diamonds, they sparkled like the dew,
You may talk about your dearest Mae and sing of Rosie Lee,
But the Yellow Rose of Texas beats the belles of Tennessee.

Unbidden, a smile crept on Will's face, as the men enthusiastically sang the Yellow Rose of Texas. In this world, far removed from the one into which Will had been born, there had been no San Jacinto and no legend of Emily West. But one night around the campfire, he had written down what he recalled of the old song, sharing it with some of his fellow officers. He'd claimed that Becky was his sole inspiration.

Within a few days, the song had caught on and it had become a favorite marching tune for the army. It joined other songs the soldiers used to entertain themselves along the march, like *The Girl I left Behind, Gary Owen,* and *Yankee Doodle.*

As the column swept along the road, Will's attention was drawn to the military cemetery east of the fort. It had swollen from just a couple of dozen graves to several hundred. Scores of dirt mounds the telltale sign of soldiers who had died in defense of the Alamo. He was starved for information. The most recent news had reached the army several weeks earlier.

The column turned from the road, heading toward the fort's gates. Moments later, the lead elements swept through the gates and into the Alamo plaza. He followed the vanguard and saw the edges of the plaza was lined with soldiers. Atop the walls, more men crowded, watching his army's return. Apparently, Johnston had managed to mobilize a sizable portion of the reserves.

He wheeled out of the line of march, as rank after rank filed into the plaza. Through the noise of traipsing boots, he heard his name called. He turned and saw Becky. In her arms was their daughter, Elizabeth. She was nearly ten months old. It startled him how much she had grown in the span of just a few months. Despite the cacophony of noises in the plaza, the little girl turned her head, following her mother's finger, pointing to Will. She giggled and laughed when she saw him. She hadn't forgotten her papa. Despite the fatigue and exhaustion threatening to overwhelm him, a lightness settled over him as he leapt from his mount and ran to his wife and child, catching them in a fierce embrace. He wiped away the unbidden tears as he took his daughter in his arms and hugged her tightly to him, as she squealed in protest.

Standing behind his stepmother was Charlie. Gone was the little boy. The youth had grown in the time he'd been away, and his head came up to Will's chin. The boy smiled when Will's eyes fell on him. With his wife clinging to his neck and his daughter in one arm, he beckoned his son with the other. Slowly, reluctantly, he crossed the short distance and let Will draw him into the family's embrace. As Charlie buried his head into Will's shoulder, he felt the boy shudder then heard the muffled sound of him sobbing. Confused, Will looked to Becky. She shook her head, leaned in and whispered, "Oh, Will, it was horrible! The Mexicans nearly wiped out the fort before Sidney's men came to our rescue. Poor Charlie was helping to defend the chapel, at the last."

He was shocked at how close things had come to a complete disaster. How close he had come to losing the people who had come to mean everything shook him to the center of his core. He vowed he would never let anything befall his family, nor let them come so close to disaster. After a lengthy moment, he disentangled himself from his family. Ignoring decorum, he planted a kiss on his wife's lips, and plopped a wet kiss on his daughter's forehead, then he took Charlie by the shoulders and looked him in the eyes, "Son, you'll be alright. When time permits, we'll talk about what happened. Okay?" Charlie brushed tears from his eyes and nodded.

21st April 1842

He sat in the same chair he'd called his own some three months previous. Across the desk from him sat General Johnston. The two had talked late into the previous evening about the relief of the Alamo. Will had wanted to learn of how he had managed to bring such a sizable relief force to the fort.

Now, after sleeping with Becky for the first time in far too many nights, he said, "I know I've said it last night, Sid, but I cannot tell you enough how grateful I am that you saved my family from falling into the hands of the enemy."

Johnston was clearly uncomfortable with the praise. He cleared his throat before replying. "Ah, hell, Buck, it's not anything you wouldn't have done for me, and we both know it. But, as God is my witness, I wish we would have arrived before Woll and his troops got inside the Alamo's walls. We could have saved more than two hundred lives."

The detailed casualty reports of the Alamo's defenders lay on the desk, at Will's fingertips. He glanced down at the sheaf of papers. "What madness has descended upon Santa Anna, Sid? It wasn't enough that they killed our wounded within these very walls, but to execute prisoners in Reynosa, after honorably surrendering. It violates every rule of war. Has Santa Anna lost his mind?"

Johnston's eyes drifted down to the casualty report on the desk then hardened when he looked up. "We shouldn't rest until we've strung his "bastardness" up from the highest tree in Texas, Buck. While I agree with your assessment from last night, that we can't kill every Mexican who surrenders, but by God, they're going to have to pay for this."

A knock at the door ended the conversation and several other officers entered Will's office. Colonel Seguin led the way, followed by Sam Houston, acting as colonel of militia. Behind him came Majors West and Wyatt. Behind them appeared a nervous looking Sergeant Julio Mejia. The last to enter, and close the door behind him, was Captain Hays.

As the men found seats around the desk or leaned against the walls, Will looked at the Tejano sergeant. He was thin to a point of gauntness. His freshly laundered uniform, sported several patches and new seams where the cloth had been mended. The Alamo's supply of uniforms had been depleted by Johnston's reserves. Unfortunately, Mejia was hardly the only soldier making do with a uniform badly in need of replacing. His well-mended uniform hung loosely on his frame and his eyes were sunk deep in his head. Will wondered, *"What must he have endured?"*

Will coughed, cleared his throat, and said, "Sergeant Mejia, I know you've made your report to other officers, but I would like to hear it directly from you, what happened at Fort Moses Austin and afterwards?"

Mejia had replayed everything over in his mind countless times. Recounting the events for the officers in the room flowed smoothly from his lips. Until his narrative carried him to the massacre on the road south of Reynosa. He choked up, as he recounted the brutal execution.

Every man in the room was visibly angry as he struggled to give testimony to the events on that fateful day on the road south of Reynosa. He pushed through and described the deadly cat and mouse game he and the Mexican sergeant had played. He downplayed killing the other man and concluded with his arrival at Fort Brown.

Will shook his head. The sergeant's ordeal was the stuff from which legends were born. He made a mental note to write up a recommendation to send to congress regarding the need to create awards. There was no doubt in his mind that if anyone deserved a Congressional Medal of Honor, it was Sergeant Mejia. "I've read the remainder of your report, Sergeant. I commend you for your gallantry in bringing word of this … crime home to us. Thank you. You're dismissed."

After the sergeant left, Will said, "We're at war, gentlemen. Let there be no doubt in any of our minds this recent incursion by General Woll was a direct threat to our sovereignty. The reason I've asked you all to join me is to determine how do we best respond to it?"

Johnston played with the corner of his mustache, considering the question before he said, "We have mobilized our reserves, sir. As we're all aware, a significant portion of them are present here in the fort and in town. Based upon our best estimates, we outnumber Woll's Army of the North. We should pursue his army and destroy it."

From his place along the back wall, Captain Hays nodded. "Just give us the word, General, and we'll ride down there and kick their teeth in."

Sitting on the corner of the large desk, Colonel Seguin held up his hand, as though trying to stop someone. "I share General Johnston's opinion that we can destroy Woll's army. The problem is behind that army, Santa Anna will be sending a second, and perhaps even a third. If not this year, then next."

He stood and grabbed a map tube from a corner of the room and rolled a map across the desk. It showed all of Texas and part of northern Mexico. "The oath-breaker would rather send armies north than acknowledge the treaty of Bexar. Before we race down to the Rio Grande, let's take stock of the situation. We have nearly the entire regular army assembled here," he pointed to San Antonio on the map, "but less than half of the reserves have arrived. My counsel is that we should wait, replace our losses, transfer from McCulloch's militia the best he has into our active reserves, and continue training our soldiers. And then, once we have done those things, we go after the head of the snake himself, Santa Anna." He took the penknife he'd used as a pointer, and drove the tip into the desk, below the map, where Mexico City would be if the map continued to the south.

The room erupted into pandemonium. As they shouted back and forth across the room, Will gaged that his officers were evenly split between Johnston's proposal and Seguin's. When the men settled down, Will asked, "Sid, how many men could we move to attack General Woll's army, if we set off tomorrow in pursuit?"

Johnston stopped twirling his mustache as he pulled a notebook from his vest pocket and hastily wrote some numbers down. After a moment, he looked up and said, "Probably around twenty-six hundred men. At best guess, Woll's got a little more than two thousand."

Will looked thoughtful. "That's not bad. It would be the largest command we have ever fielded. But we've got two proposals on the table and I'd like for you to review it, too. If we wait and rebuild our regulars and train up our reserves, while picking the best of the militia to expand the reserves, how many men would we be able to field?"

Johnston's chair creaked in protest as he leaned back and stared at the ceiling as his mind worked out the details. After a long delay, he said, "If we were to wait until the autumn to attack, we could probably mobilize as many as twelve infantry battalions."

Around the room, the other officers wore looks of incredulity at Johnston's calculation. Will was tempted to side with them, but for Johnston's reputation for careful and deliberate thinking. "How do we manage that, Sid? Today, we've got five battalions between our regular and reserve infantry."

Johnston dipped his head in acknowledgement. "Fair enough, General. But let's examine what's available to us. To borrow a phrase I've heard you say more than once, before this shitstorm, McCulloch had done an excellent job building our reserves, and now, he's working on assembling the militia in defense of the republic. One problem he's faced, I've learned, is that

Tom Rusk, who has been in nominal command of the militia since the end of the revolution, hasn't done much to ensure all able-bodied men are enrolled. My point is that by McCulloch's calculation, he's found that more than six thousand men are not enrolled in the militia. I'd hazard a guess that many of them have no idea the law requires their enrollment in their district. Rusk was pretty passive about his job."

Will nudged him, "Where do we get the other men, Sid?"

"We expand the reserves. We'll transfer as much as half of the existing militia to the active reserves while McCulloch tracks down and enrolls all those missing men."

Will scratched at the stubble on his chin, thinking through Johnston's numbers. "How much time will we need to train all these new reservists?"

Johnston was quick to reply. "Give me through the end of the summer and we can have twelve battalions of infantry ready to invade come this autumn."

Watching his enthusiasm, Will ribbed him. "Sid, did you change your mind? Do you prefer Juan's plan now?"

Johnston smiled ruefully. "I'll allow that I had my dander up, and it's possible I was a might hasty earlier. But Juan's idea is sound. Where does this leave us?"

Will pulled the penknife from the desk and handed it back to Seguin. "I believe this belongs to you, Juan. In addition to the infantry we've discussed, I want you to figure out how to expand to eight troops of regular cavalry as well as an equal number of reserves."

He scanned the room, his eyes settling on Captain Hays. "I'm not sure if there's time, but I want to expand your special Rangers from one to three companies. I'll be recalling most of Major Caldwell's Rangers from our frontier along the Red River, and you'll pick from among them first, and then from the ranks of the regular and reserve services next. But I want eyes and ears south of the border when we invade, and that means more men like yours."

Hays preened at the news. Will could see the wheels spinning as he began to mentally make plans for building out his specialized force.

Seguin also smiled, "With those Rangers from Caldwell's frontier battalion, we'll have three battalions of cavalry. That'll be more than a thousand men."

Will returned the grin and sketched a mock salute in Seguin's direction. "Indeed, General Seguin. They'll be your responsibility. Jack will also report to you." Seguin's earlier smile faded when he realized how much work lay before him.

Will's features grew somber, as he brought up the third branch of the army. He turned to Johnston, "Our two batteries of field artillery are not going to be adequate to the role they'll need to play. I want a battalion of six batteries of field artillery in our invasion force. Some of those guns are going to need to be large enough to knock holes in walls. Let's bring Captain Carey back from our coastal forts."

An idea sprang to mind, "Also, let's use some of our contacts back east and see if we can talk a few officers from to the United States into joining our army. If I can get the president to agree, maybe we can sweeten the offer with some land or a cash bounty."

Most of the men knew officers who were actively serving in the United States Army, and Will could see they were building their own lists of men to invite. Hopefully, that would provide more officers. If he and the other men in the room were able to pull this off, more trained officers were a must. In a roomful of butternut uniforms, Major West's navy-blue jacket stood out. "I've not forgotten about your Marines, Major. Until we're ready to invade, I want you to work with General McCulloch on adding a few more reserve companies that can bolster our coastal defenses. But when it's time, you and your six companies will be part of our army of invasion."

Ever the professional, West saluted. "Yes, sir!"

His list nearly complete, Will turned to Sam Houston, "Last and certainly not least, General Houston." Will acknowledged his rank from the Texas Revolution.

Houston returned Will's smile with a thin one of his own. "It's about time, Buck. You'd think your Cherokee allies were more important than that."

Will winced at the sharp comment. There were times when interacting with Houston that he wanted to wipe his smug expression from his face. Instead he said, "I was under the impression these fine soldiers under your command were our citizens, not our allies, Sam."

Houston's thin, forced smile continued, "Well, that's what I meant, Buck. They've answered the call to arms, in greater numbers than other Texians. They deserve that recognition."

Houston was cagey, like a politician. Will wasn't certain if the former general really meant that he deserved the recognition or if it belonged to his Cherokee volunteers. "Of course, I'm grateful, as is every other man here, of their willingness to serve. But that brings me in a circle back to you, Sam. Are you going to stay the course with the army or do you plan on taking another shot at the presidency?"

The last six years had taught Will that even a soldier, especially one in command of the Texas army needed to develop some political chops or the politicians in congress would run him over. If there was a value that Will, as a product of the twenty-first century, innately shared with his nineteenth-century compatriots, it was that no officer should make a run for the presidency without resigning his commission in the army. He had subtly reminded Houston, he would have to choose between the two.

Houston laughed. "Had you boys decided to go punish Woll's army, I'd happily lead my Cherokee warriors into battle, but alas, as you so kindly reminded me, President Crockett's term nears its end, and you're right, I do intend to challenge *Señor* de Zavala for the office."

Will barely managed to keep a grimace from his face. Since Houston's defeat nearly six years earlier, he'd wondered if the former general still harbored a desire to seek annexation. His voice would hardly be alone. Many Texians from the southern states advocated annexation. Adding two senators from another slave state would shift the balance of power in the United States. But Will didn't know Houston's mind. Instead, he nodded and said, "Congratulations on your candidacy, Sam. I'll be issuing orders transferring them from the militia to the active reserves shortly. Who would you recommend to command them?"

Houston nodded and said, "That's fair enough, Buck. You've met Stand Watie. He's my second-in-command, and he'd make a damn fine colonel for the battalion." He fell silent, as though in thought, before he continued, "My Cherokee warriors are good men, Buck. Give them the opportunity to prove themselves and you'll not be disappointed."

While a Houston presidency chilled him, when he thought about how Sam Houston had gutted the army of the republic in the world in which he'd come, but Will could see Houston was speaking earnestly from the heart. The man, known affectionately by the Cherokee as the Raven, loved his adopted people and wanted them to prosper. With a genuine smile, Will struck out his hand and said, "You have my word, Sam."

He scanned the room, looking at each officer, thinking of their roles in the coming days. Everything which could be resolved now had been. "I believe we've set things in motion here, gentlemen. My next step is simple. Our government must bless this endeavor. I'll be traveling to Austin tomorrow. I suspect our government will respond to Woll's invasion and the treacherous murder of our men with a declaration of war."

Chapter 22

2nd May 1842

Hell, Will decided, would be eternity rocking along in a stage coach with only Sam Houston as his companion. Fortunately, Charlie shared the seat beside him as the coach swayed back and forth, as it ate away at the distance between San Antonio and Austin. It's not that Houston was an intransigent companion. Far from it, Houston regaled Charlie with many stories from his own youth spent living among the Cherokee. But Will's earlier support for Crockett during the previous election acted as a barrier of amiability between the two men.

Will tuned out the conversation and looked out the open window, as the prairie rolled by. New stagecoach inns had opened, and with fresh mounts available at regular intervals, the coach made good time. What had once been a two-day trip, could now be made between sunrise and sunset, at least during the summer.

A ferry now crossed the Guadeloupe River along the most direct route between the two cities, and it had been while crossing the languorously flowing river that he had noticed the frame of a wooden truss bridge spanning the river a few hundred feet upriver from the ferry. He'd read that a company billing itself as the Texas Central Railroad was responsible for the grading of land and this bridge. Unfortunately, the company was undercapitalized, and the last he had heard, the principals were trying to find new investors back east. If they ever completed the line, it would shorten the time needed to travel between San Antonio and Austin to only a couple of hours.

After twelve hours in the coach with Sam Houston, even Charlie perked up when the coach rolled up to the Stagecoach Inn in Austin. After they climbed down, Houston extended his hand to Will and said, "General, I know my interest in running for the presidency makes you about as comfortable as a whore in church, regarding how you and I see annexation, but rest assured, if I win, you'll have my unwavering support for the coming campaign against Mexico. That trumped-up dictator must be made to pay the price of his crimes against Texas."

Will shook the outstretched hand. "Sam, I appreciate your sentiments. They are my own. Should you win, I'm glad to know the military will continue to enjoy the government's support."

Charlie stretched after stepping from the coach. While Mr. Houston had regaled him with plenty of stories, he was glad to see the former general's backside as he crossed the street. He had said he was staying with a friend.

He picked up his bag and followed his pa into the inn's lobby, where Will checked them in. Charlie leaned against the staircase banister and watched. Twilight's last gasp, sent tendrils of weak light to compete against the lamplight basking the lobby in a soft glow. While his pa fished a few cotton-back notes from his pocket, he followed a particle of dust, eddying and sifting in the cooling air currents from the open doorway.

After Will signed the register, Charlie forgot about the dust and followed him up the stairs to their room. After dropping his bag on the floor, the boy plopped down on the bed. "Pa, I had no idea that Mr. Houston could talk that much. Do you think he'll win an election against *Señor* Zavala?"

Will chuckled, as he walked over to the window, and pulled the curtains wide, tying them back with a cord. Red and orange light danced across the western sky. The sun had only slipped below the horizon a few minutes earlier. As he answered, he raised the window, letting in a slight breeze. "I don't reckon anyone knows yet, Son. *Señor* Zavala has been a good vice president. But a lot of newcomers may be biased by his Mexican heritage, even though we both know there's no better Texian than Lorenzo de Zavala."

Charlie shrugged out of his jacket and let it fall to the floor next to his carpet bag before asking, "Do you like Mr. Houston? You were real quiet on the coach ride."

"Pick your jacket up and hang it in the wardrobe. Set your bag in there too. I can't image what Becky would say if she saw a mess like that." As Charlie reached down and grabbed his things, Will asked, "What do you mean by 'do I like him?'"

After hanging his jacket up, Charlie shrugged, "I don't know, but he did all the talking during the ride up from San Antonio. It seemed like you don't like him much."

As Will hung his jacket up next to Charlie's, he offered an apologetic smile, "There's a bit of history there, Son. Ever since I helped your Uncle Davy get elected, General Houston has resented me just a bit. I think he expected things to go different back in '36. He expected he'd lead the army to victory over Santa Anna and win the presidency in a landslide. As you know, things didn't work out that way, and he resents it at times, I think."

After dinner in the inn's common room, they returned to their room, where they prepared for bed. After shimmying into his nightshirt, Charlie climbed into bed. As he drifted off to sleep, he dreamed he was living among the Indians, carefree and having adventures, just like Mr. Houston had when he was a teenager, living among the Cherokee.

The morning breeze rustled the curtains. The soft noise woke Charlie and he opened his eyes and wiped the sleep from them. His pa was already up, standing over a wash basin placed on top of a wooden stand. He splashed cold water on his face, muttering unpleasant words about freezing parts of his body off. The boy stifled a giggle, as he recalled a similar situation a few years earlier. Then, while his pa was splashing his face with water, Charlie had heard him griping, "damned if I'm not going to invent an electric water heater one of these days."

He remembered asking, "Isn't electricity what Benjamin Franklin discovered, pa?"

Pa had explained, "He discovered that lightning and electricity are basically the same. Did you know that he invented the lightning rod?"

Charlie had asked, "What's that?"

His pa patiently explained, "Tall buildings attract lightning. A lightning rod, helps to conduct the current into the ground, and defuses the electrical charge. Without it, the building is more likely to catch fire when lightning strikes."

As Charlie swung his feet out of bed, he realized, Pa had distracted him with the lesson about electricity. He had had never answered his question about how to use electricity to warm water. As he fished his clothes from the carpetbag, he thought one of these days, he'd ask about it.

His pa's brown dress uniform was draped over the bed, as he stood in front of the little mirror hanging on the wall above the wash basin. His face was covered in a lather, as he used a straight razor to scrape a few days' beard growth from his face. Charlie didn't think it looked fun. He ran his fingers across his face, feeling soft, downy fuzz above his lip. As his pa finished and dried his face with a towel, he beckoned Charlie over to him, where he pretended to size him up and eyed one side of his face then another. "Hmm, won't be too much longer before I'm teaching you how to get rid of that peach fuzz over your upper lip."

He made as if to bring the blade to Charlie's face, as the boy danced away. As Charlie continued getting dressed, his pa shrugged and smiled. "It was probably just some dirt smudged on your face. Make sure you wash it clean." Charlie scowled at his pa. Sometimes Pa could read him so well.

As Will slipped on a waistcoat, Charlie was trying for the third time to tie the ascot's bow. Becky had packed his Sunday-go-to-Meeting clothes, and he hadn't mastered how to tie the damned thing in a bow yet. When he swore under his breath, he caught his pa looking at him. For a moment, it looked like Will's lips were twitching upwards. Finally, exasperated, Charlie held out the white ascot and his pa took it and came around behind him and wrapped it around his throat before saying, "Best not let Becky hear you talking like that. Stand still and I'll have it done for you."

Charlie beamed after it took his pa two attempts to tie the bow in the current fashion. His pa glanced at his pocket watch and slid it back into the pocket. "We've got a bit of time yet before we need to head over to the Capitol building, Son." He sat on the edge of the bed and patted the space next to him. "I wanted to ask you about how you're doing? We haven't had time yet to talk about what happened a couple of weeks ago in the Alamo's chapel."

Charlie sat next to him and shrugged. "I dunno, Pa. I guess I'm alright now. But I ain't ever been that scared before. I thought we were all going to die."

His pa wrapped his arm around him and gave his shoulder a squeeze. He hadn't felt as safe for the past few weeks as he felt right then. "Believe it or not, Son, I have a very good idea how you felt. The most scared I ever was, was when your Uncle Davy and I were fighting some Mexican lancers in an arroyo south of the Nueces River. I had fallen on the ground, and this huge Mexican was standing over me with a long lance in his hands, pointing it at me. I thought I was a goner, for sure. But your uncle killed him and saved my life. I've been in my fair share of scrapes, and bar none, that was the most scared I have ever been."

Charlie leaned against his pa's shoulder and said, "I've heard Uncle Davy tell the story, but the way he told it, it didn't sound as scary."

His pa laughed. "Your Uncle Davy has a way of spinning words, Son. Hell, that's part of what makes him such a good politician. He's never been one to let a few details get in the way of telling a good story."

Charlie had heard Uncle Davy tell more than a few tall tales, and he joined his pa, laughing at the president's well-earned reputation as a raconteur. His pa continued, "But what I was saying, is that it's okay to be scared when you're caught up in a fight. That's how we know we're brave is when we can take that fear and still do the right thing. Just like you did, Son."

The boy glanced up and saw conflict in his pa's eyes, as though there was more he wanted to say. He looked back at the boy, searching his young face, as though looking for something. When he found his voice, he said, "Charlie … Son. What you did, protecting Becky and your sister, made me very proud of you. What you did was very brave. But I don't want to ever lose you. Between you, Liza, and Becky, y'all are my whole world. What I'm trying to say, is that I love you."

Charlie felt tears welling in his eyes, as he listened to his father. He reached around and hugged him as hard as he could. "Thanks, Pa. I love you, too."

Near the Colorado River stood the lone church in Austin with a steeple. From its single bell, it tolled noon. Will listened as the bell rang twelve times. He and Charlie stood in the Capitol building's House of Representatives' chamber, behind a rope cordon separating the gallery from the desks behind which the peoples' representatives sat. The back of the room was crowded with several hundred people, waiting to hear the president's speech.

Nearly every senator and representative had returned to Austin over the past couple of weeks, once it was evident Mexico's latest foray into the Republic had been turned back. Additional chairs had been brought in, allowing the senators to share desks with their counterparts from the House. There was a buzz of conversation as they made small talk with each other, waiting for the president's arrival.

The air was growing stale at Will's spot near the rope, which stretched from one side of the room to the other. Even though every window in the chamber was open, what little breeze came through failed to stir the air at the back of the room. As the temperature climbed, Charlie tugged at the ascot around his neck, Will resisted the urge to unfasten his jacket's top button, silently cursing the need to maintain the formal image expected of him as commander of the army.

The door, near the speaker's podium swung open, and the chamber's sergeant-at-arms stepped through. The chattering died off, as he announced the arrival of the president. To a man, the representatives and senators stood as David Crockett strode through the door. He wore a somber expression, which was far removed from the normal joviality that was his stock-in-trade.

He stepped up to the podium and adjusted the black silk cravat tied around his throat. It matched perfectly the black suit and black waistcoat he wore. Will thought he looked like he was dressed to attend a funeral.

He chased the thought away. Heaven help him if it were so. The president opened a leather portfolio and glanced down at a prepared text. As he spoke, Will focused intently on his words.

"Gentlemen of the House of Representatives and the Senate. Mr. Vice President, Mr. Speaker, and Mr. President Pro-Tem." Crockett's gaze swept over the assembled men in the room before settling briefly on the three men to his right. Lorenzo de Zavala, as Vice President sat next to the podium, and beside him sat the Speaker of the House, Colin McKinney, and last was the president pro-tem of the senate, Richard Ellis.

"Thank you for the opportunity to address this august body regarding the state of relations that exist between the Republic of Texas and the United States of Mexico. On the thirteenth of March, the Mexican Army of the North crossed over the treaty line at the Rio Grande and attacked elements of our army at Fort

Moses Austin. At dawn on the thirtieth of March, the same army attacked without provocation elements of our active and reserve army at our primary military fortification, the Alamo.

"Were it not for the fortuitous arrival of brevet General A.S. Johnston's relief column, the Alamo would have become like Thermopylae of old, a holocaust of fire and death. Circumstances cast our beloved Major Almaron Dickinson in the role of Leonidas, leading his own three hundred Spartans, in defense of sacred duty." Crockett paused, looking up from his prepared statement and gazed around the room at the assembly, looking many of them in the eyes before continuing.

"There are those in Mexico, who claim that we are a band of pirates, when they are not busy demarking our boundaries at the Nueces River. Let us set aside such rank hypocrisy and examine how we have come to this moment. When Santa Anna overturned the lawful constitution of 1824, he made himself a dictator and an enemy of democracy. Rather than live under Santa Anna's bootheel, we threw off the shackles of despotism and declared our independence. Texian arms were victorious and Santa Anna was captured. As the leader of the Mexican nation, he negotiated the Treaty of Bexar, in which both nations agreed our shared boundary would be the Rio Grande River to its headwaters.

"The oath-breaker had no sooner stepped foot on Mexican soil than he repudiated the treaty. The office of the president is tasked as the executive of state with overseeing the territorial integrity of our great nation. To that end, I have instructed our secretary of war to use our army to secure our border with Mexico. We have established border forts at the mouth of the Rio Grande and at Laredo, and most recently at Ysleta. Every action taken has been in the spirit of the Treaty of Bexar, which the Senate of the Republic ratified six year ago."

Crocket turned the page and looked up as he continued, "The lawless instability within the factions vying for control of the government of the United States of Mexico has allowed Santa Anna to seize power yet again. Even if his only crimes against Texas were the envelopment and surrender of our garrison at Fort Moses Austin or the attempted sacking of the Alamo, we would be acting in righteous fury in retaliating. But it is with heavy heart I must inform members of congress and the people of Texas that on the third of April, sixty prisoners of war from Fort Moses Austin were murdered in cold blood on the orders of Santa Anna." Crocket paused again, his eyes red with emotion.

Word of the massacre outside of Reynosa had not become widespread yet, even among Texas' representatives and senators. Most were hearing of this for the first time. Stunned silence descended upon the chamber, as the news registered among Texas' elected officials.

First to his feet was the honorable representative from San Antonio, Francisco Ruiz. He slammed his hands on his desk, yelling, "Down with Santa Anna!"

Other politicians leapt to their feet, shouting for revenge for their murdered soldiers. The president stood at the podium, his hands tightly clasped to its sides, as the pandemonium ran its course.

"I trust I speak for each man who hears my voice or reads of this in the newspapers in the coming days, when I say, we have suffered the indignation of watching our fathers, sons, and brothers butchered by Santa Anna for the last time. It was for this reason I asked to address you, in a joint session of congress of the Republic of Texas. I call upon this august body to jointly issue a declaration of war against the government of Mexico. We will not rest, we will not tire nor flag in our resolve until Santa Anna has been brought to justice for his crimes against Texas!"

Every congressman and senator, every man, woman, and child packed into the public gallery stood and cheered as Crockett closed the folder, tucked it under his arm and turned and nodded to the men to his right, and exited quickly by the same door he had entered fifteen minutes earlier.

After he and Charlie escaped from the crush of people in the gallery, Will strode down the hallway and took the stairs two at a time, and arrived on the landing outside Crockett's office. The door was closed but not locked and he let himself and his son into the small executive office.

The long table he and the president had used to plan their capture of Santa Fe was gone. The large, wooden desk was back in its normal place and near the door, a couple of chairs faced the desk. Crockett's black felt jacket was haphazardly draped over one the chairs. The president sat behind his desk, a pen in his hand swiftly scratching across a piece of paper. When he finished, he set the pen down and looked up. "It's good to see you, Buck. I'm right glad you're back from Santa Fe. I do wish you'd brought Becky and the baby with you, though. I miss them mightily."

His smile widened as he turned to Charlie, "Damnation boy, what's my Becky been feeding you? You've shot up like a weed. A few more inches and you'll be as tall as your pa, I believe."

Will sank down into the open chair opposite from Crockett and waved to the other chair, "If you'll move your Uncle Davy's jacket there, have a seat. Your uncle and I have a war to plan."

Crockett took the jacket from the boy and set it on the desk before responding. "It might not take that long, Buck. I've read the report you sent over last night, and damned, if you haven't put together a fine plan of action. There's only one or two items I'd recommend differently, but that can wait.

The president had always taken Will's plans in his stride and adopted them as his own, when pushing them through congress. "One or two things" was a departure for Crockett. Will cocked his head to the side, and looked keenly at his commander-in-chief, "Ah, what kind of changes do you have in mind, Mr. President?"

A crooked smile lit up Crockett's face and filled Will with dread. "Oh, hell, David, what have you gone and done?"

Crockett smiled impishly. "Oh, ye of little faith. Where's your trust, can't you extend your father-in-law a little credit?"

Not liking the direction the president was taking the conversation, Will drily replied, "In God we trust, everyone else pays cash, David."

Crockett guffawed, "That's a delightful bit of blasphemy, Buck. I'll have to remember it. It's only a slight change I'm looking for. I couldn't help but notice that your plan includes a large expansion in the number of reserve battalions. I'd normally never interfere with who you pick to command these units. However, in the case of one of them, I made an exception, and taken the liberty of appointing a colonel to one of them."

Will gave the president an icy glare. Afraid he knew the answer, he was hesitant to ask. But Charlie piped up, "Who'd you pick, Uncle Davy?"

With a twinkle in his eye, he smiled wide and said, "Me!"

Will leapt to his feet, knocking his chair over backwards, and shouted, "You can't do that! You're the president! Who's going to run the government if you're gallivanting around Mexico with me?"

The president looked back at him as though Will had a screw loose. He then tapped the paper on the desk and said, "This here letter says that tomorrow Lorenzo becomes president. At least until elections in the fall. And don't bother asking him. It took me long enough, but I convinced him that this is for the best."

Will picked the chair back up and slammed the legs back on the floor before sitting down again. "What are you thinking, David? The republic needs you."

Crockett leaned back in his chair until it creaked and shook his head. "No, what the republic needs is another six years to grow stronger. I've had my ears in certain places and I learned a while back that Sam Houston is planning another run for this here desk. And Sam's not a bad sort. Hell, he'd make a decent president if he'd get over that tomfoolery about annexation. I'll never understand that man. He spent the last six years giving the Cherokee everything he had. And if he won and got us annexed, the United States would do their best pull the rug out from giving the Cherokee a fair shake."

Will was startled by the revelation. "He only told me a few days ago. How'd you find out so quickly?"

Crockett smiled conspiratorially and said, "Come now, Buck, I ain't no blushing bride on her wedding day. I learned a long time ago to keep my friends close and my enemies closer. It's a gamble, but I figure if I can give Lorenzo a few months to transform himself into a wartime president, that folks won't want to change horses midstream, and elect him to his own term. With any luck, he'll send Sam back to live among the Cherokee again."

Will had always held Crockett in the highest of estimation, but this revelation made him ratchet up his opinion even higher. Shaking his head, and laughing a little at his friend and father-in-law's machinations, he asked, "And what do you gain by commanding one of a dozen battalions going south into Mexico?"

Crockett leaned across the desk and conspiratorially whispered, "Buck, who said anything about me going south?"

New Traditions

Set between the end of To the Victors the Remains and book 4 of the Texas Reloaded Series, New Traditions is a stand-alone short story.

August 1842

In the Capitol building, the small corner office of the president felt cramped, even though President Lorenzo de Zavala and Captain Jim Boylan were the only men present. The president's desk was piled high with correspondence, and several law books were perched on its edge. Zavala ran his fingers through rapidly graying hair.

Since David Crockett's resignation earlier in the spring, the full weight of running the executive branch of the government weighed heavily upon him. It didn't help that he should have been campaigning. Instead, he was a prisoner to the demands of the office. The reason for Captain Boylan's presence was simply one of dozens of irons he was trying to manage. He rummaged through one of the stacks on his desk until he found the item he was looking for.

"Captain, thanks for coming up from Galveston. As I indicated in my letter, the republic of the Yucatan has informed us that Mexico has taken possession of two new ships that pose a serious threat to both our nations' trade. At the moment, those ships, as well as others in the Mexican fleet have moved in to blockade the Yucatan coast."

The naval officer tilted his head, acknowledging the news. Zavala continued, "It serves Texas' purpose to see that Yucatan maintains her independence. Should Mexico reconquer the Yucatan, then Santa Anna would be free to turn his entire attention on us. This is why you're here."

Boylan leaned forward, focusing on the president's words, "I want you to take three of our four ships to Campeche and lift the blockade. If you can draw the Mexican fleet into battle, all the better. If we force their ships back into port, then we can force a blockade of the Mexican coast.

"Mr. President, I have heard of the two new steamships the Mexicans have procured. The last I heard, they were under the command of English mercenaries. Would defeating these ships damage our relationship with the English?"

Zavala frowned, "You've heard that rumor, too. I believe Britain's sale of those ships to Mexico has far more to do with challenging the United States than intending to put a dagger at our heart. If something happens to those ships, it's possible it could impact our relationship with the British, but it's equally likely, that destroying them may alter the balance of power with the United States, in a way that plays to our advantage. Either way, I think the reward is worth the risk."

Zavala turned his attention to the paperwork on his desk and Boylan took his leave and was deep in thought, planning the campaign as he left the Capitol building.

The gentle swells of the Gulf of Mexico rocked the ships of the Texas Navy as they rode at anchor a few miles north of the Yucatecan port of Campeche. A midshipman aboard the squadron's flagship, the *Fannin*, raised a signal flag, ordering an officer's call. In response, longboats were swung out from the *Nueces* and the *Austin*, and a short time later, each ship's captain and Marine officer were ferried between the ships.

Lieutenant Oliver Porter grabbed the sides of the pilot ladder and climbed up the rope ladder, until he swung his feet over the gunwale and felt the solid wooden decking under him. Despite more than a year's service in the Texas Marine Corps, Porter preferred standing on dry ground to the rolling and pitching of a ship's deck. He saluted the ship's ensign, flying aft of the ship, then saluted the officer of the watch. A midshipman, no more than fourteen or fifteen years of age, guided him to the wardroom where the other officers were assembled.

Captain Boylan, acting as the squadron's commodore, nodded to him as he entered, and indicated toward an empty chair. Porter hurried over, and took his seat next to Captain Gabriel Gibson, the commander of the *Fannin's* Marine contingent. Boylan remained seated as he spoke, "Gentlemen, now that we have arrived on station, I'm at liberty to divulge our plans. Of course, you all are aware that we have been tasked with breaking the Mexican naval blockade of the Republic of Yucatan's port.

"The Mexican fleet has been augmented with a couple of new warships they purchased from the British. The *Montezuma* and the *Guadalupe*. Either of them is the equal to the Fannin, and from what I've heard, both are clad with iron plating. The reports I have from our spies in Mexico is that they're crewed by British officers and a mix of Mexican and British sailors."

The captain paused as he searched the table around which they were seated. He found what he was looking for and continued, "In addition to these two steam frigates, the Mexican fleet consists of the *Regenerator*, a steamship the Mexicans have converted to carry some guns, and two schooners and two brigs. Were it not for the ironclad ships, we'd sweep their fleet from the gulf and be its undisputed masters."

The captain from the *Nueces*, Henry Thompson asked, "What about the armament of those ironclads, Captain?"

Boylan's face settled into a frown. "The British-built ships carry Paixhans guns. For those who may not be familiar with them," he said with a sidelong glance at the Marine officers, "they're designed expressly for firing exploding shells. Our best guess is that both are equipped with a half-dozen of these guns. Of special note, though is that both ironclads are equipped with a 68-pounder pivot gun, mounted on the bow. Against that, the Fannin's got one twelve-inch bow-chaser that can fire a two-hundred-twenty-five pound shell, as well as her twelve 42-pounder carronades."

Captain Gibson leaned back in his chair, rocking it back on its back legs, "The Fannin sounds like she can give as good as she gets, what have you got planned."

Boylan stood to his feet and leaned over the table and in a conspiratorial whisper shared his plan.

The rhythmic sound of water lapping against the longboat's hull did nothing to sooth Lieutenant Porter's nerves as the crowded boat sliced through the waters of the Bay of Campeche. Twenty men, a mixture of sailors and Marines were crowded onto its benches. Three more longboats kept pace and in formation with Porter's boat, as they rowed through the heavily overcast night's inky darkness.

The crew had been rowing for a couple of hours, following a compass reading, which according to Yucatecan sources would take them to where the Mexican fleet rode at anchor outside the harbor of Campeche. Porter turned from his place near the bow, and watched his men silently pulling on their oars, as though willing the boat to go even faster.

Despite the cloud covered night, when he turned and faced forward, he saw silhouettes materializing in the distance. The tall masts of the Mexican fleet came into view. He prayed his men would make no noise other than the steady oar strokes. If the sailors aboard the Mexican ships became aware of them while they were still more than a mile away, they could turn the heavy guns on them and reduce their boats to kindling. He shuddered as he thought about what would happen to his men should that occur.

Porter motioned to several Marines, who were sitting in the middle of the boat. They had been waiting for that signal. He heard the soft snicking sound of their bayonets being pulled from leather scabbards. Locking the sharp weapon on the barrel's end, they edged forward in the boat. They were tasked with securing the gunwale on the midships of the *Guadalupe*.

When Porter realized he'd been holding his breath as the boats neared their target, he exhaled and tried to breath normally. Or at least as normal as his nerves would allow. As the ship's silhouette became more distinct and he could make out the iron plating, he started looking for the best place for his men to throw their grappling hooks.

The boat glided alongside the ironclad, as the men shipped their oars, raising them up. Two men leapt past Porter, as they threw a set of grappling hooks over the gunwales amidships. The set of hooks were attached to a rope ladder, and as they dug into the wood on the gunwales, a Marine slipped by the lieutenant and scurried up the side of the ship, with his rifle slung over his back.

Pounding on the wooden deck and enraged shouts split the night air. A decidedly British voice called out, "Beat to quarters! We're attacked!"

Following behind the handful of men who had already climbed the ladder, Porter leapt up and grabbed onto a rung and started climbing. He hadn't reached the top when the sharp report of a rifle echoed in the night air. If anyone hadn't been aware they were aboard before the gunshot split the night air, they were now.

DREW McGUNN

As he wrapped his fingers around the wooden gunwale and pulled himself over the side, he heard scuffling and cursing. When his head cleared the side of the ship, Porter saw two of his Marines wrestling several sailors, who were armed with truncheons and knives. A beefy, tattooed sailor slipped between the Marine's rifles and slammed his club against a Marine's head, dropping him like a stone.

Alarmed, Porter jerked his revolver from its holster and pointed it at the sailor. "Drop it or you're a dead man."

The sailor saw him, and the young lieutenant could tell the other man was weighing his options. After a long moment, in which several more Marines clambered onto the deck, he dropped the weapon and slowly raised his hands.

One man down, Porter thought, and more than a hundred fifty to go. Fights had broken out across the midships, as his marines were joined by men from the other boats, who had swarmed over the side, and added their weight to the battle raging across the ship's deck.

More sailors were surging up from below decks, even as the boarding parties from the four longboats washed over the port side gunwales. Porter grabbed Marines by their collars, and shouted above the din of melee combat, "Form a Goddamned line!"

Amid the din on the deck, a thin line of Marines formed, stretching across it until reaching the starboard side. Porter stood behind the riflemen, "Aim at the hatchway!"

"Fire!"

A score of bullets riddled the sailors who had rushed up the ladder from the berth deck, momentarily stopping the surge onto the main deck. As the sailors still fighting amidships were subdued, more men joined the battle line of Marines.

The hatches to the berth deck were slammed shut and bolted closed. The score of Texian sailors, who had arrived with his Marines, scurried up the ratlines, and loosed the sails, and unfurled them as several marines attacked the thick ropes wrapped around the capstan. The ship was pulling against its anchor when the rope snapped, and the ship lurched forward.

Porter ran over to the gunwale and looked behind the ship, as the *Guadalupe* picked up speed when her sails filled. Despite the heavy cloud cover overhead, he saw lights illuminating the other ships in the Mexican squadron, as they came to life, reacting to the Texian navy's cutting out the iron hulled ship.

Marines forced the captured sailors on the main deck below at gunpoint. A young midshipman was in command of the Texian sailors, and because they only controlled the above deck section, no effort was made to build up a head of steam, as that would have required forcing their way to the engine room. Porter had little regard for the mixed crew of British and Mexican sailors, but until they surrendered, he disliked further risking his men's lives by forcing their way below decks to the engine room. As it was, two Marines had been killed when they had boarded, and several more were seriously injured.

Porter looked aft and saw the Mexican flag flying from the yardarm. He strode by the pilot house and drew his sword, cutting the line. The rope slid through the pulley, depositing the flag on the deck. He pulled the Texas ensign from a leather pouch he wore and beckoned a couple of Marines over. They took the flag and with help from a sailor aloft, rigged a new line and raised the Texas flag over the captured ship.

Behind the *Guadalupe*, Porter thought he could see a black smudge in the night sky, billowing out of the *Montezuma's* smoke stack, as the other ship's boilers began building up pressure to power the side-paddlewheels in their iron casements. Other sails unfurled behind the enemy ironclad as the rest of the Mexican squadron followed in pursuit.

At best, the Texians had gained a mile before the *Montezuma* started gaining on her. Porter stood next to the pilot house, aft of the ship and watched the sun rise behind the other ironclad. The distance continued closing, and as though the thought of being fired upon would trigger the action, a puff of smoke appeared in the *Montezuma*'s bow, following a moment later by the report echoing across Campeche Bay. A few seconds later, the shell splashed into the water less than a hundred yards astern. When a Paixhans gun fires a shell, a fuse is lit. A wooden sabot protects the shell and keeps it from exploding prematurely. After the shell splashed behind the ship, a moment later, a geyser erupted where it exploded.

Five minutes later, the gun fired again, and this time, the shell fell short less than a hundred feet from the *Guadalupe*. When it exploded, water cascaded onto the ship's stern. Porter turned to yell at the sailor in the pilot house but was interrupted by a cheer from the

Marines on the deck of the *Guadalupe*. Steaming from the west were the *Fannin*, *Nueces,* and *Austin*.

A deep rumble reverberated across the water as the twelve-inch bow chaser on the Fannin fired. The two hundred twenty-five-pound shell landed between the *Guadalupe* and *Montezuma*, throwing up a mountain of water when it detonated.

The enemy ship veered to starboard and presented its broadside to the fleeing ship. The three guns on the starboard battery disappeared behind a cloud of smoke, as their 42-pound shells screamed downrange toward the *Guadalupe*. One fell short, another long, but the third slammed into the side of the ship. The iron plating held, even when the shell exploded, and sent a sheet of flame up and over the gunwale above where the shot struck home.

Before the *Montezuma* could fire another broadside, the heavy bow chaser aboard the Fannin fired again. A fountain of water hid the enemy ship from view when the shell fell short.

The distance between the captured ironclad and her sister ship grew, as the *Montezuma* took evasive action against the *Fannin*. But the *Fannin* was under full steam and carried every stitch of canvas she could safely carry. She flew across the water, passing the *Guadalupe*, and fired again on the *Montezuma*, which was attempting to turn back toward Campeche.

The Paixhans guns were designed to make wooden sailing ships obsolete. The counter-technology to the Paixhans was an ironclad ship, like the *Montezuma*. When the British had built the ships for the Mexican navy, the means of propulsion were twin paddlewheels on the side of the ship. It was an obvious weakness. The solution was more iron plating. Against a 42- or even a 68-pound shell, the ships' builders had properly shielded the vulnerable paddlewheel. When the lucky shot from the twelve-inch gun slammed into the iron casement and exploded, the rivets holding the iron plating sheared off, and the iron plating was shredded. The wooden paddlewheel was turned to kindling, sending a wave of splinters across the deck. Dozens of sailors went down, in bloody heaps, as the ship slowed, without the steam-powered propulsion.

From his place along the *Guadalupe's* gunwale, Porter watched the mighty *Fannin* slice through the water, nearing the crippled *Montezuma*. Before its large bow chaser could fire again, the Mexican flag dipped, and the second ironclad surrendered.

With both ironclads in tow, the other ships of the Mexican squadron fled, carrying every piece of canvas they could handle. The small, wooden-hulled steamer, the *Regenerator* surrendered without firing a shot. While the sun was still high in the midday sky, the three ships of the Texas navy sailed into Campeche harbor, with the three captured ships of the Mexican fleet.

October 1842

Charles Elliott, appointed chargé d'affaires to the Republic of Texas a few months before, was uncomfortable in the hard-backed chair. As a career diplomat he had represented the Empire's trade interests in China before the Opium War had tarnished his reputation, at least that's what the rumors had said.

He was disinclined to doubt them, having been exiled to this mosquito-bitten, pretentious republic. Tired of ignoring the pain in his back, he stood and walked over to the glass-paned window.

This house, owned by a wealthy merchant, had been given over to today's meeting with Secretary of State, John Wharton. No doubt Wharton had chosen this location and this room to deliver a point. The docks of the Port of Galveston were clearly visible from the room, and tall masts crowded the wharves as trade flowed in and out of the republic's principal port. At the moment, the ships alongside the docks failed to interest him. What caught his attention were the two ironclads anchored in the Galveston channel. Next to them was the steam frigate *Fannin*.

He bit his lip until he tasted blood. Since arriving during the summer, things had gone better than he had anticipated, until the battle of Campeche. He was dismayed that two of the most powerful warships in the world had fallen to the third-rate Texas navy, and had done so while under the command of British officers, even if they were on loan to the Mexicans.

That should have been the worst of it, he thought as he shook his head in dismay. Word had reached him only a few weeks ago that the British bankers who had underwritten the loan to the Mexican government for the purchase of the ironclads had petitioned to the crown for redress. The Earl of Aberdeen, Minister of Foreign Affairs had written to him that the Crown's position on the matter of the captured ships is that the loans for the ships were in default and to press the Republic of Texas for their return. Elliott grimaced, recalling that the Foreign Minister's note said nothing of the two hundred British sailors rotting as prisoners of war on this very island.

The door swung open and John Wharton strode through, followed by General William Travis. With a perfunctory nod, Wharton took one of the chairs at the table and waited for Elliott to return to his seat. General Travis took the chair between the two diplomats.

"Mr. Elliott, thank you for meeting us on short notice. My apologies for the delay, but my meeting with your counterpart from the United States ran late."

Elliott masked his surprise at the news. What could that upstart Fletcher Webster want with Wharton?

He cleared his throat and decided these Texians would prefer to dispense with the normal diplomatic pleasantries. "The Crown requires the return of her property, Secretary Wharton. When can she expect to take possession of the two ironclads?"

Wharton appeared nonplused, as though something had hit him between the eyes. He coughed until General Travis retrieved a pitcher of water from a small table against the wall and poured him a drink. When he finally recovered, he said, "I am not aware of any British ships. Now, if you're talking about those two Mexican ironclads, I'm not sure there's anything Texas can do. They were captured after a state of war was declared between our country and our southern neighbor. They were flying the Mexican flag and were provisioned by the Centralist government in Mexico City. As to their provenance, if indeed they were funded by London bankers, well, sometimes you've got to write off a bad investment."

While it wasn't what he wanted to hear, Elliott hadn't expected any other answer. Having satisfied his imperial duty for the moment, he moved on to his own item. "Setting that aside, then, that brings me to the next issue at hand. You are in possession of more than two hundred of Her Majesty's subjects. As Her representative to them, I require access to determine if they are being properly cared for."

Wharton glanced at Travis before responding, "I'm not familiar with any British subjects in Texas prisons. If anyone from the British Empire has lawfully entered our country and has been charged with a crime, we will certainly give you access, as is customary."

Elliott resisted the urge to shout. He tamped down his ire. Diplomacy, like chess, was a game of skill. He changed tack "Come now, John, let us not maintain any fiction here. You and I both know that when Britain sold those ironclads to the Mexican government they required competent seamanship. British sailors were contracted by the Mexican government."

Wharton smirked upon hearing Elliott's admission. "Frank talk is a rare commodity, Charles, especially in the circles in which we travel. But let me speak plain, Her Majesty's government has caused us offense by selling and crewing the ships of the Mexican navy. Neither I, nor the president, is blind to the reality that the British Empire gets to operate by a unique set of rules."

Elliott liked hearing others acknowledge that the British Empire was first among equals. "Then, I'm sure you're interested in remaining in Her Majesty's good graces. Let me arrange for the transportation of our sailors back home."

Wharton was about to respond when General Travis placed his hand on the other's arm. Travis smiled at Elliott. It reminded the Englishman of a wolf about to take a bite out of a weaker animal. "Good graces. What an interesting expression, Mr. Elliott, it covers a multitude of sins."

Elliott eyed the young general, skeptically, as he continued, "Was it Her Majesty's good graces that caused your government to be the last significant European power to recognize our independence?"

Without waiting for a response, General Travis continued, "Mr. Elliott, were we to release men who had served our mortal enemy, it would make us unpopular with the citizenry of Texas. Now, if you're prepared to ask us to make a politically unpopular gesture, I'm sure you can appreciate we need something significant in return."

The chargé d'affaires had expected something else, a retrenchment in the Texian position, based upon Travis' reputation. But he implied an accommodation could be worked out. "What do you have in mind, General?"

Travis turned and looked out the window at the ships loading and unloading their cargo along the wharves below. "In the balance of power in the western hemisphere, Her Majesty's government has, at every opportunity, tipped the scales in Mexico's favor. Are you aware that even the Czar of Russian beat your government by five years in recognizing our independence? May I suggest that the British empire would do better to show that we are in her good graces by extending to the Republic of Texas most favored nation status? This would, I believe, result in lower tariffs for British goods coming into Texas as well as expanding British textile markets by offering more Texas' cotton exports to Britain."

Elliott nodded thoughtfully at Travis' words. "I'm not authorized to make such significant trade policy actions, but I'll be glad to present your proposal to the Foreign Ministry. In the meantime, as a sign of good faith, I would like to visit your prisoners from the Battle of Campeche."

Travis slid his eyes back to Wharton, who responded. "Of course, Charles. I'll provide you a pass before we leave today. On an unrelated note, I do have a proposal for you, regarding the disposition of a couple of ships we captured from the Mexican navy."

Elliott leaned forward. Wharton's machinations intrigued him. Denying any action regarding the British bankers and now, he wanted to talk about them as though they belonged to Mexico. This would be interesting. Elliott indicated he was listening.

"The 'Crockett Doctrine' remains Texas' official position regarding unsubstantiated rumors that the new administration is seeking terms of annexation from the United States. Despite many in the American South and not a few in East Texas who are clamoring for annexation, we are committed to our independence. Rest assured the Clay administration approves of our position. It serves the interest of all three of our nations to quiet such voices of annexation. The best way to accomplish this is for Texas to step out onto the world's stage and make a clear commitment to peace in the western hemisphere."

Elliott chuckled, "Those are odd words coming from a nation who not half a year past declared war on your southern neighbor."

Wharton smiled wryly. "In fairness, we were invaded, Charles. Give us our due, please."

"What have you in mind, John?"

"Texas has extended an offer to the United States offering our fair city of Galveston to host a conference between the United States and Great Britain for the purpose of settling your boundary disputes." Wharton leaned back, looking expectantly at him.

This wasn't what Elliott had expected. It was a novel idea, but why would Her Majesty's government allow a no-account nation play host to a conference. "That's an interesting idea, John, but why should we agree to this?"

Wharton stood and went to the window, and pointed toward the channel, where the ironclads rode at anchor. "Why, Charles, I believe we have something your government would like returned. If your government will agree to our hosting a conference then as a sign of good faith, we will release those ships back to your bankers."

TO THE VICTORS THE REMAINS

Stay tuned for the continued adventures of the Lone Star Reloaded Series, book 4 in the Q2 of 2018.

Thank you for reading

If you enjoyed reading To the Victors the Remains please help support the author by leaving a review where you purchased the book. For announcements, promotions, special offers, you can sign up for updates from Drew McGunn at:

https://drewmcgunn.wixsite.com/website

About the Author

Drew McGunn lives on the Texas gulf coast with his wonderfully supportive wife. He started writing in high school and after college worked the nine-to-five grind for many years, while the stories in his head rattled around, begging to be released.

After one too many video games, Drew awoke from his desire for one more turn, and returned to his love of the printed word. His love of history led him to study his roots, and as a sixth generation Texan, he decided to write about the founding of Texas as a Republic. There were many terrific books about early Texas, but hardly any about alternate histories of the great state. With that in mind, he wrote his debut novel "Forget the Alamo!" as a reimagining of the first days of the Republic. To the Victors the Remains is the third in the series.

When he's not writing or otherwise putting food on the table, Drew enjoys traveling to historic places, or reading other engaging novels from up and coming authors.

Made in the USA
Columbia, SC
14 September 2023

22865431R00186